Moonlight

&

A Marine

Book 3: Semper Fi in Love

Danette Fogarty

Dear Readers:

This is the 3rd installment of my Semper Fi in Love Series and I am so excited to be sharing it with you. This book is a little different in that Abi and Gav have basically been told they're to be married. Only one problem……they've never met. Not exactly true but you'll have to read the story to find out what I mean.

I wanted to extend a huge thank you to our friend, Gunnery Sgt. Roy Wright III, otherwise known as Trae. This exceptional man answered so many of my questions without complaint or exasperation. His lovely wife Tami didn't think it was completely odd that he would get texts from a writer at all hours of the day and night so she should be up for sainthood. Anyway, thank you both for making this book as accurate and great as it is.

The wonderful thing about a series is that you really get to expand on your characters. The interplay between Eryn and Chase (A Marine to Remember) is awesome and I had so much fun with them. It's like a family reunion in some respects.

This was originally going to be the last book in the series but I couldn't close it out without giving you Emma Cantrell's story. As you'll find out in this book, Emma is…….very "man savvy." So wouldn't it be so much fun to have her finally meet her match? Look for A Marine and Her Sensibilities; due out March, 2014.

As always, thank you to our serving men and women in the Armed Forces who make it happen every day.

With Much Love and Gratitude,

Semper Fidelis

Danette Fogarty

Chapter 1

Abi was running late...again. She hated running late but that seemed to be her MO these days. There were some issues at work and, since she was covering for both her OIC and NCOIC, at times, it was pure hell.

Tonight signaled the end of a very hectic week and she needed to get her butt over to the hotel in Honolulu for a dinner. She was getting ready to leave work when she realized she left her wallet at Bryan's house this morning when she went to work. Dammit, she needed her wallet if she was going to drive.

Pulling up in front of Bryan's apartment, she wondered if she should've called first but, seeing his car, she sighed in relief. She didn't have a key after six months of dating and was kind of surprised but she figured Bryan just wasn't ready for that step. She wasn't either on some levels so it didn't bother her as much as it might've bothered other women. She and Bryan had a good time together and that should be enough for now.

She got out of her car and started walking towards his front door. She heard the music before she reached the door and wondered why he had it turned up so loud. She knocked and, hearing no answer, walked in. He probably couldn't hear her over the noise.

"Bryan!" Abi called out.

She heard no reply so she went into the kitchen and picked up her wallet. When she looked at the table, she saw a purse there and wondered whose it was because it didn't look familiar. He probably found it. But if that was the case, then why did she have a bad feeling creeping up her spine?

Abi walked back to Bryan's bedroom and heard noise. She was a smart woman so she knew what she'd find when she opened the door but had to do it anyway. It was like a dream moving in slow motion as she pushed the door open and stepped into the room.

They were on the bed and having a pretty good time by the sound of it. She stood there for about ten seconds before she said anything.

She spoke loudly, "Well, are you guys having fun?"

Bryan almost jumped off the bed. The woman grabbed the sheet and crouched up against the headboard. Abi thought the whole thing was almost comical, except that it was happening to her.

"Abi," Bryan said, "I can explain."

Abi thought that was ridiculous that he would think he could explain this. "Funny thing, Bryan," she started back out of the room, "I really don't give a damn."

Not waiting for him, Abi left the room and walked out the door. Unfortunately, stupid tears were streaming down her cheeks and she was pissed that she couldn't stop them.

The drive into Honolulu passed in a blur of emotional pain and she was glad she actually made it in one piece. She pulled into the hotel's parking lot and grabbed her makeup bag, needing to make some quick repairs so people wouldn't think she looked as awful as she felt. Looking in her visor mirror, she figured she couldn't fool everyone but she'd sure give it a try.

Walking into the Hale Koa lobby, Abi scanned the area looking for anyone familiar. The dinner was a pre-wedding shindig for the families of the bride and groom to meet before the wedding which was the day after tomorrow. Being one of the bridesmaids, Abi was invited and was expected to show up.

The bride and groom were her good friends, Eryn and Chase, and they both happened to be her bosses up until about three months ago. Chase decided to retire from the Marine Corps so he and Eryn could get married. Their story was a long one, spanning over ten years, but Abi was glad they finally were able to make their peace and find one another again. Now they were getting married and Abi was so happy for them but really upset with her own current situation. She put on her game face and followed the signs to the ballroom where they were having dinner.

By the time Abi walked in, the party was in full swing and the place was crowded. She looked around trying to find someone she knew. Finally, she spotted her fellow bridesmaid, Emma, and walked over to her.

"Em," Abi said with a smile, "how are you?"

Emma looked up and smiled at her friend, "Abi," she gave Abi a quick squeeze, "I'm good, a little jet-lagged, but good."

Once they pulled back from their hug, Abi felt uncomfortable because Emma was looking at her way too closely.

"You're upset," Emma said calmly.

Shaking her head, Abi smiled. Now was not the time to dwell on that ass she'd been seeing. "Nothing too bad."

Emma could tell Abi didn't want to talk about whatever was bothering her and she could relate. Sometimes you just needed to work it out in your own mind. "Okay," she found a passing waiter and grabbed two glasses of wine from the tray he was carrying, "this will help."

Abi gladly accepted the glass and took a drink, "Thanks."

"Hey," Emma took a sip, "what are friends for?"

It was hard to stay down when you were around upbeat people so Abi decided she would try to not let her present emotional state affect the festivities. After all, they were here for a pretty awesome reason.

Abi and Emma made their way around the room, speaking to a few people they knew from Eryn's family. Her parents thanked them for being in the wedding party and were very kind. Everyone was really happy so it was easy for Abi to relax. Of course, the wine certainly helped. She wasn't drunk, but feeling a little more mellow.

Everyone started finding seats and Abi smiled when she saw Chase's Best Man, Mitch Frinnel, get up to talk. She'd only met him once, in passing at a ball years ago, but heard a lot about him through Eryn and Chase. She sat down at the table with Emma and listened to the toasts.

Chase introduced the wedding party so they were forced to stand up so everyone could see them. Abi felt like a monkey on display but she did it for Eryn and Chase. She didn't pay attention to the other names; she only felt sorry for them. Relief washed over her when they were done and Chase announced dinner would be served.

Once the dinner started, everyone talked about the wedding and the people they met. A few of the guests at her table asked her questions about the base and sightseeing recommendations. The conversation was easy and it was nice for Abi to stop thinking about Bryan and his bullshit.

After dinner, everyone scattered to the dance floor or went to find other people they wanted to speak to. Abi hung back, preferring to watch and listen. She was scanning the dance floor when she saw Eryn dancing with Mitch and wondered what was going on. The body language between them said "tense." She was going to walk over to Chase and ask about it when Emma came up beside her.

"Have you seen Eryn's cousin Katherine?" Emma asked while handing Abi another glass of wine. "The woman is gorgeous!"

Abi smiled, "Are you jealous, Em?" She thought her friend, Emma was very pretty.

"Hell yeah," Emma said. "She's a blonde version of Eryn and about two inches taller."

Looking around, Abi tried to spot the beauty Emma described. When she didn't see anyone fitting that description she shrugged. "I guess I'll meet her later or tomorrow night at the rehearsal dinner."

Emma nodded. "Are you feeling any better?" She didn't want to pry but she wanted Abi to know she was offering an ear.

Nodding, Abi looked at her friend. They met through Eryn a few years back and stayed in touch since. Emma was a great woman and a phenomenal Marine. She understood how it was to be in a primarily male field and made no pretentions about her thoughts. Abi considered her one of the best women she knew.

"Well, if you want to talk about that ass who you dumped you let me know." Emma squeezed her arm and walked off.

Abi shook her head, how did the woman know?

After wandering around for a little while, and refusing a couple of requests to dance, Abi wound her way over to where the bride and groom were standing. She was glad to see that Eryn didn't look nearly as stressed as she looked earlier when Abi saw her dancing with the Best Man.

"Hey, you two," Abi said as she came up to them. She kissed Eryn's cheek then Chase's.

Chase smiled, "Hey, you."

Eryn looked at her closely, "Is work running you ragged?"

It was as good an excuse as any, "Yes," she said, but she didn't want Eryn to worry, "but nothing your wonderful Crash Chief can't handle."

"Amen," Eryn said. She wondered if her friend thought she was fooling anybody.

Chase looked around, "Hey, where's Bryan? I thought he'd be here with you?" His questions stopped when he received an elbow to the rib. "What?" he asked Eryn.

Abi looked at Eryn and shrugged. It was not the end of the world but it sure did a number on her ego right now.

"Let's not worry about him right now; is there anything I can help with before tomorrow night?" Abi asked, hoping to change the subject.

Eryn shook her head no, "Just meet us at the Clubhouse tomorrow evening at six."

"Okay," Abi tried to sound upbeat, "I'm off to cruise for guys, I guess."

Chase started to say something but the look Eryn gave him must have stopped him. He smiled at Abi.

He looked at his bride-to-be and asked, "What's going on?"

"She and Bryan broke up earlier today," Eryn whispered. She knew because Emma pulled her aside earlier to say something was up and they figured it was Bryan.

Chase nodded, "Oh, I'm sorry."

Eryn was very glad she found the man she was going to spend the rest of her life with, "You didn't know, sweetie." She looked up at him and smiled. Only two more days until they were married.

Chase looked at their friend and sighed, "What's with all the drama going on in our wedding party anyway?"

The man was amazing, Eryn thought. "I know, right!" Eryn said, "Why can't they be calm and collected like us?"

"Yeah," Chase said, shaking his head. "That's us alright."

Abi went out onto the patio off the ballroom the party was held in and stared out into the night. She could hear the ocean waves as they came onto shore but she couldn't see them. The night enveloped the ocean and tucked it into a secret place.

Even with the wine, Abi knew she would still think about what went wrong. Why did Bryan feel like he had to keep dating other people when she thought they were exclusive? She supposed she should've asked if he was dating other women but why should she have to? When you were dating someone, you gave a commitment. At least that's what she did. She stood on the patio for a long time, letting the tears roll down her cheeks. This was all she would allow herself; no more crying or pitying after tonight.

As soon as she could, Abi excused herself from the party.

She opted to stay at the hotel and bunked with Emma since her room had two beds. They stayed up late talking smack about the jerks they dated over the last couple of years and Abi felt better.

When she really thought about it, Bryan and she weren't going anywhere. Their arrangement was comfortable and that was okay with her. Looking at Eryn and Chase, she realized any feelings she had for him were not even in the same ballpark as what her friends shared and so it was for the best. She just wished he would've broken up with her in a more respectful manner.

On Friday morning, the girls got up and showered. Abi had to get back to the base to get some work done before she took off for the weekend. Emma was staying at the hotel and doing some shopping with some friends she knew here and doing last minute errands for the wedding.

Abi drove back to Crash Crew and parked outside. She was a little late but nothing major. With Eryn on leave and no NCOIC, everyone would look to the Crash Chief to handle daily operations. Abi knew she was more than capable but her head wasn't in the game today.

"Gunny," Sgt. Matthews said as she walked in. "I have some papers for you to look over."

Nodding, Abi kept walking, "Sure, just put them on my desk and I'll read them after I've grabbed some coffee."

Sgt. Matthews smiled, "Aye, Gunny."

Abi went into the lunchroom and poured herself a cup of coffee, adding way too much sugar, and went into her office. She looked at the desk and cringed. There were the papers the Sgt. dropped off but about a dozen phone messages she needed to return. Oh well, Abi thought, no time like the present.

Three hours later, Abi came up for air. Her desk was cleared and she met with the Section Leaders to give out last minute assignments for the weekend. Even though she was attending the wedding, she was still technically on call. She trusted her staff to handle it so she was able to leave Crash Crew with a clear head.

She drove to her barracks and thought she had a little time for a nap before she had to get ready for the rehearsal dinner. Walking into her room, she sighed. It might not be a big sprawling house, but it was hers.

She was really lucky to have a nice suite in the barracks. There was a sitting area with a kitchenette and a bedroom off to one side with a private bath. The higher ranking NCO's were treated pretty well so Abi decided to stay on the base. A lot of her friends lived off base but Abi never really saw the need. When she was dating Bryan, she went over there if they wanted alone time. Oh great, she snarled, him again!

Determined not to be a whining little girl, Abi tossed her bag onto the couch, kicked off her boots, and took off her flight suit. Comfortable in her shorts and tank top, she laid on the bed and drifted off to sleep.

Her alarm went off and Abi opened her eyes. She took a second to figure out what she was doing. She slept hard, obviously needing the sleep. Looking at the clock, she figured she better get ready so she wouldn't be late for the rehearsal dinner.

An hour later she was pulling into the Clubhouse parking lot. She waved at Emma when she pulled in. It looked like everyone was already there. She got out quickly and smiled as she walked up the sidewalk.

"Hey," she said to Emma, "where are the bride and groom?"

Emma gestured toward the golf course, "Out there at the ceremony site talking to the minister."

Abi nodded, Eryn was nothing if not detail oriented.

The two women walked up to where the majority of the wedding party were gathered. Eryn's mom introduced everyone and played hostess until Eryn and Chase came over.

Emma and Abi stood next to one another and exchanged looks when Eryn's cousin, Katherine, was introduced. Emma was right, Abi thought, the woman was a stunner.

The minister came over and asked everyone to gather round. The group, although playful, was respectful and followed the directions. They lined up in the processional and started the walk down the aisle.

Abi did her duty and smiled while she watched Eryn and Chase do a quick run-through of tomorrow's ceremony. It was hard to be cynical when you were surrounded by love.

The rehearsal went off without a hitch. Abi was paired up with Chase's brother and thought he was a really sweet guy. She figured his wife thought so too and smiled sweetly as they made their way back to the Clubhouse for the dinner.

Everyone laughed when they walked into the room the group was using for the dinner, it was a cheesy Hawaiian party motif complete with plastic grass skirts and blow up palm trees. Abi laughed with Emma as they ate pu pus (Hawaiian finger foods) and drank mai tais.

The bride and groom gave out gifts and Abi hugged Eryn when she looked at the gold pendant engraved with her name. It was a sweet gesture and very like Eryn to think of it.

Abi was talking to one of the groomsmen when she noticed Mitch and Katherine get up and leave. She also noticed Eryn's look and knew, without a doubt, something was going on there. If she couldn't find time to corner Eryn before the wedding, she definitely wanted details when Eryn came back to work after her honeymoon.

Emma came over after everyone got up to leave and they were talking about possibly going out to a club when the guys walked outside. They were ribbing Chase about decorating the car and Mitch herded them out, probably to threaten them with bodily harm if they tried anything. She saw Eryn's cousin, Katherine standing alone and walked over to her.

Smiling, Abi nodded, "So, you're an artist," she said to Katherine.

Emma walked up to join the conversation.

"Actually," Katherine said, "I'm a fashion designer."

Interesting, Abi thought.

"Oh really," Emma said, "What's your brand? Maybe we've heard of you."

Abi shook her head, leave it to Emma to make the woman look even more cornered than she did a minute ago. Eryn's cousin looked like she was ready to bolt out the door.

"Oh, I go under the brand Katie Fred," Katherine said calmly.

What! Abi was shocked! Katie Fred was one of her favorite labels. "Are you kidding me?" she asked the woman, not really sure if she believed it.

Katherine looked at them directly, "Yes, why would I lie about that?"

They didn't mean to insult her. Emma was gushing over her now and Abi thought Katherine wanted to be anywhere but here. She thought about it for a second and had to ask, "How come you didn't design our dresses?"

Katherine didn't miss a beat; she answered quickly, "Because I wasn't asked to."

Okay, Abi thought. Eryn's cousin was definitely not one for small talk or subtlety. But she was a phenomenal designer and she was drop-dead gorgeous. Although Abi wanted to dislike her in some way, she found it pretty much impossible. Damn! As if that wasn't crazy enough, Katherine's next statement almost made Abi pass out.

"I'd love to show you some sketches of my upcoming designs if you'd like." Katherine smiled.

Oh My Lord, Abi thought. She was obviously paralyzed with awe. Not only was she talking with her very favorite designer, but the same designer was showing her sketches of clothes that weren't even for sale yet. Hell yeah!

The three women sat down with Abi and Emma pouring over Katherine's phone like it was a lost treasure. The drawings were fabulous, of course, and Abi was struck by how much creativity it took to design clothes. When they were done looking at the sketches, they asked some questions and Katherine was kind enough to patiently answer them.

Katherine took her phone when they finished and put it away, "Why don't you both make sure I have your addresses before I leave and I'll make sure I get you both tickets to my next show in New York."

It was like winning a lottery jackpot in Abi's mind. "Yes, sure," she said breathlessly. She wanted to hug Katherine but was afraid she'd frighten the woman with her excitement.

Eryn and Chase came back in so they all walked over to them and made sure there wasn't anything else to do before they went back to the hotel. Abi was riding with Emma and leaving her car at the Clubhouse for tomorrow.

Once the group parted ways, Abi and Emma went out to get Abi's things from her car and put them in Emma's. They were pulling Abi's bags out when they saw Mitch come up to Katherine beside Chase's jeep. Abi was about to say something when Katherine kissed him. Abi turned to say something to Emma but her friend was looking at the couple already.

"Well, I didn't see that," Emma said.

Abi smiled, "I did." She shook her head when Emma gave her a shocked expression. "I guess I didn't know "THAT" was happening but I suspected something."

Emma swatted at her playfully, "Get into my car and tell me everything."

Abi got in and they started to head toward Honolulu, discussing the very interesting situation between Katherine and Mitch and how it might affect Eryn. It was good natured gossip. Once they got back to the hotel, Emma suggested they go downstairs to the bar and see if there were any guys there.

Abi wasn't really tired and didn't have anything else planned so she nodded. They were getting ready when Abi's phone rang. She looked at the caller ID and saw it was her mother.

"Em!" she yelled into the bedroom, "my mom's calling, I'm going to step out onto the balcony and take it."

Emma yelled back, "Okay, No problem!"

Abi opened the sliding door to the balcony and stepped out as she hit accept on her phone, "Mama, how are you?"

"Abigale," Elena Rochelle said warmly.

Abi smiled, "Mama." She always worried that she lived too far away from her parents, who lived in New York City.

Elena smiled, her girl sounded funny. "We are good, mah-yo sohl-neesh-kah."

She smiled and warmed instantly when she heard the childhood endearment her Mama always used. It meant "my sunshine" in her parents' native Russian and Abi could never spell it but always loved it when her parents used the loving words. It was hard to not be her parents' little girl.

"Mama, is Papa good?" Abi asked while she looked out across the dark Pacific. The breeze felt good.

Elena spoke in Russian to her husband, then spoke into the phone, "He is good, he misses you."

A constant battle between her and her parents was the cultural bubble her parents lived in there in New York. Abi joined the Marine Corps to get away from it.

Andrei and Elena Rochelle immigrated to the United States when Abi was only a year old, but continued to live and socialize with many other Russian immigrants. There was nothing wrong with that, Abi just knew that there was more to life and wanted to see what that was.

Danette Fogarty

During her senior year of high school, a Marine Corps recruiter came in and talked about the travel and job opportunities. Her parents wanted her to go to college and marry some nice Russian boy who lived in her neighborhood but Abi had other plans.

As soon as she graduated, she got on the bus and left. She didn't speak to them all through boot camp so everyone had time to forgive and adjust to the change in plans. Even though her parents seemed to accept her choices, Abi never really thought they got over her leaving the way she did.

Now, they were getting older and always spoke of grandbabies their friends had and always asked when Abi was going to settle down. She figured that's what this call was about too.

Elena tried to be calm, "I am calling to see how you and the young man you are dating are doing."

Leave it to her mother to get right to the point. "Mama, we are no longer dating." Abi didn't see the need to sugar coat it.

"Oh," Elena said and turned to speak to her husband again in Russian.

Abi could pick out words here and there but since she didn't hear it all the time, she wasn't fluent. Her mother's tone didn't sound exactly positive though.

"Hey," Emma stuck her head out the patio door, "you ready to go?"

Shaking her head no, Abi pointed at the phone, "You go on, I'll come down when I finish."

Emma nodded, "Okay, but don't be pissed off when all the boys pick me."

Abi laughed but stopped when she heard her mother's tone.

"Abigale," Elena wanted her daughter to listen. "Your father and I have let you go on long enough moving here and there and finding your job, but we are done."

Her mouth dropped open, did her mother just tell her that they wanted her to leave the Corps and come home?

Andrei Rochelle grabbed the phone, "Abigale," his tone still heavy with his native Russian after living in America for thirty years, "it is time you should marry and have babies."

If she wasn't in shock, Abi was pretty sure she would've started to laugh. Though she knew her parents and they were not kidding. Not one bit.

"Papa," she started.

Andrei silenced her with a loud, "NO!" He did not like yelling at his baby but enough was enough. "You stop this now and you come home and you meet your husband!"

Okay, now she worried that her father was delusional. "Papa," she kept her voice soft, "I don't have a husband yet."

His temper rising, Andrei started speaking in Russian and using bad words so he handed the phone back to his wife. She would have to make their little one see reason.

Elena picked up the phone, "Abigale," she tried to soothe, "we have your husband here and he is waiting for you."

Abi couldn't help it now, she started laughing. "Mama, what do you mean he is waiting?" Did her parents know how ridiculous they sounded?

"Your husband is Gavriil Maslov, you are promised to him and you will marry him." Elena used her sternest voice. She loved her daughter above all else but Abigale was not fulfilling her obligation to marry and carry on their family.

Okay, enough was enough. This was just crazy talk. Abi took a deep breath, "Mama, I am attending my friend Eryn's wedding tomorrow so I have to go now but I will call you on Monday and we'll sort this out, okay?"

Elena knew her daughter was avoiding them. "Abigale, you will call me on Monday?"

Anything to stop this conversation, "Yes, Mama."

Nodding, Elena held her hand up to calm her husband. "You tell your friend we send best wishes and you call your Mama on Monday."

"I will," Abi said and ended the call.

She stood out on the balcony for a long time after that and wondered how her parents thought she would ever come home and marry someone they picked out for her.

Once Abi finally made it downstairs to the bar, she only had to look for the group of guys to find Emma. Her friend attracted men like flies to a backyard barbeque. They just found her irresistible and hovered. Abi wasn't exactly jealous but she wondered what Emma's secret was.

"Hey!" Emma yelled and waved her over.

Abi walked up to her friend and her current collection of men. "How's it going?" she asked even though she knew it was going pretty well from the looks of things.

Emma laughed, "Okay, this is Derek, Blaine, Chris, Jon, and Phil."

All the guys nodded when Emma said their names and Abi was in awe. Emma was like the "guy whisperer."

The group sat in the bar for a while, drinking and talking. Abi should've been having fun, but she kept thinking about what her parents said about getting married and a blanket of guilt and anger enveloped her.

It wasn't like she didn't want to get married, she just hadn't found a guy she wanted to marry. Bryan sure wasn't the right kind of man. But besides that, who was this guy her mother said was her husband? Gavreel? Is that what her mom said his name was? What kind of guy said he'd marry a woman he never met?

"Earth to Abi," Emma said.

Shaken out of her inner monologue, Abi smiled, "Yes, ma'am."

Emma knew something was up, "Are you okay?"

"Sure," Abi answered. She looked around and didn't see any of Emma's man harem, "Where are your devoted followers?"

Laughing, Emma waved her hand, "They were excused from class."

It amazed Abi how her friend looked at guys, "You didn't like any of them?" she asked. Some of them were really cute.

"Sure," Emma mimicked Abi's earlier response, "but tonight is about us girls and getting a good night's sleep so we look "super hot" at Eryn's wedding tomorrow."

It was a very good point, "That's good, now let's get a glass of champagne and toast our friend and her good fortune." Abi didn't want to tell anyone about her friggin odd conversation with her parents. At least not until she cleared it all up.

"My sentiments exactly," Emma said and motioned for the waiter to come their way.

Chapter 2

Saturday was gorgeous. Abi and Emma woke up early so they could get in some sun before they met the other wedding attendants for brunch with Eryn. A girl needed a nice tan if she was going to be a bridesmaid. They giggled like school girls as they went down to the beach in front of the hotel. The sun was warm and the breeze light; a perfect setting for relaxing.

Abi would have liked to be relaxed but the phone call with her parents played over and over in her mind like a broken record. She even dreamed that she was walking down the aisle toward a big hairy Russian man who scared the hell out of her. There was just no way that her parents could make her marry someone!

"Turn over," Emma said and nudged Abi's arm.

Nodding, Abi turned over and put her sunglasses on. "I am tired."

Emma picked her head up and looked over, "How can you be tired? We went to bed before twelve and we didn't get up until eight." She smiled, "I've gotten a lot less sleep than that."

"I'll just bet you have," Abi said snottily. "No, I didn't sleep well."

Sitting up, Emma faced her friend, "Anything to do with you yelling "No, Mama" in your sleep?"

Oh Lord, "I did?" she asked and knew full well she did.

"Yes," Emma said, "Listen, we haven't talked about that jackass Bryan. Did your parents take the news badly?" Emma didn't think Abi's parents ever met Bryan but maybe they were attached.

Abi shook her head, "Oh no," she didn't know what to say, "I walked in on Bryan "still dating" someone else."

It didn't take but a second for Emma to catch on, "That son of a-"

"It's fine," Abi interrupted her friend's name calling, "I mean, it's not fine but it wasn't true love."

Emma was pissed enough for them both, "Even so, Abi, to just sleep around, that's low."

Abi nodded, "Yes, my parents want me to settle down and are pressuring me."

"Parents sometimes do that," Emma responded. "My parents lay on the guilt every once in a while."

Chuckling, Abi laid back down, "Well, they'll all just have to wait."

"Exactly," Emma stated and pulled her hat low over her eyes.

They went back upstairs a while later and got ready for the brunch. Everyone was meeting in the lobby at nine-thirty and riding over to a nearby restaurant.

When Abi and Emma arrived, they greeted Eryn's mom first.

"How are you girls doing?" Beverly Fredricks asked.

Emma smiled, "We are bright eyed and ready to go, Mrs. Fredricks."

Abi thought that was laying it on a little thick but she'd go along with it.

Eryn came downstairs with her cousin, Katherine, a few minutes later. They waited until her sister, Sarah, showed up and then all the ladies piled into two cars to go to brunch.

The atmosphere was light and everyone was in a great mood. They toasted to the bride, who then made a toast to them and made everyone cry. Abi was seated between Emma and Eryn's future mother-in-law, Rebecca Johnson.

"Are you enjoying your stay?" Abi asked Chase's mother. The woman seemed a little lost.

Rebecca nodded, "We are; everyone has been very sweet." She looked around then leaned in, "I think I just feel a little left out." She placed her hand on Abi's, "Don't I sound ungrateful."

Abi didn't think so, "I understand, Eryn's mom is pretty much in charge."

Smiling, Rebecca looked embarrassed, "Shouldn't I be happy I didn't have to deal with all the details?"

Shaking her head, Abi looked at Chase's mom sincerely, "No, the details are what make it special." She could see Rebecca tearing up a little, "why don't you do something during the ceremony that you and your husband did to bring your side into it a little more?"

Rebecca thought for a moment, "That's a great idea."

She watched Chase's mom make a quick phone call and look a lot happier. After she hung up, she walked over to Eryn's mom and whispered in her ear. Beverly nodded excitedly and the two mothers hugged. It was hard not to think about weddings when they were about to be in one. Abi looked over and watched Eryn. She was talking to Emma about something Chase did.

Honestly, Abi wasn't very sure that Eryn and Chase would get their heads on straight enough to make their relationship work. Anyone could see they loved one another but watching it play out the way it did was almost painful. Abi tried to help where she could but, in the end, it was up to them to choose the path. She was sure they chose the right one and couldn't be happier for them.

"Hey," Emma said in her ear.

Abi lifted her head and peered over at her friend, "Yes?"

It was time for Abi to quit daydreaming. "Get your head in the game, Rochelle," Emma said playfully.

When Abi looked around, everyone was getting up to leave. She turned red, knowing she was busted.

"Coming, your Highness," she said sarcastically to Emma and grabbed her purse.

The group loaded up in the cars again and drove through Honolulu. They were going to get their hair and makeup done in Kailua so they were closer to the base in case anyone was running late. If Eryn's mother had anything to do with it, they would all be there hours early. Abi smiled, thinking her mother and Eryn's mom were a lot alike.

When she was a little girl, her mother and father doted on her. She wondered why she was an only child but was never brave enough to ask.

Her childhood was filled with love and stories about her parents' native land. She certainly didn't remember anything about Russia but her parents' descriptions made her think maybe they regretted leaving. She always heard stories about the little village her mother, Elena, lived in with her family. How they took her to the large city of Yahutsk so Abi's grandfather could find more work. That's when Elena first saw Abi's father, Andrei. He was a college student who happened to be eating at the same restaurant as Elena's family.

Back then, Abi's mother explained, a boy couldn't just ask a girl out; he had to get permission from her parents first. The concept seemed so odd to Abi but it was also kind of romantic. Elena talked about how Andrei had to meet with her parents on more than one occasion and earn their trust before they would let him take their daughter out. Andrei didn't necessarily agree with the custom because he was from the city where the customs weren't as strict. But he always said how, when he saw Elena for the first time, he knew she would be his wife.

The car pulled into the parking lot and Abi decided she needed to stop daydreaming about her parents and all the crap she was dealing with. This was Eryn and Chase's day. She needed to be a good friend and do what they needed.

It took hours for everyone to have their hair and makeup done but the bridesmaids seemed especially happy with the results.

"I'm happy if I don't have to mess with my hair," Emma said as she inspected the complicated twist in her hair.

It was nice to have it done and not curse your way through it; at least that's how Abi saw it. She hated doing her hair up for nice occasions, it never stayed. "I'm with you." She winked at Emma.

Emma nodded her head toward Katherine, "She is gorgeous," Emma whispered.

"Yes she is," Abi said but turned back to Emma, "but no more gorgeous than you are."

Blushing, Emma looked back at her reflection, "Not like her," she sighed.

It occurred to Abi that maybe Emma wasn't as confident with herself as they all thought. Plus, she was as beautiful as Katherine or any woman around. It was a shame she didn't see it. Not wanting to get into a debate about beauty, Abi hugged Emma quickly and went in search of Eryn.

Once everyone was done up and looking fabulous, the group drove to the base. The Clubhouse was bustling with staff members setting up for the reception so the ladies tried to stay out of their way. There was a designated dressing room for the group with a sitting room. The wedding coordinator was there waiting when they arrived and smiled.

"Hello, ladies. We have some light food here for you and some bottled water," she looked at Eryn for permission, "and some champagne if the bride is okay with that."

Eryn nodded and everyone cheered. The champagne was poured and everyone chatted happily until the photographer showed up.

"Show time," Emma announced when the photographer came in and started setting up.

Abi laughed, "Oh, like you don't looooveee to have your picture taken."

Emma tried to look sheepish, "Not love, maybe like a lot."

Her friend was a breath of fresh air. How could Emma not see how great a person she was?

They were shooed out of the sitting area and instructed to change.

The dressing room was roomy and everyone had plenty of privacy. All the dresses were hung up and they each grabbed theirs.

The dresses were beautiful; a pale pink with thin straps over the shoulders. The fabric flowed so when the girls moved, the fabric shimmered. Abi wasn't a "pink" kind of girl normally but she loved the dress the first time she saw it in the bridal shop. She and Eryn looked for them since everyone else lived so far away.

Abi started to feel the pressing of tears thinking of Eryn's face when she saw the dress. How she said she just knew it was perfect for all of them.

"No tears yet," Emma whispered.

She nodded but noticed that Emma was feeling a little emotional too. They helped each other get dressed and laughed as the photographer pestered Eryn about stopping and posing. Abi was glad it wasn't her having to do that.

The ladies were getting in line at the Clubhouse when they heard the pre-ceremony music start. It was a lovely mix of love songs that spanned many years. Abi remembered her parents dancing to one of the songs in their living room when she was a child. The memory made her smile and wish her parents weren't so intent on having her married and popping out kids like a PEZ dispenser.

She saw Emma and Katherine move over to Eryn and looked at the bride. She was stunning. Her dress was fabulous, one of Katherine's creations, and she couldn't remember ever seeing Eryn look this happy. Walking over, she touched her hand to Eryn's and squeezed.

"Good luck, you look gorgeous," Abi said softly, trying not to cry.

Eryn smiled, "Thank you."

There wasn't any reason to say anymore; the wedding coordinator ushered them back into line and the processional music started.

Emma started down the aisle first, moving slowly and looking like a beautiful rose. Abi waited for the cue from the coordinator, then started moving forward. It was uncomfortable, being on display for everyone but she tried to smile and look like she was enjoying herself. She got close to the altar and could see Chase smiling like a big dope. His friend, Mitch, was right beside him looking pretty hot in his uniform. 'Don't look at that one,' she said to herself, he's taken.

She sighed with relief when she made it up front without tripping, Abi turned to watch the rest of the ladies come down the aisle. Sarah, Eryn's sister, was right behind her. The woman was about six months pregnant but looked so wonderful in the dress she wore. Finally, Katherine made her way down and Abi's breath actually hitched.

As she watched Katherine come toward them, she finally saw what Emma meant. The woman practically floated down the walkway. She was part ballerina and part Greek goddess all rolled into one. Abi's eyes moved over to see Mitch watching Katherine and she wanted to look away when she saw the raw need in his eyes. If a man looked at her like that, Abi would be able to die a happy woman.

'Stop it!' She yelled at herself. They were here for Eryn and Chase, not because Abi wanted to throw a personal pity party.

When Eryn started toward her groom, the guests stood. Abi watched Eryn's mom, and Chase's too, dab at tears. This family loved. It was refreshing to see.

After Eryn made her way up to Chase and her father gave her away, everyone sat down and the ceremony started.

It was short but very sweet in Abi's estimation. The bride and groom did not wear microphones and recited their vows to one another quietly. It was intimate and very romantic. The mothers stood and came up to the couple. Eryn's mother took a ring out of a small bag and looked at her new son-in-law.

"This is us, giving you our hearts. You are now our son," Beverly said, she put the ring on Chase's right hand and kissed Chase's cheek.

Rebecca, Chase's mother, removed a bracelet she was wearing and put it around Eryn's wrist, "This is us, giving you our hearts. You are now our daughter." She kissed Eryn's cheek.

The mothers went back to sit down and everyone was crying. Abi wondered if that was what Rebecca and Beverly decided to do during the brunch earlier. If so, that was so cool.

The recessional music started and everyone was lining up to walk down the aisle toward the Clubhouse. She patiently waited her turn and met up with Chase's brother, Spencer, to make their way toward the receiving line.

"My mom told me what you did," Spencer whispered as he tucked Abi's arm in his.

What? Abi was on alert, "What did I do?" she asked, desperate to know if she insulted Chase's mother somehow.

Spencer smiled, "She was feeling a little left out and you told her to do something that would bring our family into the ceremony." He squeezed Abi's hand, "She talked to Eryn's mom and asked if they could each present a family heirloom to the couple from the families since that's what my parents had at their wedding."

Awww, Abi thought. "I'm glad she found something."

They were coming up to the rest of the wedding party so they got in line and met the guests as everyone made their way into the reception hall.

Abi shook hands, accepted thanks and congratulations, and even took some kisses. This was not her most comfortable situation but she took it in stride. She'd make Eryn pay up when she got back to work. Smiling, she was relieved when the last guest passed.

"Pictures," the photographer said loudly.

Groaning inwardly, Abi pasted on a smile and followed directions. The photographer was so tough, he made her Squadron Commander look like a puppy. Not wanting to endure his wrath, Abi was obedient. Sometimes you just had to know when to take orders.

Finally, the pictures were done and the group went into the Clubhouse. Luckily, they weren't being "introduced" as they entered so everyone was able to go right to the table and sit down.

Rubbing her foot under the table with one hand, Abi took a drink of water with her free one. Why did looking gorgeous hurt so much? She chuckled to herself and was relieved that dinner was a sit down affair where the wait staff served them.

The groom stood and made his speech, which made her want to cry again. Damn it! Then Mitch stood up and gave his speech. It was a great mixture of humor and sincerity. Abi knew she liked him. Everyone clapped and then settled down to eat.

Abi enjoyed the food and especially enjoyed the atmosphere. Happiness swirled around the room and lifted you up into its folds. A nice change from everyday life.

Once the tables were cleared and the music started, everyone gravitated toward the dance floor. The music was fast-paced and fun. Abi slipped off her heels and got a pair of slippers from a little bag she and Emma set under the table. They were Marines so they were prepared.

A drink made it to the table in front of her. Abi looked up and saw Emma smiling. She sat down beside Abi.

"Drink up, sister," she looked around the room, "we are going to find some trouble to get into."

The woman was an animal; of course, Abi never minded finding a little bit of trouble.

Picking up the glass, she drank. Whew! "That's something," Abi said when she could speak again.

Emma slammed her glass down, "Nothing like a good shot of whiskey."

Is that what they were drinking? Abi thought it was definitely not what she would've chosen but it was a special occasion. She laughed and motioned for a waiter.

A few minutes later, and two more shots, Abi and Emma were laughing at everything. There was an announcement that the wedding party was going to have a dance. Oh Lord!

"I do not want to dance,"Abi said in a conspiratorial whisper.

Emma laughed, "Well, you'll sure be loose."

Nodding, Abi looked around, "I guess we'll have the guys to hold us up."

Putting her arm around Abi's shoulders, "Yes we will." Emma said in a mock-serious tone.

They got up and walked to the edge of the dance floor and waiting for the groomsmen to come over.

Abi felt good thanks to the alcohol. She never drank as much as she had in the last couple of days. She waited for Spencer to take her hand and lead her onto the floor. He was about the same height as Chase but had longer hair and a bigger frame. She watched him as they moved around the floor. She thought he was good looking enough but he didn't carry himself like a Marine. She always dated Marines. Maybe that was her problem?

"Do I have something on my face?" Spencer asked Abi. She was looking at him closely and he was starting to feel uncomfortable.

Startled out of her thoughts, Abi blushed. "I'm sorry, I was just comparing you to Chase."

That was a little rough. "Oh, don't do that," Spencer smiled. "We are like night and day."

"What do you mean?" Abi asked. She was sincerely curious.

Spencer moved across the floor smoothly with Abi in his arms. "Well, I don't exercise and wear my hair nearly as short; too much regimentation in his world." He laughed, "Of course, now that he's retired, we'll see how that goes."

Abi was starting to feel a little offended on Chase's behalf. "Do you think he'll stop being a Marine even though he retired?"

Oh, he touched a nerve with Chase's friend. Spencer looked sheepishly, "No, I'm sorry if my teasing offended you."

"I'm sorry," Abi said quickly, "I just don't think we stop being Marines when we retire." She smiled at Chase's brother, "I'm sorry I was defensive."

Spencer nodded, "Apology accepted." He moved to avoid another couple, "I've always been a little jealous of Chase, I guess."

An interesting perspective. Abi's eyebrows raised, "Really?"

Chuckling, Spencer looked serious, "Really. The guy," he nodded in Chase's direction, "is loyal, caring, and is in excellent shape."

The last part was meant to be funny and Abi laughed. "You are right," she said and relaxed again.

When the song ended, she gave Spencer a peck on the cheek and thanked him for the dance. He walked over to where his wife was standing and took her into his arms with a flourish. He was smooth on his feet, Abi thought.

She walked back over to the table and plopped down. The sense of being lonely came over her again and she was getting pretty pissed that it wouldn't leave her in peace. Never could she remember being so introspective about her life. She loved her life! She loved her job, she loved traveling, she loved the freedom, and she loved the Corps.

"Would you like to dance?" Corporal Wright asked. He wouldn't normally ask his Crash Chief to dance but she sure did look pretty tonight.

Abi looked up and saw Eryn's assistant, Corporal Wright, standing with his hand held out. He was being sweet, she knew, and tonight she would accept that.

Placing her hand in his, Abi smiled, "I'd be honored."

The couple moved to the dance floor as the next song started. It was slow, for which she was thankful, and she was surprised when Cpl. Wright took her into his arms with a flourish. He smoothly moved them across the floor and Abi felt swept up. The kid could certainly dance. She watched him expertly maneuver them around and tried not to yelp when he spun her.

"Wow," Abi said in a breath when she was back in the Corporal's arms.

Cpl. Wright smiled, "My mom told me that the key to impressing a woman was making sure you could dance."

Smart advice, Abi thought. She was certainly impressed.

They moved around and around and Abi felt like she was flying. The alcohol combined with the Cpl.'s expert moves made her feel like a little kid. She was actually disappointed when the song ended.

"That was so great," Abi said loudly.

Cpl. Wright laughed, "Thank you, ma'am."

Abi kissed the Corporal on the cheek, "No, thank you." She walked slowly back to the table, smiling like a silly school girl.

Emma took the seat beside her, a dopey grin on her face. "Hey that guy really has some moves," she said and waved at the Corporal.

Shaking her head, she slapped at Emma's arm, "He's too young for you and way too inexperienced to handle you."

Wearing a fake pout, Emma took a sip of water, "Yes, but it's the young ones that surprise you."

Now Abi really did slap her arm, "Behave yourself, Emma!"

Wiggling her eyebrows, Emma stood, "NEVER!" she yelled and went about to dominate the single males in the room.

Abi watched Emma work the room and wondered how on earth she was able to have the blatant confidence and sexuality around men. Within two minutes, she had at least four guys following her around like puppies. It was strangely interesting to watch. She kind of felt bad for the men; they didn't know what they were in for.

Looking over, Abi saw Katherine and Mitch sitting at the far end of the table and carrying on an intense conversation. Yep, something was going on there. Scanning the room, she saw Eryn and Chase talking to guests and laughing. She hoped their wedding was all they wanted it to be.

A little while later, Emma was waving wildly at Abi, motioning her to come onto the dance floor. As soon as she got next to Emma, she was yanked into a huddle.

"Okay," Emma said in a whisper, "we are going to catch that bouquet."

Abi couldn't help it, she laughed. Emma was pretty intense about this. "Okay," Abi answered.

The DJ got on the mike, "Okay, girls, get ready!"

The other single women poured out onto the floor trying to figure out where the bouquet would land.

Katherine was reluctant to step out until Emma practically dragged her to where they were standing. Emma set the woman in front of them and shrugged at Abi's questioning look. It was plain to see Katherine did not want to join in the fun. Abi was always up for a competition; she really didn't care what catching the bouquet meant, she just wanted to win.

"One, two, and three!" the DJ yelled.

Eryn threw the bouquet up and all the ladies screamed. It was high and to their right so she figured they wouldn't catch it. But as it came down, Emma jumped and smacked it toward them. Abi reached but it was too high. When she looked again, the flowers were sitting in the arms of a very surprised Katherine.

Everyone cheered and Katherine looked like she wanted to be swallowed up by the ground. Poor girl, Abi thought. Emma came up behind her and looked mad.

"I'm sorry," Abi said, "I tried."

Emma nodded, "I know, I'm just wondering why the one who's already snagged a man needs the bouquet."

Her poor friend. Abi put her arm around Emma's shoulders and guided her towards the bar. "You poor baby, I'll get you another whiskey and you'll feel better." She tried to sound motherly.

Emma laughed, "Okay that will probably help."

They got to the bar and toasted to one another, downed the whiskey, and watched the men try to catch the garter.

Once the reception started winding down, Abi spoke to Eryn's mom and asked what she could do.

"We're doing okay here; we've got Mitch roped into helping," Beverly said as she nodded to the gift table. Mitch and Victoria were gathering up gifts and cards.

Abi smiled, what a gentleman. "Okay, well, I'll see you tomorrow."

Beverly nodded, "Yes, and, Abi," she smiled, "thank you again for being such a nice friend to Eryn."

Without thinking, Abi walked over and hugged Eryn's mom tightly. When she pulled away, she had tears in her eyes, "Mrs. Fredricks, it's me who's lucky to have Eryn as a friend."

Abi kissed Mrs. Fredricks' cheek and walked out of the Clubhouse before she melted into an emotional pile of tears.

Chapter 3

Sunday morning was bright and sunny and Abi hoped it helped improve her current mood. She got home at a decent hour and went to bed right away and, still, she woke up feeling drained and empty.

After sitting up in bed, she looked around and saw her bridesmaid dress hanging on the back of the bathroom door. Even now, just on a hanger, the dress was gorgeous. Today, she'd put it in her closet and probably never pull it out again. Even that thought made her depressed and want to cry.

She looked at the clock and saw it was time to get ready to head to the hotel for the gift opening.

After showering and putting on a nice sun dress, Abi did her hair up loosely. She applied her makeup lightly so she looked fresh but not over-done. With a quick check in at work to make sure there were no hiccups, she grabbed her purse and left her room. She was just about to her car when she heard someone.

"Abi!" Bryan yelled from his car.

Not now, Abi thought as she turned around slowly. He was making his way toward her and looking pretty friggin good. Unfortunately.

There was no way she would forgive him or get back together but she was now very well aware of how much his actions hurt her. When he was a few feet away, she put up her hand to halt his progress.

She wanted to be nice, "Bryan," she smiled sweetly, "how nice of you to stop screwing that girl long enough to come and talk with me." But...we didn't always get what we wanted now did we?

Bryan flinched, "I know I screwed up, Abi," he wasn't sure what he could say.

Nodding, Abi snarled, "Well, I think that may be under playing it a little bit but if you want to use that description, okay."

"I know," He stepped closer, "Baby, I was just being stupid and it was a lapse."

It took every ounce of restraint for Abi to keep from beating the crap out of him. "A lapse is...I don't know; forgetting my birthday, or not calling if you're going to be late." She poked him in the chest, "Getting into the bed you just had sex with me in a mere eight hours before is not a LAPSE."

A few people were walking by and noticing their exchange.

Bryan waved his hands in an effort to get her to lower her volume. "Baby," he put his hand on her waist.

Without hesitating, Abi grabbed his arm with her free hand, shifted her weight and flipped him around so he was up against the car next to hers. She was behind him holding his arm up and used her elbow to press against a nasty pressure point that did not feel good. Thank goodness for her martial arts training. With a sneer on her face, she leaned in closely so only he could hear her.

"Don't ever touch me, call me, text me, email me, or contact me in any way." She smiled and nodded at some guys who were walking by. They didn't seem to know if they should laugh or intercede. "I don't give a rat's ass what you think you did. I know you cheated and I deserve better than that."

She let him go and he turned around quickly, obviously embarrassed.

"Fine," Bryan said and smoothed his shirt, "you're such a bitch!" he said through clenched teeth as he walked away.

Abi sighed and said calmly, "Yes I am."

She got into her car and drove to Honolulu.

After arriving at the hotel, Abi texted Emma to see where she was. Emma texted her and let her know they were going down to the restaurant/lounge where the lunch was going to be held and gave Abi the directions.

When Abi walked in, she saw a lot of people. This was not what she was expecting at all but she figured with this many, maybe she wouldn't be expected to socialize. After her little run in with Bryan she felt better, until the adrenaline dissipated. Now she felt awful, like she wanted to cry or something.

"Hey," Emma said when she walked up to Abi.

Abi smiled, "Hey, how was your night?"

Looking closely, Emma knew something happened. "I'm thinking it was better than yours, sweetie."

Nodding, Abi walked over and sat down at one of the tables. "Mine was fine."

There was going to come a time very soon when Ms. Rochelle was going to have to spill, but now wasn't the time so Emma let her friend have a little space.

"I'll be right back," Emma said and went over to the bar.

When she came back, she took a sip out of one glass and handed the other to Abi. Eyeing the glass, Abi took a tentative sip. "Yum...white soda."

Emma wrinkled her nose, trying to be cute, "Only the best for you."

They chatted for a little bit until they saw Eryn and Chase come in. Everyone swooped in for a minute or two of face time with the newlyweds so Abi hung back. She worked with Eryn so she would see a lot of her when she was back from her honeymoon. Plus, she really didn't want to put her own sour mood onto their day.

Everyone found a place and sat down to eat. Someone was passing around pictures of the reception for the guests to look at. Abi glanced at them, smiling and commenting, until she came across one that was of her and the young Corporal dancing. She stared at the photograph and wondered, once again, why she wasn't really happy. Without another thought, she handed the pictures to Emma.

After lunch, the bride and groom moved to another part of the room where the gifts were set up and they started opening them. The guests made the appropriate comments and were having a good time. At that point, Abi was just too depressed. She got up and walked over to where the bar was.

Abi ordered a drink and downed it in just a few seconds. She ordered another drink but figured she should at least wait a few minutes before downing that one. Her father always told her that alcohol might make you feel better but you'd better be prepared for the after effects.

Out of the corner of her eye, she noticed Mitch sitting at the other end of the bar. He did not look happy.

Mitch looked over to where Abi sat and saw her look like she was trying to drown her sorrows, "Hey, Gunny," he said.

Abi smiled then saluted Mitch, "Master Sgt.," and downed the shot. Man it went down smoothly.

He asked her if he could bring Katherine over to Crash Crew the following day for a tour. She didn't see any reason why she couldn't fit in a little tour; she liked Katherine.

"No problem, Master Sgt." She picked up the next glass and downed the liquid.

Mitch eyed her curiously, "Not to pry, but you're putting those down pretty quickly." He moved over so he was on the barstool next to hers.

"Yep," she leered, "I was systematically dumped this morning and I feel like drowning my sorrows."

Mitch nodded and leaned in, "Well, we'll drown our sorrows together then." He motioned for a beer.

They sat there for a minute or two then Mitch looked at her, "This morning?" he asked. He didn't see her with anyone the last couple of days.

Okay, she was exaggerating, "Not really, actually I walked in on him and another woman in a...let's just say compromising situation on Friday," another glass went down. "I put his sorry ass up against a car this morning and that just solidified the whole dumping thing for me."

Mitch chuckled, he liked this lady, "Good for you, Gunny."

Abi nodded, "Yes, sir, he was really embarrassed that a girl got him too. That was the funny part."

He clapped Abi on the back and nodded, "I'll bet it was."

"You know," Abi looked at Mitch and smiled. He was such a nice man, "I don't even know why I thought he would be faithful." She looked back down at her drink, looking for the answers in the caramel colored liquid. "I don't seem to inspire a lot of loyalty."

Mitch didn't agree, "Abi," he nodded to the bartender when he set down a fresh beer in front of him, "I know what you did for Chase and Eryn. I have no doubt you inspire loyalty."

"Just not in the men I date, I guess." Oh, she sounded like a whiny kid.

Mitch was torn because he knew what she felt right now. He was so confused about Katherine and their situation that he could empathize. "Don't underestimate yourself, Gunny."

Abi smiled, no wonder Eryn and Chase loved Mitch, "I won't. Thanks, Master Sgt."

They were done talking for a little bit and just sat there drinking.

"You know," Abi started after her brief silence, "I'm too good for him anyway."

Mitch nodded. He put his arm around her shoulders to show his support. He listened as she went on about this ass who cheated.

Abi really appreciated Mitch's support. She was going to say more foul things about Bryan when she heard Mitch say hello to Katherine, who was now standing on the other side of him. Ooooohh, the lady didn't look too happy.

Trying to help Mitch, she said, "Katherine, Mitch was just listening to me go on about my recent ex-boyfriend." Smiling sheepishly, she hoped her explanation helped.

Sitting there, Abi watched Mitch pay his tab then walk Katherine over to a corner of the room, away from the other guests. She hoped she didn't get him in trouble. Unlike the ass, Bryan, Mitch was a gentleman.

After a minute or two, Abi saw Katherine's father walk over to the pair. Oh geez, this guy was full of himself, Abi thought. He was antagonizing Mitch and, to Abi's surprise, Mitch took it. If she had to guess, that was only for Katherine's benefit. What was with these fathers? First Eryn's, then Katherine's, thinking they could "handle" their daughters?

Well, smart ass, she said to herself, isn't your dad doing the same thing? Isn't he saying he's now taking over and making your life go a certain way?

That thought sobered Abi up quickly. Crap! She put her hand up so the bartender knew she didn't want a refill. Enough was enough.

She settled her bar tab, grabbed her purse, and then made her way over to Eryn. The gifts were done being opened and everyone was starting to clean up.

"Well, Mrs. Johnson, how are you feeling?" she asked Eryn.

Eryn smiled wide, "I am quite well, thank you." She tipped her head, looking closely at Abi, "But you aren't, are you?"

Now Abi knew why she counted Eryn as a friend, "No, but you can help me with it when you get back from your wild honeymoon with cutie over there," she nodded in Chase's direction.

"Count on it," Eryn answered and gave Abi a hug. "Don't think you can't call me either next week if something comes up."

Abi raised her eyebrows, "I don't think so but thanks."

They laughed and hugged again. Abi helped get some of the gifts out to the car and called a friend to come and get her. She was still feeling the alcohol and knew driving was not a wise thing to do.

Finding a comfortable over-stuffed chair in the lobby, Abi sat down and waited for her friend. She checked her mail through her mobile apps and replied to a few emails from friends. Her head was starting to ache now that the alcohol was wearing off. She went up to the front desk and asked if they had any aspirin. The front desk clerk was kind enough to hand her two and a bottled water. Abi nodded her thanks and turned when she saw Mitch coming over.

"Master Sgt," Abi smiled.

Mitch knew she wasn't feeling too hot. He didn't say anything, just put his arm around her shoulders and walked her outside.

Abi leaned into him, she didn't know him all that well, but she needed a shoulder. "My girlfriend is picking me up; she'll be here any minute."

He was relieved Abi wasn't driving.

They walked out to the circular drive in front of the hotel and stood there. After less than five minutes, a blue car pulled up. Abi smiled, gave him a smile of thanks, and got in. He watched the car leave and turned to go inside.

Abi's friend, Sheri, picked her up and started back to the base. "What about your car?" she asked.

"Emma will bring it by tomorrow afternoon and I'll get a ride to work," she replied, hoping the aspirin would kick in pretty soon.

Sheri nodded, "I heard about Bryan."

News travels fast, Abi thought to herself. She only nodded.

"I also heard you put him up against a car this morning," Sheri said in a smart tone.

Abi snorted, "Damn straight."

They drove to the base without speaking of her loser ex-boyfriend again. Abi nodded off for a little while and woke up when the car stopped. She was surprised they were outside her barracks.

Looking at Sheri, Abi felt embarrassed, "I'm sorry I fell asleep."

Sheri smiled, "No problem. I didn't mind." She hugged Abi, "Call me this week and we'll have dinner."

"Okay," Abi said and got out of the car.

She was smart enough to remember to get her room key off the key ring when she gave her set of car keys to Emma. Now she just had to find the stupid thing.

After dumping almost the entire contents of her purse out, Abi finally found the key and was unlocking her door when he phone started ringing. Great! It was in the pile of stuff from her purse. She propped the door open with her foot and rummaged to get the pile back into her purse and answer her phone.

Dropping her phone, Abi yelled, "Dammit!" then picked it up. "Hello," she growled into the phone.

Gavriil Maslov frowned at his phone, "Hello? Is this Abigale?"

"Yes," Abi said shortly, "this is Abigale."

Clearing his throat, Gavriil wasn't sure what to say, "Yes, I'm Gavriil Maslov." She didn't say anything. "I'm your future husband."

Standing in her room, Abi dropped everything in her hands, including the phone. Oh crap!

Gavriil heard rustling and didn't know what was happening on her end of the phone. Was she in danger? He didn't hear voices, "Abigale?" he asked worriedly.

"Listen," Abi said when she finally got the phone picked up and wasn't going to trip over the contents of her purse, "Gavriil?"

Gavriil interrupted her, "It's pronounced, Gav reel, but you can call me Gav." His words were rushed and he was embarrassed.

Sighing, Abi plopped down in the nearest chair. "Okay, GAV," she annunciated slowly, "I am sure you are a very nice man but you are not my future husband."

Her father warned him that Abigale would be resistant to the arrangement. "I'm sure you think that now, Abigale; we've only just met and over the phone no less." He tried to sound calm even though his gut was churning, "Once we meet, you will change your mind."

Okay, who was this guy and what mental institution did he just get released from? What the hell! Abi didn't know what to say so she just remained quiet. Maybe he would get the hint and hang up. If her parents yelled at her for being rude, oh well.

There was silence, but Gav knew she was still on the phone. He could hear her breathing. "Abigale, I am not a crazy person, I assure you."

Well, he was lucid enough to know what she would be thinking. "Good to know," Abi said dryly.

He couldn't help but laugh, her mother told her about this side of Abigale as well. The sarcastic and independent side. When he heard her sigh, he figured he shouldn't be rude.

"I'm sorry," Gav said quickly, "I thought you might feel this way and that's why I asked your parents for your phone number," he took a quick breath, "I wanted to contact you directly."

Abi clenched her jaw. If her head wasn't banging around like a drum and her mouth didn't feel like she'd spent the last month in the desert, then maybe she would be open to a calm, adult conversation. But the truth was, she wasn't.

Looking absently out her window, Abi considered her options. "I'll tell you what," she said softly, "I'm calling my parents tomorrow and then I will call you tomorrow evening if that's okay and we'll see what the resolution is."

Her willingness surprised him. He didn't believe for one minute she was giving in; he figured she was just buying time. He had time so he'd wait. "Okay," he answered.

"Bye, GAV," She said emphasizing his name.

Gav smiled, "Bye, ABEEGALE," he said in the same sarcastic way.

Abi hung up her phone and let out a breath. What the hell was going on? She didn't even want to think about a husband when she was still really pissed about the jack wagon who screwed around on her. But, she thought as she pulled off her shoes, this Gav guy did have a nice voice. And, she had to admit as she crawled into bed, he didn't sound like a deranged serial killer. Two good points, she contemplated, as she drifted off to sleep.

Monday morning, Abi's alarm went off and she cracked her eyes open. She went to bed after getting back from Honolulu yesterday and slept all the way through until this morning. She had to use the bathroom so ran in there to get ready for work.

She was in the shower, washing up, when she recalled the conversation with her "future husband." Against her will, a smile started. The way he said he was her future husband; like it was a foregone conclusion or something.

Scrubbing her scalp a little harder than necessary, she remembered how he said her name, punctuated with a Russian accent. It was crazy but she thought that was cute.

After stepping out and wrapping herself in a towel, she wiped the fogged mirror and looked at her reflection. All of that notwithstanding, the man was a stranger...that her parents picked out for her...to marry. It was all insane!

She finished getting ready for work and wished this was all just a bad dream. All of it with the exception of her and Bryan being over with. That particular thing she wouldn't regret. Thinking about it all now, Abi knew he would cheat because she checked out of the relationship emotionally weeks ago.

When she pulled into Crash Crew, all of her personal stuff was shoved in a box in her mind and she concentrated on work. For the next couple of hours at least.

"Hello, Gunny," Corporal Wright said to her when she walked into the building.

Game face on, Abi nodded, "Corporal." She went directly to her office and dug in.

Three hours later, Abi leaned back and sighed. Okay, the rush of the weekend stuff was done and they were cleared to focus on today and current assignments. She was due to meet with the department heads this afternoon but had a little time now. Looking at the clock, she decided she might as well get the call to her parents over with. There was a seven hour time difference so calling them tonight would be rude. She picked up the phone and hit their contact.

Elena Rochelle picked up, "Hello," she said softly, her Russian accent sounding lyrical.

"Mama," Abi said with a smile. "How are you?"

"May-yo Sohl-neesh-kah," Elena whispered.

Abi was on edge, her mother didn't sound well. "Are you okay, Mama?" She asked.

Elena sat down and played with the edge of her apron. She always wore it when she was cooking; it was her mother's and her grandmother's before her. She hoped Abigale would ask for it when she had her own home. Now, the older their daughter became, the less Elena thought that would happen.

"Yes," Elena said with a smile.

Abi didn't know where to start so she opened up the can of worms right away, "Gavriil called me yesterday."

Oh, she could hear the temper in her daughter. Not unlike her father, this one. Trying to keep from grinning, Elena cleared her throat. "Yes," she said softly.

"Mama," Abi didn't want to hurt her parents, "you know you can't make two people get married." It came out sounding like she was talking to a child.

Unlike her husband and daughter, Elena knew when to hold her temper. "My Love," She said in bright tone, "you are promised to Gavriil."

Frustration was flowing over her in waves, "How can you promise your daughter to someone?" She was feeling like a car on Craigslist.

"Abigale," Elena said in a short tone, "we do this for your own good." She took a breath, "We do this so you will be happy and have babies."

Feeling like she was just tossed back into the nineteen fifties, Abi clenched her teeth. "Mama, I am not going to marry him." Why couldn't her parents see how absurd this whole thing was?

Her patience failing, Elena couldn't help it, "Abigale, you will marry Gavriil!" Trying to calm down, she said a quick prayer, "You will honor your parents!"

Okay, enough was enough, "Mama, I love you and Papa so much," she started to cry, "but I can't do what you are asking me." She had to hang up, "I'm at work so I'll call you soon."

Elena shouted, "Abigale!" but it was too late, her daughter already disconnected.

Sitting in her kitchen, Elena prayed that her daughter would listen to them and do what was right. She prayed that it would all work out.

Getting up, Abi high-tailed it to the women's head (bathroom) and took a few minutes to compose herself. She looked in the mirror and couldn't believe what her parents were asking her to do. The crying thing had to stop so she dabbed her eyes, made sure her makeup was okay and walked back to her office.

An hour later, she was miserable. Guilt was ripping up her conscious and she was still angry over the situation. Her rampaging thoughts were interrupted by a knock at her office door.

"Enter," she said roughly and regretted using that tone.

Mitch entered the office, smiling, "Hey, Gunny," he said.

Oh crap, she forgot about showing Katherine around today.

Katherine followed Mitch in and stood there looking uncomfortable so Abi got up and gave her a quick hug. It probably put Abi more at ease than Katherine.

"Is this a bad time?" Katherine asked. She noticed that Abi looked distracted.

Abi waived her hand, "Not at all," she set the papers on her desk in a neat pile and turned to them, "I believe I owe you a tour."

For the next hour, the three of them toured the building. Abi explained the jobs of the different departments, being sure to break it down into civilian talk so Katherine wouldn't be confused. The military used so many anagrams so it was difficult for someone outside to get all the lingo.

When they finished the tour, Abi walked them to the door of the Crash Barn and said goodbye. She made sure to remind Katherine to send her the info on her upcoming show. A girl never tired of fashion. She waved them off and went back into her office to sulk.

The afternoon was spent meeting with the department heads and taking detailed notes for Eryn. She got the word from Headquarters that their new NCOIC would be arriving in a few weeks. Thank goodness, Abi said to herself on the way out of her office for the day. She said goodbye to everyone she passed. She liked to be cordial with everyone since they had to rely on one another when dealing with an emergency.

She stopped on the way home and picked up a pizza. It was her Monday night ritual. A small with sausage, onions, extra cheese, and black olives. The smell of pizza permeated her car and, by the time she pulled into the barracks parking lot, her stomach was growling.

Abi locked her car and grabbed the pizza box. She was determined to get out of her flight suit, catch up on her DVR'd TV shows, and just veg.

As she was opening her door, her phone went off. Damn! She hoped it wasn't work but, if it was, then she'd handle it. Without looking, she answered the phone.

"Hello," she said as she put down the pizza box and dropped her purse onto the desk.

Gav smiled, she always sounded like she was busy, "Hello, Abigale," he said softly.

The sound of his voice made her stop dead. There was something about the way he said her name, "Hello, Gav." She answered. Oh boy!

Chapter 4

Well, Gav thought, she didn't hang up. That was a good sign. "I was wondering if you were able to speak to your parents today." He undid his tie and threw it on the dining chair on the way to the kitchen in his apartment.

"Yes," Abi squeaked, "I'm mean yes," she said in a more even tone.

Her tone didn't go unnoticed. Gav smiled as he opened his refrigerator and pulled out a bottled water. "So?" he asked.

Resigned to stop this nonsense right now, Abi started, "Listen, you sound like a nice guy and all but this just isn't going to happen." There, she said it plainly.

Gav couldn't stop smiling. She was saying one thing but he was pretty sure she wasn't as confident about it as she was trying to sound. "Really?" he asked.

Was this guy a moron? "Yes!" Abi yelled, "Hello," she couldn't hide the sarcasm dripping off of every word, "we don't even know one another."

"I thought that's what we were doing, Abigale." He said it calmly because he knew it would get at her. She seemed like a lady who was used to setting the rules. It was an attractive trait.

How could he be so calm? Didn't he find this whole thing friggin crazy? "Why are you calling me?" She wanted to hit something, she was so mad. "Why would you want to?"

Sitting in his living room, the water bottle on the table beside him, Gav looked around and knew exactly why. "Because, we were promised." It really was very simple.

"Okay, I am hanging up now. Please don't call me again." She almost cried. She was just this side of being scared and that was not an option.

Gav nodded, "I understand." He would just have to try another tactic, "I won't call."

Abi had a feeling she was missing something, "Thank you," she said.

"Goodnight, Abigale," Gav said softly and hung up the phone.

Abi sat there for a long time, staring at her phone, and wondering why on earth she got goose bumps every time the man used her name in that way. By the time she regained her emotional footing, the pizza was cold. Too bad, she ate it anyway.

The rest of the week flew by in a flurry of getting everything just right so Eryn could come back and not have to be too stressed. Luckily, they didn't have an emergency so the paperwork was manageable. She was out of work on time Friday evening and looked forward to her dinner date with her friend, Sheri.

They were going to a place in Kailua so they could get off the base. Sometimes you just wanted to have a good meal somewhere where everybody didn't refer to you as Gunny.

Abi showered and changed and was ready to go by six which was when she was meeting Sheri. They both lived in the barracks but at the opposite ends so they didn't see each other all that often. Sheri worked with one of the squadrons as an administrative specialist. She didn't mind being a "paper pusher" as long as she was around the planes. At least that's what she told Abi.

It wasn't like Abi didn't like the planes; she did. She just liked them a lot more when they landed safely. What a crazy thought!

There was a knock on her door and she opened it to a smiling Sheri.

"Are you ready?" Sheri asked.

Abi nodded, "Yep, just let me grab my purse." She made sure her phone was inside the clutch and they left the room.

The two ladies went down and got into Sheri's car. Abi was glad she didn't have to drive. Sheri made it to the restaurant in under fifteen minutes. They must have got in right before the dinner crowd because they were seated right away.

"Whew," Abi said as they settled into their booth. "We were lucky."

Sheri nodded, "Uh, yeah, I figured at least a thirty minute wait for a table." She picked up her menu.

They ordered salads and Sheri picked the salmon while Abi chose mahi mahi. After they placed their order, they started talking about their week at work. It was good conversation and Abi had every opportunity to talk to Sheri about the crazy situation her parents were putting her in but she couldn't talk about it. Not yet. The more she thought about it, the more nervous she got. That was a conflict in itself; her thinking about it so much.

Who, these days, actually entered into an arranged marriage? No one she knew. No one's parents she knew; not even her own parents. So why did they think she should do it?

"Anyway," Sheri interrupted Abi's zoning, "are you going to tell me what's going on with you?"

Abi laughed, "Nothing, why?"

Shaking her head, Sheri took a sip of her soda, "Really?" She sighed, "Abi you are nothing if not pretty expressive."

It didn't occur to Abi that she was so transparent. "It's just my parents." She was trying to say something without saying something.

Sheri nodded.

"They are just disappointed that I broke up with Bryan," she said the words and hoped her friend bought it.

Her eyebrows raised, Sheri shook her head. "Do they know the jerk cheated on you?"

Abi looked chagrined, "No, I couldn't tell them."

"Abi," Sheri whined, "you need to be honest with them." She tilted her head. "Why would they be upset anyway? I thought you said they never met him."

Her friends were too smart, Abi decided. "They didn't, I think it's just that they want me settled down."

Nodding, Sheri smiled, "I know, our parents seem to want the best for us but don't get that we may have some inkling about what that is."

Laughing, Abi knew Sheri was a keeper, "Yes, let's toast our parents and their good, if not slightly misguided, behavior."

"I'll toast to that," Sheri said and lifted her glass to Abi's.

The two friends enjoyed the rest of their dinner, their parents set aside for now. Sometimes breaking away from your family's expectations could weigh heavy, especially for daughters.

After Sheri dropped her off a while later, Abi plopped down on her bed and stared at the ceiling. Gav hadn't called her back after Monday and she should be relieved, but she was curious. Saying his name over in her head. Gavreel, what an unusual name. Was he unusual in other ways too? Well, that was a silly question. The man was willing to marry her and they'd never met; that doesn't exactly equal a sane person.

Turning over onto her side, Abi lay there for a long time wondering what would happen. Sometime in the darkness, she drifted off to sleep and dreamed of a mysterious man.

Monday morning was a little cloudy which matched Abi's mood exactly. Her weekend was fine, doing errands and catching up on her recorded TV shows. But now she was restless and didn't have a clue why. By the time she got to work, she was ready to blow up. It was weird because Abi was always the calm one, the one who everyone else turned to. She wasn't the prettiest or the skinniest or the tallest or the best dressed, she was just Abi.

Eryn just got back from her honeymoon on Friday and was eager to jump back into work. She should have known Abi would have handled everything just fine. There wasn't anything pressing on her desk, just items to review. The woman was phenomenal. Eryn hoped she was promoted to Master Sgt. soon because she definitely deserved it. Of course, when she saw Abi come in on Monday, she was worried; her Crash Chief didn't look too happy.

"Good morning, sunshine," Eryn said brightly as she poked her head into Abi's office.

Abi was surprised since usually she reported to her OIC's office, not the other way around. "Hi, would you like me to come to your office and we can go over everything?" She wasn't exactly prepared but she could wing it.

Sitting down across from Abi, Eryn shook her head no. "I'm fine here."

Her boss wasn't saying anything so Abi felt kind of uncomfortable. "Um, did you want to go over the papers on your desk?"

"Nope," Eryn said quickly. If she could wait ten years for Chase Johnson to marry her, she could wait a few minutes for Abi to tell her what was wrong.

Abi tipped her head, "Okay, what did you want to discuss, Warrant Officer?" She thought maybe Eryn was in work mode. They made a pact a long time ago that work was work and friendship was friendship.

Eryn got up and shut Abi's office door. When she sat back down, she leaned back in the chair, "Well, I just got back from a very relaxing honeymoon to see that my Crash Chief, and very good friend, looking a little upset."

Abi looked down at her desk, the next week's work rosters were very interesting.

Really? Eryn asked herself, "Well, let's start this way." She leaned forward, "Hello, Warrant Officer Johnson, how was your honeymoon?" Eryn smiled sweetly, "Well, Gunny, it was great, thank you for asking."

There was no need to mock, Abi thought. "Okay, okay, how was the honeymoon?"

It was obvious to Eryn that something was eating at Abi. It may take a while to worm it out of her, but Eryn was pretty confident she could do it. She was about to start her interrogation when there was a knock at the door.

"Enter," Abi said quickly, relieved for the excuse to put off this conversation. She knew she was being a jerk but she just wasn't ready to explain it.

Corporal Wright entered the office with an extremely large bouquet of flowers in his hands.

There were so many roses that Abi couldn't see who was carrying them. She looked at Eryn, "Well, your husband must have enjoyed last week," she winked at her friend.

Corporal Wright put the vase on the Gunny's desk, "Gunny, they are for you," he said quietly.

Eryn watched her assistant and figured out that the guy was mad. She suspected the young man had a little crush on Abi but she didn't think it was serious. Obviously the flowers weren't from him. If Eryn was right, he was mad that he hadn't thought of getting them himself.

"Thank you, Corporal," Abi said. She was shocked. Who would send her flowers? Oh, right. Bryan.

Corporal Wright looked from the flowers to Gunny Rochelle and then back to the flowers. Jerk, whoever he was! With a nod to Warrant Officer Johnson, he left the office and closed the door quietly behind him.

Eryn stood up and looked at the flowers. They were gorgeous! There were several different colors and the arrangement was intricate.

Big expense! She looked at Abi, who was still seated, just staring at the flowers like they would bite her.

"Aren't you going to look at the card?" Eryn asked as she plucked it from the little plastic holder at the mouth of the vase.

Abi shook her head, "They're probably from Bryan." She didn't want to touch them.

Nodding, Eryn sat back down, "Yes, we didn't discuss that, I'm sorry."

Looking out the window, Abi shook her head to dismiss it, "He's an ass."

"Well, if he hurt you, of course he is." Eryn felt it was pretty cut and dried.

It dawned on Abi that she didn't tell Eryn what happened because of the wedding. "The Friday before your wedding, when you and Chase had the dinner," she sighed, "I left my wallet at his place so, when I went to get it, I found him in bed with some skank." She hated using the vile word but it seemed appropriate.

"What!" Eryn said loudly, her face red with anger.

Abi didn't want it to be a big deal, she got over his crap easily enough. "Yes, these are probably his 'I'm sorry' gesture."

Eryn grabbed the card and waited for Abi to nod before she read the writing. Her face looked confused when she handed the card to Abi.

"Who's Gav?" Eryn asked, confused.

What! Abi grabbed the card and read it, her heart pounding fast. Her eyes scanned the words a couple of times before she set the card down on her desk.

Abi,

I'm not calling.

Gav

"Okay," Eryn grinned, "obviously I'm missing something here."

There was way too much information for Abi to start this up at work and she didn't want to talk about it anyway. "Not here," she said firmly.

Eryn nodded, "Okay but you are coming over to the house for dinner tomorrow night and we will discuss this."

She was hearing the boss side of Eryn and knew it was no use to resist. "Yes, ma'am." She smiled and took a deep breath when Eryn got up and left.

The whole day was a test of Abi's patience. She generally thought of herself as laid back and solid, but every time she looked up to the enormous bouquet of flowers on her desk, her mind went crazy. What was he thinking? You didn't send flowers, much less that many flowers to someone you didn't know!

And, of course, every person who passed by or came into her office HAD to comment on them. Ugh! She wanted to punch somebody by the end of the day. When four thirty came around and she was able to go home, she grabbed her bag and high-tailed it out of the office. The flowers stayed at work; she didn't want them to come home and she needed peace.

When she got to her room, Abi threw her bag onto a chair and walked into the bathroom. She was a bundle of nerves and she had to figure out something or she would start screaming. After changing into workout clothes, she went to the gym.

Abi signed in and went to the area with treadmills and elliptical cycles. Maybe an hour working out all her frustration would help. Luckily, there weren't that many people here so she didn't have to wait for a machine.

Getting the settings right, Abi started out on the elliptical. That way she could use both her arms and legs. If she could just exhaust her body, maybe her mind would shut down.

She was on her second mile, twenty minutes later, when she looked up to see Bryan. Oh great, she thought sarcastically. Now what?

Pretending she didn't see him, Abi just kept going. She concentrated on the music in her ears and the display screen. Her speed was increasing, probably due to the rush of wanting to get away from Bryan and his BS. Unfortunately, when she looked up again, he was making his way over to her.

Fantastic! She was sweaty and tired and now she was supposed to make nice with the ass who cheated on her. Could this get any worse?

Bryan walked over to where Abi was working out, "Hi," he said quietly.

All she got was a "hi"? Well, that was just pitiful. Looking at him, she had to refrain from punching him in the face.

"I suppose I deserve your ignoring me." He was nervous because he hoped they wouldn't end up hating each other. She was a nice girl, just not what he wanted.

Abi looked pointedly at him, "Listen, Bryan," she stopped moving so she could talk to him, "I know," she wiped the sweat from her brow, "we were at a point where we were just biding time."

Bryan nodded, she was right. Obviously she was smart enough to figure it out; he felt like a jerk for hurting her.

"But, you could've just broken up with me and that would have hurt less than the cheating." She looked around to make sure no one was close enough to hear their conversation.

He looked at the ground, knowing she was right and hating it. "Yes, you're right."

She figured he needed the closure, and maybe she did too. "Let's just part now and wish each other a good life."

Bryan respected Abi for her honesty. She was a good woman. "Thanks." He smiled and went over to the free weights.

Abi felt better after Bryan walked away. It was like that whole thing was now neatly filed away in her mind, stamped completed. She started the machine up again and go through the rest of her workout feeling better.

Once she was back in her room, Abi showered and got her comfy pajamas on. She sat on the couch, a bag of light popcorn in her hand, no salt, and put in a movie. There was something to be said for closure.

Halfway through the movie, Abi shut off the TV and went to bed. Again, she dreamed of a mysterious man with roses.

Tuesday was better, weather wise, and so was Abi. She got to work and stopped when she opened her office door and saw the flowers. Her whole office smelled of a beautiful perfume from the roses. It was so nice. She sat down at her desk and stared at them. What kind of man sent a woman such beautiful flowers and a playful note to match? Without thinking, she picked up her phone and dialed the number on her caller ID.

Gav was just returning to work from a working lunch with a client, when his phone rang. "This is Gavriil Maslov," he said in his no-nonsense business tone.

Another side to the enigma that was Gav, Abi thought. "Hi, this is Abigale Rochelle." She felt silly for calling.

Stopping, Gav turned away from the door he was about to enter. He didn't want to have a personal conversation inside his place of work. "Well," he smiled, "you must have gotten the flowers."

No games, Abi liked that. "I did and thank you," The words were sticking in her throat for some reason. "Why did you send them?"

His smile faded, "Were they bad? Are you allergic? I didn't ask that, sorry." Now he was embarrassed.

Abi laughed, "No, they are gorgeous," she lifted her fingers to touch the softness of one of the petals, "I was just wondering why you sent them."

Outside on the busy street was not the best place to have a quiet conversation but he would wing it. "Because, you didn't want me to call but I didn't want you to stop thinking about us."

Through the haze of sweetness, Abi started to get upset. "What 'us'? There is no 'us'." she said, the tone of her voice turning colder.

Wrong move, Gav, he thought. "Abigale, I just want to get to know you."

But why? Abi asked herself. She didn't understand him wanting to invest in something that wasn't going to happen. She shook her head in frustration. "Can you promise not to send any more flowers? My co-workers have been asking questions for two days."

"I didn't mean to embarrass you with the gift," Gav said.

Now she felt awful, he was being nice and she was basically saying it was bad. "I love them, they're beautiful. Just don't send anymore, okay?" She hoped he felt a little better.

Gav smiled, every little bit of ground gained, was good. "I will not send you anymore flowers," he nodded to a co-worker as he passed by, "am I still not allowed to call you?"

The man was very frustrating! What did she say? "Can I think about it?"

An inch, but an inch it was. "Yes."

Abi saw one of the Section Leaders at her office and knew she needed to go, "Thank you for the flowers," she said softly.

"You're very welcome, Abi," Gav said slowly and hung up. He walked into the building with a big smile on his face.

Abi answered the Section Leader's question and took a deep breath when he left. That conversation was odd on some levels. She looked at the flowers. Maybe she needed to do some investigating of her own on this Gav guy? Maybe if she knew who he was and what he wanted, she could figure out why he would want to even think about marrying her.

After work, Abi went home and changed, eager to get over to Eryn's house for dinner. She knew there would be an interrogation from Eryn and probably from Chase too. He was like a big brother to her and she loved him for it. They worked together for months before Eryn was stationed here and they developed a good rapport. When she met him, she knew he was someone from Eryn's past but she never let that affect her working relationship with him. Everyone deserved to be treated fairly based on their own merit.

She drove off the base and headed into Kailua toward Eryn and Chase's place and thought about what she just thought. If everyone deserved to be given a chance, then why was she so reluctant to give this Gav guy a chance? Because, she yelled to herself, he's a civilian who lives in New York and he's someone your parents picked out!

By the time Abi pulled into the driveway, she was an emotional mess inside. She checked her appearance in the mirror and hoped she would get through this.

"Hello there, Gunny," Chase said as he came outside the house.

Abi waved, "Hello, Chase." It sounded weird not addressing him with his rank. They decided to do that once he retired.

When Abi walked up to the house, she was enveloped into a hug. She and Chase didn't really hug so it was a little odd at first. When she looked up, she could see Eryn probably filled him in on what was going on. She only hoped he didn't pity her, she was just fine.

They walked in the house and went straight to the kitchen. Eryn was tossing a salad and looked up, "Hey there," she said as she dropped some cherry tomatoes into the bowl in front of her.

"Hello, boss," Abi said sarcastically. She liked that they could tease each other outside of work.

Eryn shook her head, "No boss tonight; this is dinner." She made a flourish of putting the salad on the table.

Yeah right, Abi said to herself. She looked to Chase and smiled, "Are you rested from your honeymoon?"

Chase laughed, that was a loaded question, "Yes," he said with a sly smile to his wife, "I'll finish the chicken on the grill." He walked out the sliding doors to the lanai.

Eryn looked at Abi and was so glad they were friends. "Well, here's some water, let's sit down and you can tell me what the heck is going on."

Faster than Abi thought, but it was good to get it over. "You know most of it," Abi answered as they sat down outside on some chairs.

"Most being the operative word here," Eryn said slowly. She looked at Abi, a gleam in her eye, "Who is Gav?"

Abi looked from Eryn to Chase, who was now standing there looking at her. She hadn't been this nervous since she was called up to the Squadron Commander's office to explain an emergency last year. Actually, that was less intimidating than this was.

There was no point in stalling as it would come out eventually. "Well, it's a long story," she sipped her water, "Why don't we talk about the wedding first. Did you get the pictures yet?"

Eryn snorted, stall tactics? Really? "We will talk about the wedding and I will show you the pictures but I'm asking about Gav." She looked at her husband, "The guy who sent her a huge bouquet of roses with a cryptic note."

"Yeah," Chase frowned, "he made me look bad." He winked at Abi to show he was teasing.

Abi couldn't help it, she smiled. "I told you about Bryan." She looked to Chase to see if Eryn updated him on that little humiliating incident. He nodded so she cleared her throat, "Anyway, when I told my parents we broke up, they kind of went a little nuts."

Eryn looked concerned, "What do you mean nuts?"

Sighing, Abi shifted in her chair, "They were just like, "Abigale, you need to stop fooling around and get married and start having kids" and I was blown away."

Eryn and Chase looked at each other, not sure what to say.

"I never thought of myself as any kind of failure for still being single but they really made me feel that way." She made the admission without realizing she'd been thinking that.

Chase walked over and sat down beside Eryn, "Abi, you are not a failure." He wasn't sure what to say; this was kind of a chick discussion.

Abi nodded, "I know, I'm proud of my career and what I do. I just felt like I was really letting them down."

Eryn could relate all too well, although she always felt she let her father down with her career choice. It was still the feeling of not quiet living up to something. It weighed heavily on you and could keep you from taking chances. She looked at her husband and still felt the pang of regret for her mistakes with him. When he looked at her, she knew he was thinking the same thing.

"Listen," Eryn said as she squeezed Abi's hand, "I understand all too well that part but I don't understand what this Gav guy has to do with it."

The hard part, Abi thought, was explaining something to someone else that she didn't understand herself. "Well, my parents apparently arranged a marriage between us."

The words were out and hung in the air. Abi watched her friends trying to digest her explanation. This whole thing was so archaic that surely everyone would think it was as ridiculous as she herself did.

"I'm sorry," Eryn said after several awkward seconds. She wasn't sure what to say, "They arranged a marriage for you?"

Abi nodded, she didn't really know what else to say. Would her friends think her family was a bunch of fanatics? Would they think she was weird because of what her family did?

Chase looked from his wife to their friend and back again. "That is so cool!" he said loudly. Only they were both looking at him like he lost his mind so he figured that was the wrong thing to say.

Chapter 5

"Have you lost your mind?" Eryn asked loudly. The question was directed at her husband.

Yep, he had said the wrong thing. Chase tried to smile, "Well, I was just thinking it was interesting to have your parents pick someone out for you."

Abi watched Eryn and wanted to laugh. She was almost ready to beat her husband up, she looked so upset.

"Do you think my parents should have picked someone out for me?" Eryn asked Chase.

Chase sobered, "No, Eryn, I think you misunderstood me." He wanted to explain.

Not wanting to start a fight between the newlyweds, Abi interrupted. "Okay, we're not going to argue over this." She calmed her tone when they both looked at her, "I did not come here to dredge up old hurts with you two," she wanted to cry, "I think it's all very out-dated and embarrassing."

Eryn felt bad. Abi was right, Chase's comment opened up an old wound for her and they were supposed to be listening to a friend's problems, not bickering. "I'm sorry," she smiled at Abi, "you are not going to go through with it then?"

That was the million dollar question, "No," Abi said seriously. "I honestly cannot understand how Gav can consider it either."

"Wait," Eryn said, "So Gav knows this is an arranged marriage and he's on board with it?"
Abi nodded.

Chase hoped his question would be okay to ask, "Abi, have you met him?"

"No," Abi said, "I've never even seen a picture of him." She took another drink of water hoping the liquid would help soothe the knot in her throat. "I've never even heard of him before my parents told me."

This was very odd, Eryn thought. "Have you expressed your opinion to your parents?"

When Abi nodded, Eryn was flabbergasted. She, Eryn, had never met Mr. and Mrs. Rochelle and knew from what Abi told her that they were Russian immigrants. But that being the case, this was really an unusual situation.

"So," Eryn said questioningly, "he knew and he sent you flowers?"

This was confusing, even to Abi, and it was happening to her. "Yes, he sent me the flowers because I told him not to call me."

Okay, Eryn thought, the card made sense now. The guy had a sense of humor. Of course Eryn didn't know him but she had to give him some credit for making the usually unflappable Abi look pretty nervous.

Abi watched her friends watch her and felt funny. "I got a call from him and he sounded nice but it's all a little too creepy for me so I told him not to call." She gestured to the grill since the chicken was smoking and laughed when Chase jumped up.

"It's not bad," Chase announced and they all walked into the house to eat.

Once dinner was set and the three of them started to dish it onto their plates, Abi noticed Chase eying her curiously. "What?" she asked.

Chase knew he shouldn't have listened to this; now he was in it up to his ears and he was friggin curious. "I was just thinking that maybe your parents know something you don't."

Abi looked at Chase intently. What did he know? It was hard to not scream out in frustration over this whole thing.

Eryn glared at her husband who put up his hands in surrender.

"I'm just thinking," Chase said tentatively. These two could probably give him a good beating if they joined forces. "Maybe you should get to know this guy and see what your parents apparently see in him before you completely discount it."

For some crazy reason, what Chase said actually made sense to Abi. She nodded and smiled, "Chase, you do have a point."

Eryn was shaking her head, "You are both nuts." She took a bite of chicken, "but I guess it's your call, Abi." She only wanted what was best for her friend. "It may be something you need to do in order to reconcile it in your mind anyway."

Chase snickered, he knew Eryn hated it when he was right. It was something that made her seem cute to him.

Abi ate her dinner with her friends and thought about what they said. Crazy or not, they had a point and, crazy or not, Gav seemed to have some weird sense of commitment to the arrangement.

The Friday after Abi's dinner with Eryn and Chase, she was sitting at her desk going over some leave requests from the sections when her phone rang. "Gunnery Sgt. Rochelle," she answered.

"Abigale," Andrei Rochelle addressed his daughter, "this is your Papa."

Abi couldn't help but smile. Her papa was so cute the way he thought he had to announce himself when he called. She could never mistake his deep voice with the Russian accent that made it sound rough.

"Hi, Papa," she answered.

Andrei missed his little love. She was not home nearly enough and she still did not have a husband. This thought made him sad and kept him up at night. He was not a stupid man; he knew what he asked of his daughter was unusual and went against her wishes. He lived in this country long enough to know that arranged marriages were not practiced regularly and yet his Elena and he thought their daughter would benefit from such a plan. It was clear she was not able to find a man to father her babies and keep her safe.

Andrei held his wife's hand as he talked, "You have spoken to Gavriil?" he asked.

Taking a deep breath, Abi tried to remain calm. "Yes, Papa, I have."

Good, Andrei thought. The boy did what was asked of him. "Do you like him?" he asked his daughter, smiling reassuringly at his wife.

"I don't know him, Papa." She did not want to argue with her father today, "But from what I have learned, he seems like a nice man."

If Andrei knew anything, it was that "nice" didn't make a woman yearn for you. The boy would need some prodding from his parents to make sure he could make Abigale happy. "I see," he said, a plan formulating in his head.

This was too easy, Abi thought. Her father should be demanding she fly to New York and meet Gav but he was acquiescing. Very unusual indeed!

"Well," Andrei said, "I am glad to see you are learning about him. I would like you to meet him soon."

She knew it! "I cannot take time off right now, Papa." It was a lie and she knew it but she did not want to perpetuate her parents' delusion of her marrying a man she didn't know.

Huffing, Andrei was not happy. "Soon, Abigale," he said clearly. "Your Mama loves you," he said and hung up.

Abi stared at the phone and wondered how on earth her parents thought this was logical. She didn't even get to say goodbye before he hung up. Geez, what was going on around here?

After work, Abi drove to the post office to pick up her mail before going to her barracks. She tended to forget to pick it up for days and didn't know why. She was usually so organized but this was one thing that dropped between the cracks.

As usual, her mailbox was jam packed with mail. She threw it in her bag and would sort through it back at the barracks. She just got in her car when her phone rang. It was Eryn.

"You left before I could catch you," Eryn said.

Abi didn't think she forgot to do anything at work, "Did you need me to do something?" she asked. She did not want to make any mistakes at work.

Eryn laughed, "This is not work-related." She played with the pen on her desk, "Your little situation has had my husband and I talking a lot this week."

Oh, Abi's heart sank. She hoped her "problem" didn't somehow strain their new relationship. "I'm sorry," she said quietly.

"Oh no," Eryn said quickly, "it's not like that actually." She looked out the window to see Chase coming around the corner of the building to pick her up. Just seeing her husband made her heart race.

Good, Abi thought, relieved. "Then, what can I help you with?"

This was the tricky part, Eryn thought. She waved Chase into her office when he poked his head into the doorway. She smiled and motioned for him to sit.

"Well," Eryn said hesitating, "we were thinking maybe you should ask this Gav guy to come here." She closed her eyes, waiting for Abi to yell at her for butting in.

Abi stopped and frowned. This was not at all what she figured Eryn would say about this. "Really?" she asked, clearly not believing they were having this conversation.

Eryn nodded victoriously to her husband and wiggled her eyebrows. "Well, we were just thinking that maybe if he came here, then he could be on your turf and maybe he would see that you weren't willing to give up your career for marriage. And maybe," Sshe took a breath, "just maybe he would give up on it and let you off the hook."

Well, sitting in her car, Abi thought the idea had merit. As odd as this all was, they were spending a lot of time contemplating it. "How about I get back to you on that," Abi said.

Her face fell, "Okay," Eryn said. "Have a good weekend."

"You too," Abi responded. Her poor friends...trying to be so nice.

Eryn hung up the phone and looked at her husband. Lord, he was beautiful, she thought. He sat looking at her lovingly, as if she were the only person in the world right now. Watching him watch her made her body come alive; the woman inside of her wanting so badly to love the man in him. She was newly married and wanted all of her friends to be as happy as she was.

Chase stood and walked around Eryn's desk, "No go, huh?" He thought it was a long shot.

Eryn stood and hugged him. He felt so good. "Nope." Her friend would have her support no matter what. That had to be good enough for now.

"Let's go home," Chase whispered, "I have some things I'd like to go over with you."

His tone was unmistakable, "Really?" she asked.

Chase walked his wife out of her office and to his jeep, "Yes, and it may take all night to get it right."

Eryn laughed, "Well, we'll just have to be diligent about getting it right then."

She got into the jeep and watched her husband as he pulled out of the parking lot. She was so thankful for him and their love but she couldn't help remembering the pain of their separation years ago. Her father's meddling almost crushed them both. Now Abi is in the opposite position; her father was trying to bring her together with this guy and, if she didn't do something, would she have the deep-rooted regrets like Eryn had?

Abi drove to her barracks room and shook her head when she thought of what Eryn said. Not only was it ridiculous to ask someone you didn't know to travel like five thousand miles to see you, but it was even more ridiculous to try and prove to them that you were not a person they should marry.

She sat down at her desk and pulled the pile of mail out of her bag. Ugh, this was imposing but it was a necessary evil because of her "mail issue." Most of it was junk mail, thank goodness. She found a letter from her insurance agent saying her premium was going to drop a little. Great! The highlight of her week was getting a lower insurance premium. That was just sad on so many levels.

After tossing a few more credit card offers into the trash she came across a letter. When she looked at the writing, she was shocked by the return address. It said Klara Maslov. Wasn't Maslov Gav's last name? Curiosity getting the best of her, she tore open the envelope and pulled out the letter inside. The handwriting was beautiful, delicate almost. Abi read the letter:

Abigale,

Danette Fogarty

My name is Klara Maslov. This letter must surprise you as it surprises me to write it. You see, my son Gavriil is the man promised to you. I have been told by your parents that this is a surprise to you and I am sorry for any negative feelings you may have right now.

My family comes from the same village as your mother's. Our families are distantly related so we were able to spend time together during our childhood. It was not easy, living in a small Russian village in a time of great change for our country. Our village arranged marriages but your mother's family moved to Yahutsk when she was older so she was free to marry the man she chose, your father. A very wise choice in my estimation.

Abi smiled, she would have to agree with that, her father and mother always seemed very much in love. She looked back down at the paper and read on:

I was promised to a young man in our village, Isaak Maslov. I was very upset that my parents promised me to this boy since I did not know him and yet I was supposed to promise my life to him and have his children as it was my duty. I had very many fights with my parents over their wishes but, in the end, I did what they expected and married Isaak.

I can honestly say I did not love Isaak when I married him. He was only a few years older than I was but he seemed very distant. He was college-educated and worldly compared to me. He was living in the city and moved me there right after we were married.

Oh, it was such a shock, the difference in being in a new environment and having a husband. There were nights when I would cry and cry; for my parents, for my village, for myself. Isaak was very kind, never expecting too much of me. Slowly, I started to adjust to my surroundings. I was able to meet up with your mother since she lived in the city and we were reacquainted. She and your father were my only friends for a long time until I looked at Isaak one day and saw that he, too, was a friend.

For some reason, Abi started crying. The tears were for a young girl who she didn't even know but felt like she could understand.

Your parents were talking about babies and their family and how they hoped Isaak and I would be as happy as they were. I could not see myself as a woman in love but I was sitting at my desk one day and felt my child kick inside my belly for the first time. I knew then, that I loved this baby with my whole heart and his father too. (I don't know why I assumed the baby was a boy, but I did.)

When Gavriil was born and I looked into Isaak's eyes, I knew he felt the same way. We have been married for over thirty years and they have been happy years. Gavriil is our only living child; we have lost two other children since he was born, so we are very protective of him.

After we immigrated to America, we were able to meet up with your parents once again. It was a happy reunion and we were all excited that our children were playing together. Gavriil was about four and you were about three. One day, your mother and I were talking and we were discussing our relationships, as girlfriends do, and the conversation turned to our village. We talked of how the children were promised at a very young age. We both looked at you and Gavriil playing and knew it was destined. So, we agreed to promise you to each other.

Abi's heart was racing and her stomach was churning. She might throw up because the letter made her feel so odd.

We told our husbands of this agreement and they were very skeptical. Although Isaak and I were promised, we agreed that we would not enter into such an arrangement for our children. The matter was dropped after that, as both of you were so young.

Isaak's work took him away, so we moved to Europe for many years. Gavriil was educated abroad in boarding schools and went to college back in America. After he graduated, he decided to stay so we moved back to America as well.

I got in touch with your mother some years back but neither of us discussed this "arrangement" as you were both adults and pursuing your own careers. I feel women should be independent even though I am proud to be a stay-at-home wife and mother.

Last year, Gavriil ended a relationship with his long-time girlfriend from college. She was much like how your mother describes you, driven and adventurous. Admirable traits but she was not the one for Gavriil. Anyway, Isaak and I sat down after seeing our son hurt and decided we should discuss the promise with your parents.

I called your mother and, after the normal pleasantries of catching up, asked if you were married. Your mother is a very smart woman and knew what I was asking. She told me she would speak to your father and see if he agreed to the arrangement now. She called me back a few days later and said they loved you so much that they would enter into the agreement since you had not yet found a suitable husband.

Needing to breath, Abi set the letter down and went to get a bottled water out of her compact refrigerator. This could not be happening. It was literally unbelievable. This was some elaborate practical joke her parents concocted. She drank half the bottle and realized she should probably finish reading the letter before she called them and yelled in outrage.

I told Isaak about their decision and we sat down with Gavriil soon after. He was, as you probably are, very outraged with our behavior. He said that we had no right to meddle in his life and that he was free to choose the person he would spend his life with.

Yes! Abi thought, good for him. She continued reading:

We explained that we loved him enough to find him a match. He said it didn't matter. Then we explained how our marriage was arranged, he did not know of this before, and told him of how our bond in marriage was made. He listened intently and nodded but we knew he did not believe us. He was, after all, a modern thinker. But we told him that, as his parents, and as the ones who loved him the most, wouldn't we know the type of woman he needed to make his life fulfilling?

Now you are not what we expected. You are in the Marine Corps and have chosen to make it your career for as long as that takes. I do not pretend to know about military service the way it is here in America much less how it could be for a woman. My experience was not a positive one as a child but I have spoken to your mother quite a bit and asked her a thousand questions about you. You are, in our opinion, a good match for our son. We ask that you consider him as well since we believe he is the best kind of man: patient, hard-working, kind, respectful, and (at least I think so) very handsome.

Abi was thinking he must be something for his mother to write this letter...

I imagine that you will read this letter more than once, hopefully trying to figure out if your parents, and Gavriil's, are certifiably crazy. If it is crazy to choose the person you think will love your child in the way they deserve to be loved is crazy, then I suppose we are.

We wish you many blessings and hope to meet you at some point in the near future. Gavriil does not tell us what he does to introduce himself to you, only that he has contacted you. As his mother, I hope he was a gentleman and, if not, please let me know so that I may exact a mother's discipline.

Best Wishes,

Klara Maslov

Putting the letter down, Abi stared out the window of her room for a while. When she came up from her contemplation, the sun was very low in the sky. She re-read the letter, as Klara predicted, a few times and every time, she was more fascinated.

Not only was Gav's mother a very interesting person but her story deeply moved Abi. It was probably meant to be that way to convince Abi to agree to this craziness but she was moved anyway.

Reading it again, Abi realized how Gav's name was spelled. How remarkable that was, an unusual name for an unusual man.

When Abi went to bed, she read the letter one more time before turning off her bedside lamp. When she slept her subconscious filled her mind with thoughts of a little boy and little girl playing together.

The next morning, Abi read the letter one more time and decided to call her mother. She had some questions. Dialing the number, she hoped her mother was home.

"Hello," Elena Rochelle answered the phone in a light voice.

Abi smiled, her mother's voice was very soothing, "Hello, Mama," she said.

Elena smiled, "Abigale, how are you, May-ho Sohl-neesh-kah?"

Her mother would not change and Abi was kind of glad for that, "I wanted to talk to you; do you have some time?"

"For you, I always have time," Elena said. She turned off the stove so she would not be distracted by cooking.

Abi held the letter in her hands, kind of nervous about what she was going to say. "I received a letter from Klara Maslov," Abi said, and waited for her mother's reaction.

Knowing the letter was sent, Elena was not surprised that her daughter called. When the Maslov's came to her and Andrei, she knew this would not be easy for their children to understand. Sometimes she herself did not understand why they were trying to do this, but it seemed to feel so right. After many days of praying, Elena agreed that it was for the best. But now, having her daughter seem so unsure, made Elena question whether they were doing this for their children or for themselves.

"She did tell me she was sending it and what it said," Elena explained.

Good, Abi wouldn't have to go into detail, "I was wondering how you felt about all of this."

Not the question she was expecting her daughter to ask, Elena took a moment to think about her answer. "I suppose I feel good knowing that it is destined to be. My faith reinforces the decision and I have chosen to follow my faith."

Abi was torn. She had her own faith and it was not telling her to marry a guy she didn't know because her parents said she should. It would do no good in telling her mother that because this wasn't about fighting; it was about rational understanding.

"Okay," Abi said, getting frustrated, "but how do you KNOW?"

Elena sighed, "Oh, my love," she sat down at the table in her kitchen.

She remembered many hours of Abigale asking her questions such as this. Abigale always wanted to know how everything worked and how everyone felt; it was her inquisitiveness that gave Elena the strength to let her daughter go off into the world.

"There are things in this life we simply will not know." She smiled, remembering her little girl with pigtails. "Who we will meet, who we will love, who we will be," a tear slipped down her cheek, her little girl was now all grown up. "There are more times when we need to go on our faith to see us through."

Sometimes, Abi thought her mother had to be the smartest person in the entire world. "I just don't agree, Mama." She couldn't lie to her parents about something as important as this.

Elena wished her daughter were here in the room with her, this conversation would be better face-to-face, "I know." She smiled when her husband came into the room. He looked at her curiously.

"Then why are you and Papa trying to have me marry this man when you don't know anything for sure?" she asked, her voice rising.

Her heart ached for Abigale. Elena did not want her daughter to know pain. "Because I do, Abigale." She put her hands up to silence her husband. She knew he wanted to talk to Abigale.

Abi shook her head, this was just running around in circles. "I need some time, Mama, to think about this."

Elena heard the defeat in Abigale and was upset. "I understand," she said, the tears streaming down her cheeks now.

"Okay," Abi blew out her breath, "I'll call you and Papa in a few weeks and we'll talk."

There were words Elena wanted to say but she knew they would not be useful right now, "I understand," she said again, softly.

Abi was glad her mother didn't sound mad, "Okay, I love you both. Bye."

"Bye," Elena said and hung up the phone.

Andrei took Elena into his arms and held her while her tears fell. She could not help but think they were responsible for the pain Abigale was currently feeling. She finally looked at her husband and tried to smile. He looked as anguished as she was.

She walked to the stove and turned on the water for tea, "Andrei, did we do the right thing?" she asked.

Andrei wasn't sure but he was willing to follow it through, "She will come around; we just have to wait."

He rubbed his wife's back while she stood at the stove. Even in the kitchen cooking, she was a beauty. His heart still skipped the way it did years ago when he walked into the restaurant and saw the girl she was. They knew they were luckier than most and they wanted their daughter to have the same happiness.

Andrei kissed his wife's cheek, "We'll just have to wait and see."

Abi went for a run after she hung up the phone with her mom. This situation was becoming more complicated by the minute. Her parents' voices were running around in her brain, the words from Klara's letter swam through her mind like a movie trailer; even Eryn's suggestion made its way in and Gav's voice echoed in between it all.

She was hoping they would all get out of there when she got onto the track but it was no use. After two miles she was still in a big bowl of confusion. She was pulled out of it by the sound of a familiar voice.

"Gunny," Corporal Wright said when he caught up to his Crash Chief.

He got to the running track and noticed her right away. She was a pretty woman, her brown hair pulled back. Of course, he remembered how she looked at Warrant Officer Johnson's wedding; her hair swept up in soft waves, the pink dress she wore, making her look very feminine.

"Oh, Corporal Wright," Abi said, trying to make sure her breathing was regulated while she ran.

Cpl. Wright was dropped into the memory of her dancing with him and it was great. She even said he was a good dancer afterward. She seemed happy that night and now she looked upset. He wanted to help but didn't know how.

His stride slowed so it matched hers, "Are you okay?"

Not wanting to discuss anything personal with anyone from work, except Eryn, Abi shook her head no, "Yes, I'm fine."

They continued to run on the track, Abi thinking that she had to get her family and Gav out of her mind, while Cpl. Wright thinking he needed to ask her out.

When they left the track thirty minutes later, neither got what they wanted.

Chapter 6

The next couple of weeks were spent just biding time. Abi went to work, did her job to the best of her abilities, and even went out a few times with friends. At no time did she ever feel settled or really happy. It was like she was waiting for something to happen and had absolutely no idea what that would be.

At work, she watched Eryn like a hawk. Something was going on with her boss and Abi was happy for her. Eryn came into work and looked really pale most mornings. By the afternoon she was her old self and work went on as usual. It didn't take a degree to figure it out but Abi didn't want to pry anyway. Eryn would tell her soon enough about what was going on.

On a Wednesday, Abi was called to the OIC's office. She knocked and entered quietly since Eryn was on the phone. She took a seat across from the desk and waited.

"Yes, sir," Eryn said. She smiled at Abi then turned her attention back to the phone call. She hung up a few minutes later and sighed.

Abi nodded to the phone, "A problem?" She didn't particularly care for them, but they were part of the job.

Eryn shook her head, "Not really." She signed a set of papers Cpl. Wright gave her earlier. "I'll just be glad when our new NCOIC comes in." She looked around absently, "What is his name again?" she asked Abi.

Smiling, Abi looked at the notebook she kept with her at meetings with Eryn. They were notes to remind her about what they discussed. "Um," she scanned the pages, "A Master Sgt. Phillips." She looked at Eryn, "Do you know him?"

"No," Eryn said. "I'll have to call Miramar and speak to Warrant Officer Thompson over there and get the info on him."

Abi agreed. It was good to get a sense of a new NCOIC before they came on board if you could. He would hold a key position in Crash Crew and it wasn't like you could just ask someone to leave if they didn't jive with your current staff. The Marine Corps expected you to work with what you had and be productive.

"I agree," Abi said and jotted down some notes. "Is there anything you want me to do for his office before he gets here?" She wanted to make their new staff member welcome.

Eryn smiled, "You are very considerate, you know that?" Her friend was definitely a "giver."

Snorting, Abi looked away, "Nope, I am not. I just don't want him to bust my chops when he gets here." She smiled brightly.

It wasn't difficult to see Abi was trying to deflect attention away from herself. It was a shame that she didn't see how great she was. Well, Eryn would just have to remind her of it a little more often.

"Is that all you needed?" Abi asked. She still wasn't sure if this was a casual meeting or they had a specific agenda. "Or are you going to tell me the good news?"

Eryn's head snapped up. Oh, she thought, her friend was very perceptive. "What good news?" she asked innocently.

Laughing, Abi glared at her friend and boss. Well, the point would be addressed when Eryn and Chase wanted it to be. She'd bide her time and be nice until then. "Yeah," she stood up, "will that be all, Warrant Officer Johnson?"

Waving her hand in dismissal, Eryn laughed while Abi left her office. How did she get so lucky to have someone like Abi working with her?

The rest of the day was spent getting a training schedule set for next month. Abi worked closely with the Gunnery Sgt. in Training to make sure everyone was up-to-date with current requirements. It could be tricky when dealing with a variety of classes and working that in with the crews' leave requests, etc, but they wrapped up on time and Abi was satisfied with her progress.

She left Crash Crew and went to pick up her Dress A's at the dry cleaners. They were having a dinner next week for a Gunnery Sgt. in their squadron who was retiring so she needed to have her uniform in order. After that, she stopped off at the post office.

For some reason she remembered to stop there a few times a week now. Maybe she was hoping for another letter from Gav's mother? Since the talk with her mother, she hadn't heard from any of them. That shouldn't have upset her but it kind of did. If they all wanted her to marry him so badly, why weren't they pestering her more?

When she got back to her room, she put her dry cleaning away in the closet and sat down at her desk. The letter from Klara was lying there and she picked it up. She probably had it memorized by now; she'd read it so much over the last couple of weeks. But what did it really mean?

Abi stared out the window of her room. The mountains were in the distance, looking so lush and majestic. They were there for thousands of years and took on whatever Mother Nature threw at them without blinking. How awesome to be that solid! She wouldn't be able to endure like that; she was sure of it.

Hearing her phone ping, she looked down and saw she had an email. She frowned when she saw the email address of the send. It was Gav. Did she open it? After debating with herself for a few minutes, she figured she should open it and see what he said. Maybe he was backing down and letting her know she was off the hook? She hit the button and opened it up.

Dear Abigale:

I was just told that my mom sent you a letter in the mail. I want to apologize for the bombardment you are having to endure from our parents. It is not fair to you to have to feel pressured. I have asked my mother to refrain from sending you any letters unless you ask her to. She has agreed and apologized for any embarrassment she has caused you. I feel her intentions were good, just not what you need right now. I questioned myself, wondering if you would even accept an email from me at this point. I have tried to honor your request of no calling but, I have to admit, it has not been easy. I find I like hearing your voice. I understand we are strangers but that can be remedied if you choose. Again, I apologize for my mother's actions.

Sincerely,

Gavriil

Abi read the email and smiled. It was actually very sweet of him to write it. He was not happy with his mother's letter but that was really the one thing out of this situation that Abi appreciated. She figured she owed him a response at least.

Opening up her email on her laptop, she hated writing emails on her phone. She thought about what to say before she started typing:

Gavriil:

First, do you like Gavriil or Gav? Just wondering. Second, thanks for being worried about my reaction to your mom's letter. I have to say, I was a lot more than surprised when it came.

Honestly, I have read it over and over and I think I can understand what she was saying. (Her handwriting is beautiful, by the way.) Everyone has been nice enough to give me space the last couple of weeks but I'm still really leery of this whole thing. You're right, we're strangers. I don't see how we can overcome that. I live in Hawaii and you live in New York. What do you do there? You have to know I'm in the Marine Corps but I don't know what you do. Don't apologize for your mom, if there is one thing I can be sure of, it's that she loves you very much. That, at least, we have in common. My parents have always loved me so much. Thanks again.

Abi

Pushing the send button, Abi felt a little better. He seemed like a nice enough guy but this was just too weird. She closed her laptop down and went to get ready for the gym. A little work out was in order right now.

An hour later, Abi was on the cool down cycle of her treadmill. She did a little bit on the bike, some free weights, and finished up with a nice run. Sweat was pouring down her forehead and she was sure she looked like a drowned animal. The gym was not meant for looking pretty, thank goodness.

When she got back to her room, she made a salad and ate it while she was watching a TV show she liked. It was a good day all in all and she was nice and tired. After she took a shower and got ready for bed, she logged back into her email. She told herself that she was not checking it to see if Gav answered her email from earlier. It was a lie! That is exactly what she was doing.

The email came up and there were a few things in her inbox. Scanning them, a few were sales ads, one was from a friend who got out of the Corps and moved to Kansas, and the last one was from Gav. Abi opened it first.

Abigale:

I prefer Gav since Gavriil is not a common name and people mispronounce it all the time. Not to mention, it has 2 I's in it, who does that? Anyway, Gav is fine. Do you like Abigale or do you prefer Abi? Turnabout is fair play, young lady.

I'm relieved my mother's letter didn't offend you. I didn't read it but she told me she explained the reason why our parents decided to go into this "arrangement." Yes, she loves me a lot and I am very thankful for all the support my parents have given me throughout my life. She told me that your parents love you very much and that is a good thing. I've met too many people with "parent issues."

To answer your question about my employment, I am unemployed and living off the state at this time. I am hoping to get off of welfare and into a group home soon... Gotcha, I am just teasing. Sorry.

I am actually in finance and work at the same bank your dad works at. I wouldn't say I'm his boss but I do oversee some departments. He's a very hard worker and really likes his job. My parents were probably disappointed that I didn't follow my father into the diamond business; he's a broker in New York, but I really wanted to do something with finance. C'est la vie!

Let's see, I was educated in mostly private schools in Europe but decided I wanted to go to college in the US. I graduated, with honors, from Cornell and got out and found myself a job. I am well aware that you are in the military and was meaning to ask you about your job. Are you a firefighter? My parents were very vague about that, probably because they didn't understand it. I would love to hear about anything you want to share about your life. That way we can be a little bit more than just strangers.

Gav

Closing out her email, Abi sat back and smiled. He was a smart ass! She never would've pegged him as that. Cornell? That was a little intimidating. She had an Associate's Degree she earned online and was really happy with it. How on earth did their parents think this would be a good fit? The guy was a five star restaurant and she felt like an IHOP. Bad analogy, Abi, she told herself. When she was in bed a few minutes later, she was relieved she didn't agree to this marriage thing.

The next night, when Abi got back to her room, she decided to email him back. There was no big underlying reason; it was just something she wanted to do.

Gav:

Thanks for the clarification. I do go by Abi most of the time. Only my parents only call me Abigale and I like the way it sounds with their Russian accent. I laughed at the 2 I's comment. You definitely had me going at first with your comment about the group home, nice. Do you really like banking? I know my dad always seemed to but I can't think about being in a suit behind a desk all day. But then again, I am in a flight suit behind a desk most days so touché.

I am a Gunnery Sergeant which equates to an E-7, E means enlisted and 7, well, you're a smart guy so you can figure it out. My job is in MOS 7051, Crash, Fire, Rescue. MOS stands for

Military Occupational Specialty. A lot of acronyms in my line of work so make sure you ask if you don't recognize something. Being around it all the time, I forget that civilians don't always know what they are.

Crash, Fire, Rescue is pretty self-explanatory too. We are responsible for the safety of all aircraft on the airfield. We are cross-trained with the structural firefighters and some of the guys like that side but I'll stick with the aircraft, thanks. I am currently a Crash Chief so I oversee the crews that work the airfield. There are two of them, Section 1 & Section 2. They do 24 hour shifts during the week and 48 hour shifts on the weekend. I personally work from 7-4:30pm Monday thru Friday but I'm on call all the time. I have an NCOIC (Non-Commissioned Officer in Charge) and an OIC (Officer in Charge) above me at work. My OIC is a good friend of mine actually so that makes it more fun at work.

Before now, I've been a Section Leader, an Administration Clerk, I was the head of the Training Department, and worked on the crews too. You have to work your way up and it's best to do it on the job. My job can be full of a lot of paperwork but there are always training days and ways to break that up. I hope I've explained it well enough because it can be a little complicated. Thanks for asking about it.

I went to public schools and worked on my Associate's Degree in business while serving so I don't really have a clue about what you went through in college. This life fits me very well.

I will not expect a reply, but if you email me again, I'll answer the best I can.

Thanks,

Abi

Abi re-read the email before she pushed send. The last two sentences kind of said it all and she wasn't sure if she should change them. She was telling him that she wouldn't change her life but then said she would email him back if he wanted. Nothing like sending a mixed message Abi! She pushed the send button and would see what happened.

A few days later, Abi was getting ready for a physical training session with her sections. It was a Saturday so they normally didn't do it, but there were some members of her Sections that thought they could get away with misbehaving. It was times like this when she felt more like a parent than a superior. What was the saying...a few bad apples?

She arrived at Crash Crew at six o'clock and went into her office. The Sections were supposed to be in formation at seven so she had some time to kill. After answering some work-related emails, she responded to a few and jotted down notes for when she came into work on Monday. She was looking over some of her phone messages when she saw someone out of the corner of her eye.

"Gunny," Staff Sgt. Perry said inside the Crash Chief's office doorway.

Abi nodded, "Yes, what's up, Staff Sgt.?"

The Staff Sgt. pointed toward the bay, "I think just about everybody is here."

Putting her notebook in the drawer, Abi got up and followed the Staff Sgt. out to where the Sections were getting into formation.

Abi walked over to the center of the bay with Staff Sgt. Perry on her left and the other Section Leader, Gunnery Sgt. Richards to her right. The three of them stood there in the middle of the bay and didn't say anything.

It was Abi's understanding that the awareness of authority went a long way towards gaining the respect of your troops. The Marine Corps made her responsible for these men and women and it was her job to teach them the right way to represent themselves, their unit, and the Corps in the most appropriate manner. She was pretty lucky; she heard about other women not being taken as seriously in their own chosen careers and she never had to address that.

At six fifty-eight, Gunnery Sgt. Richards yelled, "Troops, formation!"

The Sections divided up and stood in formation, Abi waiting for the Section Leaders to tell her they were ready. Each Section was made up of about forty Marines. There was an Assistant Section Leader and Section Leader responsible for making sure the Sections ran well.

Abi watched quietly as the Section Leaders got their Sections to form into lines of four. The Asst. Section Leaders stood in front of the troops and the Section Leaders stayed standing next to Abi.

When the Section Leaders both nodded to her, she spoke up, "Good morning," she said loudly. "We are here today for some additional team-building exercises."

Staff Sgt. Perry tried not to smile at the Crash Chief's choice of words. She was putting it nicely.

"Since," Abi started walking between the two Sections as she talked, "some of you have decided that you don't want to follow the rules, we need to get you back on track."

It was pretty obvious that the Sections were not happy to be here. Abi and the Section Leaders planned this particular PT session when Gunny Richards' Section was off since it was some of his guys who were busted for disorderly conduct. It was a really sucky thing to be called in on your weekend off and, even though she felt a little bad for those who didn't break the rules, this was part of correcting problems.

She got back to the front of the Sections and stood between the Section Leaders again, "Our friends at flight operations were kind enough to let us do an FOD walk this morning." She could see the looks of disappointment and had to refrain from smiling. She had a mean streak and it was coming out this morning. "You know the drill, lines of five, go slow and if it doesn't grow, it must go."

FOD stood for Foreign Objects & Debris. The runways had to be checked regularly to make sure nothing could impede flight operations. Debris getting into a multi-million dollar piece of equipment did not look good. Normally flight operations handled it but today it was Crash Crew's pleasure.

The Section Leaders stepped up and directed the troops to file out and walk to the end of the runway. Abi followed the group. She listened to the whining and smiled.

The Sections were about a third of the way down the runway when Abi saw Eryn walking toward them. She wondered if something was wrong; Eryn knew about this exercise since Abi ran it by her before calling the formation.

"Good morning," Eryn said when she got close to Abi.

Abi smiled, "Good morning, Warrant Officer Johnson," she said formally.

Eryn nodded toward the Sections, "How are they doing?"

Now Abi couldn't help but smile, "They are motivated, ma'am."

Laughing, Abi looked across the airfield. She loved it out here. Spending this many years in this job, she would be crazy if she didn't. It was quiet now. Flights were suspended while the troops walked the runway looking for debris. When she looked back, she could see Eryn watching her closely.

Eryn didn't normally intrude on the training to do with the troops. She had Abi to do it for her and her Crash Chief did a great job. When she got up this morning, she wanted to come over to see how it was going and offer her support.

"Is there something in particular you needed this morning, ma'am?" Abi asked Eryn. Not that Eryn couldn't see what they were doing, it was just not like Eryn to show up.

Oh, her friend could peg her, Eryn thought. The woman was smart, which was a good thing, except when it was when Eryn wanted to be sneaky.

Smiling, Eryn motioned Abi to follow her back toward the crash barn. "Let's walk," she said.

Immediately, Abi scanned her mind, thinking she was going to be counseled for something. She could count on one hand how many times she'd been counseled by a superior during her career. It was a point of great pride that Abi did things right the first time; it was the way she operated and didn't want a hiccup at this stage in her career.

The women started to walk back to the Crash Barn. They would glance over at the Sections as they made their way down the runway, making sure they were following orders.

When they were inside the Crash Barn, Eryn turned to Abi, "You know I got the list of Gunnies eligible for promotion this year and you're in the zone." She waited to see Abi's reaction.

When you were promoted, you started your "time in grade" and earned service with your performance. After so many years, you were then eligible for promotion as long as you met the requirements for service. Abi knew she was close but didn't take too much stock in it.

Now, Eryn was telling her she was eligible and she felt excited and sick at the same time.

"Wow," Abi said and looked at her friend.

Smiling, Eryn said, "Don't be so excited," in a sarcastic tone. Being promoted was one of those things that you hoped for but were never guaranteed. Abi was a great Marine and she excelled in her job; Eryn felt sure that she would do well.

Abi tilted her head, "You know what I mean, it's my first time being eligible so it's a long shot," she didn't want to be cocky about it.

"Hey," Eryn said, thinking she should change the subject, "have you made any decisions about the situation your parents set up for you?"

That was one way to put it, Abi thought. "Actually, I've been meaning to tell you about that."

Eryn was intrigued, "Really?" She looked back at the airfield and saw the group was still walking. "Do you have time to steal away to my office for a few minutes?"

Nodding, Abi gestured for Eryn to precede her. She calculated that the Sections should be back in the Crash Barn in about thirty minutes or so. Then they would be treated to a nice five mile run.

The women went into Eryn's office and sat down on the sofa near the door.

As soon as they were seated, Eryn used her demanding voice, "Spill!" she said.

Abi shook her head, the woman had no patience. "Well," she wasn't sure where to start, "I got a letter a couple of weeks ago from Gav's mother."

"Now, Gav is the man you were promised to, right?" Eryn asked so she had the facts straight.

Nodding, Abi went on, "Well, her name is Klara and the letter was really touching." Abi remembered the way Klara's story pulled her in emotionally. "I guess my mother gave his mother my address and she thought she should explain."

Wow, Eryn thought, she didn't envy Abi in her situation. "Did she explain?" Eryn asked.

"Believe it or not, she kind of did," Abi said. "It was weird but, in the end, it didn't matter." She looked out the window for a second then back to Eryn, "I called my mom and told her I wouldn't go through with it."

Eryn held her friend's hand, "So it's decided then." She made it a statement.

Although the whole thing was odd to Eryn, she and Chase talked about it and they could see some valid points in the tradition of it. Not that they would do it, but they would support Abi no matter what she decided.

Abi nodded. "Yes, but then he emailed me a few days ago and we've been emailing back and forth a little bit."

It wasn't difficult for Eryn to recognize that Abi was interested in this Gav guy. Her friend's face and demeanor changed when she spoke of the emails they exchanged. She was pretty sure that Abi didn't recognize it yet herself so Eryn decided to keep quiet for the time being. Instead of responding, she just smiled and nodded.

Thinking it was kind of embarrassing to talk about this with anyone, Abi felt flushed, "He's pretty funny although his job doesn't seem that interesting. He works at the same bank my father works at. He got his degree at Cornell so he's smart. You know, he asked about what I do which kind of blew my mind." She stopped talking when she saw Eryn smiling wide. "What?" she asked her friend.

"Nothing," Eryn shrugged, "I was just listening to you list the good qualities you see in Gav."

Oh, she did sound ridiculous, at least to herself. Abi shut up right away. "I'm sorry," she said, looking down into her lap.

Smiling, Eryn realized her friend was starting what she did so many years ago; she started feeling something and she was scared out of her mind because of it. "No," Eryn squeezed Abi's hand. "You don't have to be sorry."

They heard noises down the hall which meant the sections were coming back. Abi knew she had to get back to her troops. "Thanks," she said and got up.

"Anytime," Eryn answered and stayed sitting on the couch for a while after Abi left, thinking about her friend.

Two hours later, Abi walked into her room and sat down in the chair. She was sweaty and tired but it was a good run. The Sections did not appreciate it at all but that couldn't be helped. Maybe some of the junior troops will think first the next time they want to get rowdy and get into a bar fight.

After a shower and a fresh change of clothes, Abi sat down at her desk and opened up her laptop. She walked around her room, glaring at the machine and not wanting to be so curious about whether or not Gav emailed her. Damn it, why was she so curious?

She logged into her email and checked her inbox. There were more sales emails, ick, so she deleted those. Another email from her friend back east who was asking about getting together in a few months when she was planning a vacation to Hawaii.

She smiled when she read an email from Katherine's assistant, Suzanna. It was about Katherine's show in a month. She was bummed that she didn't think she could make it but thought it was very sweet for Katherine to remember. Maybe Emma would be going; Abi made a note to call her soon and catch up.

Finally she saw an email from Gav. Before she even opened it, her pulse kicked up. Clicking on the line, she waited for the message to pull up.

Abi:

I cannot pretend that I didn't understand your email. I suppose we both have a lot to think about. Reading your emails makes me start to understand the person you are rather than hearing about your qualities through my parents. But really, what would you like out of this? If you're interested in just a pen pal, I'm not sure I would fit the bill. I've not even met you and I like you. Maybe I'm being a little delusional, just falling in line with what our parents are asking us to do. I'm well-educated and I think, a pretty practical person. I have a savings account, a comfortable life, a retirement plan, all the normal things that people have, and yet, I'm willing to consider this completely irrational idea. Why aren't you?

Sure, we're from different worlds on some levels. But on some basic levels, we are exactly the same. We both have parents who immigrated to America and worked very hard to give their children every advantage they could. I know we haven't spoken about religion but I'm guessing you have similar beliefs. As far as the rest, I guess I'm willing to take a leap of faith and see how we can work on that. Again, why aren't you?

Please, I ask that you just try to get to know me and see if you could consider this. I'll be honest, when I check my email and see something from you, I start smiling. When we spoke, even though it was briefly, I found I liked the sound of your voice. I asked my mother to refrain from showing me any pictures of you. I didn't want a preconceived notion of how you looked to influence my getting to know who you are on the inside.

Just think about it.

Best Wishes,

Gav

Abi read the email three times, then logged out of her computer. She just sat there at her desk and wondered about Gav asking her the questions. Should she risk getting to know a stranger? He had some valid points but...but what?

She couldn't think straight, she needed some advice.

Picking up the phone, Abi dialed Eryn's home number and she smiled when Chase answered.

Chase was walking past the phone when it rang at the house, "Hello," he said lightly.

"Chase, it's Abi." She thought her own voice sounded funny.

Smiling, Chase cradled the phone while he picked up a screwdriver he left on the table. Eryn would not like seeing it laying there. "Hey, what's up?" He stopped because Abi sounded a little off.

A tear made its way down Abi's cheek and she swiped at it, "Is Eryn there?" she asked.

Okay, Chase thought, something was up. "Sure," he looked around for his wife, "hold on."

Chase walked around the house quickly. He didn't handle upset women very well. It was bad enough he was forced into the middle of this thing with Katherine and Mitch; he didn't think he could handle another ball of drama with Abi.

"Eryn!" he called out when he didn't see her right away.

Walking into the hallway, Eryn looked at her husband. He looked like a deer caught in headlights. "What's wrong?" she asked and hoped Katie was okay.

"It's Abi," Chase whispered and handed her the phone.

Oh, Eryn thought. She must be upset. Eryn hoped it wasn't because of their conversation this morning. "Hello, Abi," she said softly when she put the phone to her ear.

Abi needed someone, "Can I come over?" she asked her friend without preamble.

Eryn looked at Chase and hoped he was okay with her choice, "Yes, come over."

Relieved, Abi told her friend she would be there soon and hung up. She made it out to her car and off the base in record time.

Chapter 7

Abi sat on the sofa in Chase and Eryn's living room feeling like a fool. Why did she come running over here like a little girl? Eryn told her to come and she made it over here like the devil himself was after her. Chase sat in a chair opposite her with a look of pity on his face.

"I'm sure you have some idea of what's going on?" Abi looked at him and tried to fight off the stupid tears that wanted to fall.

Chase looked in the direction of their home office; Eryn was sitting in there reading emails. She gave him the gist of the situation this morning when she returned from Crash Crew. He was kind of surprised that Eryn was so involved with this. He would've thought with getting phone calls from Mitch and Katherine over the last couple of days, that this thing with Abi wouldn't bother her so much. But, Chase should've known his wife would be in it; she was a caring person and defended her loved ones at all costs. That was one of the millions of things he loved about her.

Abi was wondering if her friend was judging her. "Do you have an opinion?" she asked him with a tone of accusation in her voice.

It was easy to see Abi was challenging him and he wouldn't rise to the bait. "Abi," he leaned forward and rested his forearms on his knees, "my opinion doesn't matter here," he smiled at her surprised look, "it only matters what you think."

No wonder Eryn married him, Abi thought. She loved Chase in a brotherly way and he never ceased to prove how much of a gentleman he was. She nodded to him and leaned back into the sofa.

Eryn came out of the office and stood in the doorway looking from her friend to her husband and back again. "Whoa!" she said in a breathy voice.

"I know, right?" Abi said to Eryn. This was so confusing.

Slowly, Eryn walked over and sat down beside Abi on the couch. "No," she shook her head, "I don't know so why don't you tell me?"

Blowing out a breath, Abi shored up her resolve, "I think he's really nice and funny and charming but I can't see how this could possibly work."

Smiling, Eryn looked at her husband. "Tell me how you feel, not what you think." She directed the question to Abi.

Chase nodded, that seemed to be a problem with couples, including them at one time. Everyone always "thought" about it but didn't act on what they were "feeling."

"I feel..." Abi started, then she stopped.

She could feel Eryn and Chase's eyes on her. There was no judgment in them, thank goodness. She knew they were here for support.

Clearing his throat, Chase smiled at his friend. "Now, I don't know you like Eryn does, we didn't really do "girl" things when we worked together," he tried to look innocent to stave off his wife's glare, "but, I respect you, Abi."

Abi wanted to cry for another reason now, "Thanks," she answered.

"And," He wanted to make his point, "I know that you are a rational person and if you are this confused, then there's some credence in it." He looked at his wife, "Don't let miscommunication or doubt stand in your way."

Eryn watched her husband explain and was thankful that she loved him so much. She hoped Abi listened to them and learned from their mistakes.

"Now," Eryn stood and grabbed Abi's hand to pull her up, "get up and go home so I can thank my husband for being so brilliant." She wiggled her eyebrows.

Newlyweds, Abi thought, what a great couple they were. "Ok." She looked at Chase and winked, "be sweet."

Chase nodded, "Always am."

Snorting, Eryn walked Abi to the front door, "He has to be or I'll kick his butt."

Abi hugged her friend, "Thanks."

Eryn and Chase stood by their front door and watched Abi walk out and get into her car. After she pulled out they went back inside.

Chase had to ask, "Um, was there any resolution found there?"

Oh, this poor man, Eryn thought. He still didn't know how women worked. "There will be," she answered and took his hand. She'd take him upstairs and show him how to "compromise."

Abi spent the rest of Saturday and all of Sunday wondering what she should do. Should she email Gav? Should she call him? Should she ignore him? The questions ran through her head like one of those digital banners you see at a bank or something. She didn't sleep well at all and couldn't focus on anything. It was very disconcerting and made Abi feel like she was falling apart emotionally.

At eleven o'clock on Sunday, she decided she wouldn't sleep until she did something. Considering it was like eight in the morning on Monday in New York, she figured she better just send an email. He was probably getting ready for work and wouldn't even read it until after he was home.

"Just do it," she said to herself and threw the covers off her legs.

Stomping over to her desk, she opened up her laptop and logged on. The machine seemed to take forever to load. She sighed when her email finally came up.

Gav:

I'm sorry it took me so long to respond. I've spent all weekend mulling over your emails and our situation. I am not interested in a pen pal, by the way. I like you too. You're funny and intelligent and everything but I cannot get my head around some pretty big issues having a relationship with you would bring up.

First, in case you haven't noticed, but I know you have, I live in Hawaii and you live in New York. If you've learned anything about me, it's that my career is VERY important to me. I've spent sixteen years in the Marine Corps and I have every intention of staying, at least, to twenty years so I can retire. But, depending on what opportunities are available, I can't even guarantee that.

Second, you know me by my emails and a few, short, phone calls. How could we possibly make time to get to know one another in person? I have some leave (vacation) available, but I don't think it's enough for us to take time to really get to know each other. Plus, me coming to New York, I would feel obligated to spend time with my parents, then the added pressure of meeting your parents. Just thinking about all of that gives me anxiety issues.

I guess, we should just say "It's been nice," and let it go then. Even typing the words, reinforces my resolve here. I wish you all the best and hope you find the right person for you.

Please take care,

I'll call my parents and tell them.

Abi

After pushing the send button, Abi went to bed. She was exhausted emotionally and fell asleep right away. Her dreams were about a man holding his hand out to her and then slipping away.

When the alarm went off the next morning, she could feel the remnants of tears in her eyes.

Work was the usual, chaotic Monday. Abi dug in and got some issues resolved with the Sections. She held a meeting regarding the new training schedule and worked on a project Eryn assigned to her.

At three thirty, there was a knock on her door. Without looking up, Abi said, "Enter." She figured it was one of the Section leaders.

"Gunny Rochelle," a very male voice said.

Abi looked up into the most gorgeous brown eyes she'd ever seen in her life. "Yes," she said softly, then berated herself for sounding like a teenage girl.

The man walked over and put out his hand, "Hi," he said and waited for her to put her hand in his, "I'm Bill Phillips, your new NCOIC."

"Oh," Abi said and gave herself a mental kick. This is your new boss, she said to herself. "Yes, Master Sgt. How are you?"

Bill smiled. His new Crash Chief was well respected. He didn't think they would have any problems working together. "Fine, I just wanted to stop in before I come into work next week."

Was he starting next week already? How time flies. "Yes, is there anything I can do for you today?"

Looking at Gunny Rochelle, he got the impression that she was a little nervous. Interesting. "No, Gunny, I'm fine." He looked around her office. Practical. "I'm settling into the barracks and finding my way around."

Abi nodded, "Oh, you won't be too far from me then." She wanted to kick herself again for sounding like some little love-struck teenager.

"You live on base?" Bill asked.

He had the deepest eyes, "Uh, yes," she answered.

Nodding, Bill smiled, "Maybe we can get a drink or dinner some time."

"I'd like that, Master Sgt.," she answered and tried to calm her nerves.

He stood and offered his hand again, "Thanks, Gunny," he said with a smile and left the office.

Moonlight & A Marine

Wow, Abi thought when she sat back down. Her new boss was going to look that good and take her out for a drink? Too weird for words!

It took Abi a while, but eventually she was able to get re-focused on the task at hand and finish her work. She was walking down the hall to leave when she saw Eryn's door was still open. Thinking she should stop and comment on their new NCOIC, she entered. Eryn didn't see her because she was turned away.

"I'm looking forward to meeting you too," Eryn said and turned to see Abi in her office. Her heart stopped! "Uh, I have to go, thank you," she said hurriedly and hung up her phone.

Abi tipped her head, "Are you okay?" she asked Eryn, "You look a little surprised."

Eryn waved her hand to blow it off, "I was just finishing up some phone calls and thought everyone else was gone." She put on a smile, "What's up?" she asked.

"Did you meet our new NCOIC?" Abi asked as she sat down in the chair facing Eryn.

Eryn started organizing her desk so she could leave for the day, "No I didn't," she smiled at Abi, "but I hear he's a real looker."

Abi looked at Eryn, shocked, "Uh yes." She was surprised Eryn noticed. "He's a smooth talker too."

"Really?" Eryn asked, the papers forgotten. "Why do you say that?"

Shrugging, Abi started to blush. "He just said we should get a drink or dinner."

That didn't sit well with Eryn. Not that Abi wasn't fully capable of handling herself, Eryn just didn't want to have an issue at work. When she thought about it, though, she started to laugh. That's exactly what she and Chase did!

Watching her friend laugh, Abi was confused. "Did I miss something?" she asked.

"No," Eryn said and grabbed her bag, "I've spoken to him on the phone but I'll be sure to watch him closely."

Oh, Abi thought, that's who she was talking to.

The women left the building and stood by their cars for a few minutes talking. They promised to do something fun soon.

When Abi got back to her room, she opened her email right away. Why was she so curious? Gav probably didn't even answer her. Then why did her breath hitch and her heart pound when she saw an email from him in her inbox? Not worrying about anything else, she clicked on the line and waited for the email to open.

Abi:

I apologize for my email. It may come out sounding harsh because I cannot put inflection in the words.

Who said you had to give up the Marine Corps? Who said you had to move to New York? Who said you had to meet my parents?

I don't see this the same way you do.

Gav

Abi read the email and got madder with each word. That's it? He just asks a bunch of questions and stops? If she was completely honest with herself, she would ask if she was pissed because he asked the questions or because she knew the answer; no one did.

Sitting back in her desk chair, Abi stared out the window and wondered how this all got so complicated. "What the hell!" she yelled to the empty room.

The next few days were spent getting the office ready for their new NCOIC. Abi laughed at the reaction he was having on some of the people she worked with. Not only had he been sweet to her, he was very nice to everyone he met and the subject of a lot of conversations. It would be tough to live up to that for her. Not that she was a jerk, she was just pretty stringent with her people. They were in the Marine Corps, not the Boy Scouts and the rules were there for a reason.

By Friday, she was ready with all the plans to welcome their new NCOIC aboard. She even helped one of the Corporals assigned to Admin paint his office. Not really necessary but she thought it would be nice.

As she got her office put to rights before the weekend, she heard someone at her office door. "Enter," she said automatically.

Corporal Wright opened the door and stepped into Gunny Rochelle's office. It was after hours so he figured he could muster up the nerve to speak to her. "Gunny," he said quietly.

Abi looked up and smiled, "Yes, Corporal," she wondered why he was still here, everyone else working on days was long gone.

"Um," Corporal Wright said and cleared his throat. He was so nervous! "I was wondering if you would like to have dinner with me and see a movie?"

The question surprised her, she wasn't expecting to be asked on a date, much less by one of the guys who worked with her. "Uh, Corporal, I don't think that would be appropriate but I thank you for taking the time to ask."

He knew it would be a long shot, but it never hurt to ask. "Well, is it because I'm not a high enough rank or because we work together?" He wanted to know if there was a chance at some point.

Abi put the pen she was writing with down and turned to face him. He was such a nice man. She had to be honest. "A little of both, I suppose." She motioned for the Corporal to take a seat. "The rank thing isn't that big of an issue since we're both adults here. But, you work for me technically and I think that might make it a little inappropriate."

Getting up from the chair, Cpl. Wright came around the desk and stood in front of the Gunny. He didn't believe her. "I don't work for you; I work for Warrant Officer Johnson."

Crap! He had a point, but she didn't want to split hairs. "You're right," Abi said and stood up to face him. "But still, we work together, Corporal."

"It's Peter," Cpl. Wright whispered and leaned in to kiss her.

Their lips met and held for a brief moment.

The kiss was so unexpected that Abi didn't immediately pull away. The kiss, surprisingly, was good but she just didn't feel the kick of attraction you should feel.

Abi stepped away, flushed. "I," She didn't know what to say.

Smiling, Cpl. Wright stepped back, "That's okay; I just wanted to see."

He turned around and left the office. Abi just stood there and stared at the doorway for a long time.

When Abi finally got home later that evening, she was in a haze of confusion. She didn't even see that kiss from the Corporal coming. Dropping her bag on the desk, she went directly into the bathroom to run a bath.

She came out of the bathroom a half hour later and felt a little better. The key word was "little." Sitting at her desk, Abi turned on her computer and opened her email. No email from Gav was in there.

'Why are you surprised?' she asked herself. 'You shot him down at everything.'

After closing her laptop, Abi went to her bed and plopped down. She laid there and prayed for sleep to take her away. But, of course, it didn't. After a while, she got up and put together a salad that tasted like nothing, and sat on the sofa.

Why was this happening? Why was she feeling all these things? Why was Gav the one she wanted to call and talk to about it?

She picked up her phone and pushed his number. She programmed it into her phone and didn't even want to delve into what that meant. The call went directly to voicemail, which upset Abi even more. Of course, she looked at the clock, it was like two in the morning there. He was probably out or sleeping. She turned the phone off and leaned back on the couch. This was going to be a long night.

Saturday morning, Abi was up early. She went to the track and ran three miles, then went back to her room to shower and change. A few friends were meeting up for shopping and lunch in Honolulu today. She invited Eryn but she had plans with Chase and couldn't meet the girls. Ahhh, married life. Abi was happy for Eryn and Chase so it was just an adjustment for Abi to get used to.

She drove into Honolulu and met Sheri and a couple of their other mutual friends. They walked around the mall for almost four hours. No one was looking for anything specific; they all just went into whatever store interested them. It was fun and mindless, which Abi really needed. The girls were lucky and picked up some good deals. Abi found a really pretty dress that she didn't have any reason to wear but wanted to get anyway.

"That's sexy and sophisticated," Sheri said when Abi came out of the dressing room.

Abi looked at herself from different angles in the mirrors. It was black and gathered at the side of the waist. The look was not normally something Abi considered but it looked really good on her.

Looking over at Sheri, Abi smiled, "Yes, I think I'll get it."

Abi paid for the dress and followed Sheri out of the store to meet up with the other girls in their group. Everyone ended up buying something. It was fun to laugh and be silly and Abi was really happy she went.

During the drive back to the base, she heard her phone go off. She never talked on it while driving so she let the voicemail pick up. If she was going to tell her Marines that they should be safe then she should lead by example.

Of course, then she was curious about who called her. Maybe it was Gav? She threw her purse on the floor when she got in the car and couldn't reach it so now she was just driving and wondering.

Once she was in the barracks parking lot, she put the car in park and grabbed her bag. She pulled the phone out and checked the caller ID. It was Gav! Her heart pounding, Abi hit call back and waited. It went directly to voicemail again. Damn! She yelled to herself. Maybe he was working.

She got inside her room and hung up her new dress right away. After that, she went to her desk and logged in to her email. No new mail. She sat down and started one to Gav. What did she say? The truth was embarrassing but she wasn't one to lie so why start now? The words were slow to form but she tried.

Gav:

I'm sorry about not responding to your last email. I was upset because the questions you asked were valid and I didn't want to admit that you were right. No one asked me to do any of those things. I just assumed that would be expected of me.

It's just that, thinking I would marry someone, who I don't really know, really scares me. Doesn't it scare you? And where would we live? I don't see it being fair for me to ask you to relocate for my job and I sure don't think it's fair for you to ask me to relocate for your job so aren't we really at a crossroads here?

Truthfully, I called you last night because a guy at work came into my office and asked me out on a date. I thought it was sweet but he is younger than I am and, frankly, I don't see him that way. When he kissed me, I was so surprised. Then when I got home, I was very confused. I just wanted to hear your voice. Why is that? Why you are the one I thought could help me with that confuses me even more.

I hope you're able to call or email. I know you have a whole life I don't know about so maybe you're just really busy.

Abi

After sending the email, Abi went online to pay some bills and look over some sales ads she got. Nothing too pressing but little things that kept her mind from wandering to Gav.

Hours later, when she was lying in bed, she still thought about him. About what he might look like, what his kisses might feel like. Even as sleep took her away, she dreamed about the man who would make her want......everything.

Sunday was bright and sunny so Abi went running again. She should do it more often but she always seemed to have more to do during the week with work and errands. She enjoyed it but not lived for it. Eryn and Chase made it a religion, or so she teased them both about over the last year or so.

When she got back to her room, she showered and changed. Looking at the new dress she bought, she wondered if she would ever have an occasion to wear it. Oh well, she thought, it would be waiting when she did.

After eating, she opened her email and smiled when she saw one from Gav in her inbox. As she started reading though, the smile faded.

Abi:

I'm sorry too that we've been missing each other. Having said that, I'm really mad that you kissed someone else. It sounds like you are certainly not going to consider our situation and want to prove it to me. Confused or not, I don't see that behavior as something you should participate in.

As to the other part, I have been wanting to talk to you. You're the one who said no phone calls. You're the one who shoots me down at every turn.

I apologize for the harshness of my words. I'm mad.

Gav

What the hell! Abi said to herself. The man had guts, she'd admit that. Of course, if he was standing her in front of her, she would have to punch him in the face. He made it sound like she was out sleeping around or something.

'Our situation,' he wrote. What situation? A crazy promise their parents made over twenty-five years earlier!

She couldn't answer the email. She was way too pissed off. Shutting the laptop, she turned and grabbed her phone.

In New York, Elena picked up the phone, "Hello," she said.

"Mama," Abi started in right away, "I don't want to hear about this marriage thing again." She tried to calm her tone. She did not want to be disrespectful to her mother, but she needed to get her point across. "It just won't work."

Elena listened to her daughter and knew something happened between her and Gavriil. As much as she wanted to help Abigale, this was something the two of them would have to work out together. "I see," she finally said.

That's it? Abi asked in her head. No arguments. "Okay, well," She didn't know what else to say, "I just wanted to tell you that."

Elena set her jaw, "Fine," she said.

"Tell Papa I love him and I love you," Abi said softly, "Bye."

Abi hung up the phone and felt like she just did something very bad.

Elena placed the phone back in its cradle and turned around to face her friend, Klara. "That was not good news." She walked back to the table they were having tea at.

Klara shook her head, "Sometimes these children just make us crazy!" She patted her friend's hand, "It's okay, Elena."

Looking at her friend, Elena wasn't so sure. "Is it?"

Abi started crying as soon as she put the phone down. She had a happy life before all of this bullshit, right? So why did it feel like she was making one mistake after another now? She worked too damn hard all these years to mess it up. She would need to straighten out her mind and her goals and get back on track if she was going to resolve all of this drama.

Either that or she was going to have to kick some major ass; either way, it was going to work out the way she wanted it to.

Moonlight & A Marine

Chapter 8

Abi was relieved for Monday morning. Going to work was a welcome distraction from the craziness of the weekend. She smiled at the Admin clerks when she entered the building and nodded to the Section Leaders who were talking in the Mess. Getting settled at her desk, she waited for the call for a Muster in the truck bay so they could introduce the new NCOIC to the Sections.

The knock on her door had her looking up. She nodded to let Corporal Wright know it was okay for him to come in.

"Gunny, about Friday," Cpl. Wright started, "I am sorry about kissing you without your permission."

He was sweet. He would make some woman a great boyfriend but it just wasn't going to be her. "Apology accepted."

Nodding, Cpl. Wright figured it was done and over with, he got up and left the office.

Abi was relieved they wouldn't discuss this any longer. She wouldn't mention it to Eryn; no need for the Corporal to get his butt chewed for something relatively innocent.

The announcement sounded and Abi got up and left her office. She met up with a couple of Staff SSgt's and they went out to the truck bay.

The Sections were starting to form and the different departments lined up behind them. Abi made her way over to where Eryn and Master Sgt. Phillips were standing. As soon as she was close, Eryn smiled to acknowledge her.

"I think it will be pretty straightforward," Master Sgt. Phillips said. He turned a little and noticed Gunny Rochelle coming up to them. "Good morning, Gunny," he said and smiled.

Well, Abi thought, this one definitely kicked up a little punch. She smiled in return, "Morning, Master Sgt."

Eryn looked at Abi, wondering how interesting the chemistry between them was. Abi wasn't kidding when she said their new NCOIC was a looker but she neglected to let Eryn know about the sparks that flew between them. The Master Sgt. seemed nice enough but Eryn couldn't shake the thought that he seemed like a player. Not exactly good news when the one you're "playing" with works with you.

"Attention!" the training Staff Sgt. shouted.

Everyone moved quickly and took their place. Eryn gave Master Sgt. Phillips' introduction and told the group where he was coming from. She mentioned a few of the highlights from his career so far and Abi was impressed. He seemed really well rounded in the field.

They were dismissed and Eryn motioned for Abi to follow her and the Master Sgt. back to the OIC office.

Abi started to follow them, but was stopped by a one of the Section Leaders. After taking a few minutes to answer his question, she finally made her way to Eryn's office. She knocked and entered, not waiting for a reply. Master Sgt. Phillips was sitting on the couch and Eryn was behind her desk. They were talking about upcoming assignments.

"Sorry,"Abi said when she sat down next to the Master Sgt.

Eryn nodded, "That's fine," she was pulling out papers, "we're just going over the training roster and a few details."

Abi got out her pen and pad of paper from her flight suit pocket and took notes while they talked.

The three of them spent the next hour or so going over anything relevant to Crash Crew operations. Abi mostly listened but spoke up to clarify anything that was unclear to either of her bosses. By the end of the meeting, Abi was confident her new NCOIC knew what was expected of him and knew his job well.

They were wrapping up the meeting when Eryn closed the folder she put her notes in, "Okay, you two," she smiled, "dinner at my place on Friday. You can bring a date."

Abi smiled. That was just like Eryn.

"I'll be there, ma'am," Master Sgt. Phillips said politely.

Looking between them, Abi piped up, "I'm always up for food."

They laughed and Abi and the Master Sgt. left to go back to their own offices.

A little while later, at lunch, Eryn told Chase about the new NCOIC and her suspicions about him and Abi.

"Their adults, Eryn," Chase said when she was finished.

Sighing, Eryn nodded, "I know, baby, but she's so worked up over this marriage thing with Gav." It was impossible for Eryn not to worry about her friend.

Chase knew something was up. He knew Eryn too well, "Honey, you sound awfully familiar with this Gav thing."

Not wanting to admit she was busted, Eryn tried, in vain, to look innocent. "I don't know what you mean."

His eyes narrowing, Chase knew she did something, "What did you do?"

Eryn started getting defensive. "What did she do for us?" she asked.

Chase sighed, "She didn't DO anything. She listened and tried to help us figure out what we wanted."

"Exactly," Eryn responded.

His wife was the absolute best woman on the planet but Chase sometimes wondered if she wasn't slightly certifiable.

At the end of the day, Abi locked up her office and started down the hallway. She saw that the door to the NCOIC office was open. Curious, she poked her head in the doorway. Her new boss was at his desk, doing some paperwork. He didn't notice her right away so she took the time to observe him.

He was tall and lean and had the most beautiful eyes ever! She needed to stop this, the guy was her boss and deserved her respect, not her charged thoughts.

"Gunny," Master Sgt. Phillips said. He smiled when he saw her jump. She was lost in thought when he looked up and saw her in the doorway. He could say he was guilty of that a time or two.

Feeling embarrassed, Abi stepped inside the office. "I was just peeking in and I noticed you were still here. It's quitting time."

Bill smiled, thinking she was sweet. He looked at his watch, "And so it is." He straightened the papers on his desk and got up. "We'll get out of here then," he said to her.

They walked out of the office and out of the building. After he walked Abi over to her car, he waited until she got in and waved when she pulled out.

Even though Abi knew nothing would come of it, she thought it was nice that he flirted with her. A girl needed an emotional pick-me-up once in a while.

She got home and was just putting her flight suit away when her phone rang. "Hello," Abi said as she cradled the phone in her neck.

"Hey there," Eryn said brightly, "I forgot to tell you about a class I want you to take later in the week. It's some computer course for the new updated software we're getting."

Abi frowned as she walked out of the closet, "What new software?" she asked. She didn't remember seeing anything about it in the emails she read recently.

Eryn cleared her throat, "Oh, it's a new thing from Command," she slapped at her husband's hand, "It will be Thursday and Friday this week."

This conversation was just a little too weird. "Okay," Abi said and wrote down a note so she could research it tomorrow.

"Oh," Eryn said, "I'm going to be late into work tomorrow. I have a doctor's appointment."

Smiling, Abi didn't want to snoop but she figured why, "No problem."

Smiling, Eryn nodded to Chase over the phone, "Okay, I'll see you at about lunch time tomorrow. Have a good night."

Her friend was sweet, "See ya."

Abi hung up and smiled while she made herself some dinner. Eryn was nothing if not a little transparent about her current condition. Abi would just have to wait for the big announcement to come. Maybe that's why she was having a dinner on Friday? It would make sense to announce it to her closest staff members. Plus, Abi was a friend and if Eryn didn't tell her first, there would be hell to pay.

The next morning, Abi was at her desk when she heard a page for her to pick up the phone. "Gunnery Sgt. Rochelle," she said formally.

It was the base Military Police and getting a call from them was NEVER a good thing. Taking a deep breath, Abi listened and frowned.

An hour later she was in her office with both Section Leaders and the Marines who got in trouble.

"Gentlemen, what part of 'Keep Your Noses Clean' did you not understand?" She wanted to knock their heads together, she was so pissed off.

Once of the Lance Corporal's spoke up, "Gunny, it wasn't our fault!"

Staff Sgt. Marks looked at the kid, "You watch your tone, Lance Cpl."

Abi nodded to the Section Leader. It was good for them to show solidarity when dealing with the Marines. "Then, Lance Corporal, tell me whose fault it is."

After another hour of listening to the Marines and coming to a unified disciplinary plan for them, Abi wanted to pull her hair out.

Geez, these young kids! Since when did she feel so old? Since she had to deal with crap like stealing cell phones and arguing over video games. This was exhausting! She was about to let dispatch know she was heading off to a late lunch when there was a knock at her office door.

Getting up, Abi walked to the door and yanked it open, "If this is more BS, I'm not having-" She stopped mid-sentence because it wasn't a Marine on the other side of it.

"Hello, Abi," Gav said.

Not knowing what to say, Abi just stood there. She knew, in her gut, that this was Gav but she didn't know how to handle her reaction to seeing him.

He was standing there, in khaki pants and a blue polo shirt, looking like an ad for cologne or clothing or something. He was tall, at least six foot four, so she had to look up to make eye contact. His dark hair, although long compared to Marine standards, was worn short and styled a little messy. His eyes were blue and piercing as they looked down into hers and made her feel really warm under his intense look.

Eryn came up beside him and looked at Abi, "Maybe you two should go into your office, Gunny Rochelle," she suggested.

"Uh yes," Abi recovered, but only slightly, "come in," she motioned for him to enter her office and backed up until she bumped into her desk.

Once Gav entered the office, Eryn closed the door behind him to give him and Abi some privacy. Then she turned to walk toward her office and fanned herself as she walked. Watching those two for just that half minute or so was like watching something very intimate. She wondered if it was like that for other people when she and Chase were together. She sure hoped so.

Once she and Gav were alone in her office, Abi didn't know what to say.

Gav looked at her and was glad he wasn't shown pictures by his mother. He doubted they would've done her justice. Her light brown hair was pulled back into a French braid so he wasn't sure how long it actually was. Her blue-green eyes were wide, in surprise he supposed, and staring at him. There was a dusting of freckles across her nose that she probably tried to hide with makeup but he was close enough to notice them. She stood there quietly, looking shocked, so he figured he would help her.

"I was really mad at your email," he started and took a step toward her.

That was not what she was expecting him to say, "Um, I..." She couldn't find words.

Gav took another step, "I know; we were at an impasse and I figured that if I didn't get out here and see you, I'd be in some real trouble."

Abi was trying not to laugh and cry at the same time, "Really?" she managed to ask in a soft voice. Her body was in turmoil, not sure what to do.

One more step closer, "Yes, and I don't like to be in trouble, Abi." His voice dropped lower in response to his physical reaction to her.

She was entranced, "Why not, Gav? It can be fun." The words were out before she could think.

Gav laughed, "I guess it depends then," he moved so he was less than a foot away from her, "on what kind of trouble we're talking about here."

He was going to kiss her! She knew it and she wanted it badly; almost as badly as she wanted him. There was no way to explain it. She just did.

As he lowered his head toward Abi's, Gav smiled, "We'll see," he whispered just before his lips met hers.

He was kissing her! Abi was falling into the deepest hole, filled with a churning that was taking over her whole body. She was hot, like when they were training; the heat surrounding you and making you feel so encompassed. This was the same feeling only a thousand times better. Without thinking, she raised her hands and placed them on his shoulders. When his arms came around her and pulled her closer, she thought she might melt into a puddle of craziness at his feet.

Her body was not letting her mind catch up because her lips parted to take him in deeper. Her breasts pressed against his chest, her thighs met his. This was insane and yet it felt like the most right thing she'd ever done.

Gav held her to him and steeled himself for the onslaught of feelings he knew would come. As soon as he saw her, he knew this would happen. It was just something he could not explain and really didn't want to. She felt so good in his arms.

Slowly, Abi came to the surface of her desire and realized they were in her office. When she pulled back, there were unshed tears in her eyes. Not wanting Gav to see her like this, she turned around to face the desk.

"I'm sorry, I don't know what came over me," she said as she wiped her eyes.

Gav didn't understand, "Why are you sorry?" he asked. He wasn't sorry, not one part of him was sorry for the kiss, only for the fact that they stopped.

Abi turned around to face him, her face flushed, "I don't know, I don't think I am." She sighed, "It just seemed like the right thing to say."

Moving his hands up her arms, Gav rested his palms on her shoulders, "Don't say it then because I'm not sorry." He wanted to kiss her again but this whole thing was really iffy.

Her senses were finally returning and she tilted her head, her brow furrowed, "How did you get here? How did you get to my office?" She didn't understand.

"Well," Gav moved so he could sit, motioning her to sit in the chair across from him. "I have to say I hope you won't be upset but I got your work number from your father." He smiled when he saw her face pale, "I explained that I wanted to contact you and he gave it to me. Then I called and spoke with your friend Eryn."

The situation was becoming pretty clear all of a sudden. "Really?" she asked sarcastically.

Gav knew she wouldn't be happy, but that couldn't be helped. "I told her I was coming and asked if she would bring me here so I could see you." He brought her hand up to his lips and kissed it gently. "I had to see you."

The words moved over her mind as if they were feathers trailing softly over her skin. They made her body alert and wanting. How could she be upset when he came all this way just to see her? "Why?" she asked so softly she wasn't sure he heard it.

"Because, I knew when I saw you, I would kiss you. And I knew when I kissed you, I would be lost." Gav looked into her eyes, trying to tell her with them that he spoke the honest truth.

Abi looked down for a moment then looked up at Gav. He was here, in front of her, telling her these beautiful things. It was like a dream, a wonderful dream. She couldn't answer, she just sat there looking at his beautiful face and wondered why. Why is this happening? The tears pressed for release and she let them come.

It wasn't difficult to see her inner turmoil, he felt it himself a hundred times during the flight here. He couldn't even say what exactly possessed him to get on a plane and fly five thousand miles, only that he had to do it.

"Okay," Abi said and started laughing through the tears falling down her cheeks. What the hell, if he didn't like her crying, too bad. "Well, we should probably get out of here huh?" She looked around like she'd never seen her office before.

Gav watched Abi get up and go around her desk. She put her things away and he watched her every move. She was not one to waste time; she got down to business quickly. He could appreciate that.

She grabbed a bag and looked at him, "We can go," she said and started toward the door.

He got up and followed her. His eyes never left her as they walked out of her office and went down the hallway. He wanted to see everything about her; the way her hair moved when she walked, trying to escape the intricate braid she had it in; the way her body moved, even though it was covered by the flight suit she wore. He could tell she was slim and curvy under the non-descript fabric. She walked as if she had a purpose; demanding respect, he supposed. Another admirable trait. He didn't notice she stopped and almost walked into her in front of an office door.

"Gav," She looked up into his eyes and wanted to kiss him so badly. "This is Eryn's office and I have to talk to her," she nodded to a chair across the hallway, "can you have a seat for a minute?"

Smiling, Gav nodded, "Sure," he answered. He figured Eryn was going to get an earful for her cooperation in his little "mission" but he figured Abi's anger would be short-lived.

Abi knocked and opened Eryn's office door. She set her jaw and walked in when she saw her friend sitting behind her desk and looking very smug.

"Hey, Gunny," Eryn said over-brightly, "how are you doing?"

Her face dropping, Abi snarled, "Really?" she asked.

Eryn came around the desk quickly and pulled Abi's arm to bring her into the office and close the door at the same time. "Oh my, he's gorgeous!" she said in a whisper to Abi. "He called and I had to do it, Abi." She hoped her friend would forgive her.

If her feelings weren't flying higher than an F-18, Abi might be able to stay mad but, she couldn't. "I know," she hugged Eryn quickly, "I'm going to lunch now and I won't be back."

"I would expect nothing else," Eryn smiled. "Oh, and don't worry about that class this week, it was cancelled."

Abi's face dropped, "Oh, you mean the class that didn't exist? The one you told me about so I would get all the pending stuff on my desk squared away so I could have a few days off? That class?"

Eryn couldn't help but laugh, Abi's face was priceless. "Yep, that's the one." She opened the door and smiled at a waiting Gav.

Gav stood as the ladies came out of the office. They were both smiling so he figured all was forgiven. Eryn came up to him first and gave him a quick hug. The gesture surprised him but he knew he liked Abi's friend. She was a genuinely nice lady.

Watching Eryn give Gav a quick hug, Abi had to beat down the arm of jealousy that wound its way through her belly. What was that about?

Eryn pulled away and smiled up at Gav, "Okay, dinner Friday night at our place," she winked at her new friend, "I'm sure Chase will want to meet you."

The way she said it made Gav pause for a second. Should he be worried about Chase? Eryn described him as like a big brother to Abi. Big brothers sometimes beat up guys who were interested in their little sisters.

Abi had to save him, "Okay, we're going now." She grabbed Gav's arm and pulled him out the door after her. When they were outside she laughed, "Oh, you poor guy."

He liked the way she laughed. "It's not so bad." He looked back at the Crash Crew building and hoped Abi would give him a tour while he was here visiting. He wanted to know as much about her life as she would let him see.

They got to Abi's car quickly. She unlocked the doors and opened the back door to put her bag on the back seat. When she got into the driver's seat, she looked over at him. "Have you eaten?" she asked, trying to figure out an impromptu plan.

"No," Gav said and looked at her with a smile on his face. "I checked into the hotel and came straight to you."

There were those words that made her belly tighten and her skin come alive. "Oh, well," she put the key in the ignition, "I think we can get you some lunch but first, I have to change."

Abi pulled out and headed to her barracks. She hoped she didn't leave the place too messy this morning. Sometimes, if she was running late, she left stuff out and cleaned up after work. She didn't want Gav to see her room in that kind of state.

They pulled into the parking lot and Gav looked around. The barracks were two story buildings that all looked exactly the same except for the large numbers on the corners. They were new and well-maintained, but barracks nonetheless. They reminded him a little bit of his college dorm from the outside.

As they walked to her room, Abi wondered what he thought. She supposed it wasn't like having your own apartment in New York, but Abi never had an issue with her living arrangements before so she wouldn't be ashamed of them now.

After unlocking the door to her room, Abi opened it wide and smiled. She was relieved her room was tidy. "Please," she motioned for Gav to have a seat, "I'll just change really quickly and we can go to lunch."

"Sounds good," Gav answered. His eyes watched her move to the closet and then to the bathroom. Once the door closed, he looked around her room.

It was actually pretty roomy, Gav thought. There was a sitting area with a kitchenette type area at one end then there was the bedroom area. Looking at the bed, he had to fight the urge to go over and touch the pillow where Abi slept. If it didn't sound so creepy, even to himself, he might have.

Abi came out of the bathroom and felt better. In the bathroom she took her hair out of the braid so it fell just past her shoulders. She decided to just finger comb it and let it fall so the wave in it from being up made it look fuller. She put on a little lip gloss, a spritz of perfume, and smiled.

"Ready," Abi said and smiled at Gav. How could he look so relaxed when she was like a strung out wire, ready to snap?

When he stood, he walked over to where Abi stood, looking very nervous. "You look beautiful, Abi," he whispered just before he captured her lips with his. It was a quick kiss because anything longer would make him forget he was a gentleman.

When he pulled his lips from hers, Abi stared up into his eyes. Just because the kiss was shorter than the one in her office didn't mean it was any less potent to Abi's system. She felt off-kilter as he stepped away and towards the door. Without saying anything, she followed him.

They went to a restaurant in Kailua for lunch and were seated relatively quickly given the size of the line waiting outside.

"This place must be popular," Gav said when they were shown to their table.

Abi nodded, "They have a great pork sandwich," she said and smiled as glasses of ice water were delivered to their table.

Gav followed her lead and ordered a pork sandwich.

"So, what are you going to show me?" Gav asked when they were free to talk.

She almost choked on her water. She was not expecting the question or the thoughts it brought up in her mind.

Laughing, Gav took a sip of his water too. "I'm sorry."

Abi shook her head, "Why, because I've got a dirty mind?"

Oh she was a spitfire, Gav thought. "It's not something I would mark as negative on my list."

"Good to know," Abi replied flippantly.

He sat there and waited.

It was hard not to stare at him; his features were so beautiful. She thought he wouldn't want to be called beautiful but he was. His eyes just focused on her and made her feel like she was the only thing he saw. "Well," I suppose I should ask how long you're here for first."

Nodding, Gav smiled, "Good point, I'm here until Sunday."

Short visit, Abi thought, but he still made a point of coming. "What can we do in five and a half days?" she asked.

Why did everything she said make him think of them naked and in bed? "I'm sure we can think of a few things," he answered and was only a little ashamed of his tone.

Good, Abi thought, she wasn't the only one. "Next question, where are you staying?"

Gav sat back, "I wasn't sure how you would take my surprise so I opted to stay in Honolulu." He covered her hand with his, "Are you okay with me being here, Abi?"

It wasn't in Abi to play games. She hated women who acted so shy and coy and knew she wasn't one of them. "I am happy, Gav."

Nodding, he leaned forward, "Then will you stay with me?"

The question shocked Abi. She actually jolted in her chair. "I'm sorry?" she asked, pretty sure she didn't hear him right.

"I reserved two rooms at the hotel." He figured he would need to do a little explaining. Chemistry or not, he didn't expect her to jump into bed with him. "I was hoping you would stay there with me."

So, this man...who didn't know her very well at all...not only flew thousands of miles to see her, but reserved TWO hotel rooms so she wouldn't be that far from him? Her thoughts ran rampant. What did she do? This whole thing was crazy!

When Abi looked up and into Gav's eyes, she felt like she was drowning in confusion, "Can I get back to you on that?"

For some reason he couldn't explain, her response was not a complete surprise. Through their emails, he was starting to get a glimpse into the complexity of Abi's mind. It didn't deter him, only intrigued him.

Gav nodded, "Yes you can." He grabbed Abi's hand and pulled it to his lips.

Chapter 9

Once lunch was over, Abi was kind of at a loss. She didn't really know what to say or do with Gav. Well, that wasn't completely true, she knew what she *wanted* to do with Gav but that was not something she was willing to jump into right now.

Sneaking a peak at Gav as they were walking out to her car, she thought maybe he was having the same problem.

"What would you like to do?" Abi asked when they were almost to her car.

Gav smiled, "Hey, you're the one who lives here, I'm just a tourist."

Sighing, Abi smiled, "Great! Nothing like a little pressure here."

He liked her sarcasm. "I'm pretty sure you can handle it, I've seen where you work." He leaned against the passenger door and winked at her over the top of her car.

Oh, he was a smart ass too. Lord, she could fall for this guy! None of that, she scolded herself mentally. This was just a little "distraction."

Gav watched Abi's face and wondered what she was thinking. It wasn't tough to figure out that she wanted to have a good time with him but was fighting it too because of their parents' expectations. He couldn't blame her. Most people would think they were insane to even consider an arranged marriage.

"Well, let's go then," Abi said and opened the driver's door.

They got in and buckled up. Abi was so nervous that her hands were shaking while she put the key in the ignition. Being so close to Gav was like being close to a live electrical outlet; one touch and she would get a shock. Knowing she was playing it reckless, she turned to look at him but he was already looking at her, which made her even more self-conscious.

Before she could speak, Gav lifted his hand and brushed his fingers across Abi's cheek. Her skin was soft and slightly flushed. He wasn't sure if it was from the bright, afternoon sun or from her reaction to him.

"Your skin is very soft," Gav whispered, watching his fingers as they brushed her skin.

Why did he have to say things like that? They made her belly flip flop, confusing her. "Why did you kiss me in my office?"

A surprise, Gav smiled wider, "Because I wanted to taste your lips." He looked down at her mouth, his fingers following his eyes and skimming across the soft, pink skin.

Sitting in her car and letting him touch her face, Abi felt like they were already naked in bed and making love. His touch only increased the pressure inside of her. "It was amazing," she whispered.

"Yes it was," Gav answered. He sucked in a breath when Abi took the tip of his finger in her mouth. When her tongue brushed along the sensitive pad of his finger, he thought they would combust right here in the car.

What are you doing? Abi asked herself. No answer...

Finally, Gav figured that he would embarrass them both if they didn't slow down. "Abi," he practically croaked, his voice cracked. "If we don't get going, I'm going to kiss you again."

Not knowing if he was teasing her or threatening her, Abi brought her hand up and covered his with it as he cupped her cheek into his palm. She closed her eyes and drank in the sensations his closeness brought. Lord, she was in trouble.

Abi opened her eyes and took a deep breath, "Okay," she said and turned back toward the wheel.

After pulling out of the parking lot, Abi turned to go back to the base. "I don't know what to do here, Gav," she said in a sharp tone as she was driving.

Frustrated both physically and emotionally, Gav clenched his jaw. "Pull over please," he said.

Making sure it was safe, Abi pulled the car over and sat there. After a minute she unbuckled and got out.

Gav watched her get out of the car. What the hell were they doing here? He got out and followed her.

They were near a beach; there were other people there enjoying their day and Abi was walking around like a zombie. She had no direction and no plan, she just needed to breathe.

"Abi," Gav said when he walked up beside her. She was standing at the top of a rise and looking down on a little lagoon area.

Looking over, Abi was lost in the way he looked and how his nearness made her body feel. "I can't," she said in a pleading voice.

He knew what she was talking about and they both knew it was going to cause problems. "Why not?" he asked quietly.

Anger finally penetrating the haze of awareness, Abi threw her hands up. "I'm standing here and defending the fact that I don't want to marry someone my parents told me I HAVE TO MARRY!" She didn't like it when anger got the better of her but all the conflicting emotions were too much for her.

"Is that why you thought I came here?!" Gav yelled back. "You think I came here to CONVINCE you to marry me?" He looked away and then back to her, "I came here because you telling me some guy kissed you in your email really pissed me off!"

His tone was so shocking to her that Abi just stood there and stared at him. Why she even thought she was the only one who was having trouble with this made her feel bad. "I'm sorry," she said quietly.

Gav looked down into her eyes, "I see you for the first time and the only thought I have is that I have to kiss you," he moved closer and brought his palms up to cup her neck, "and when I kiss you, all I can think about is kissing you again."

Lowering his head, he closed his eyes just as his lips met hers again. She was ready for him, opening up for him as soon as their lips came together. He moaned and moved closer. She was shorter than he was so he moved one of his hands from her neck to wrap it around her back and pull her closer.

Abi's body went limp in Gav's arms; all her energy was focused on kissing him. Gav's lips possessed hers with his and she was helpless to stop it. But, she didn't want to stop it anyway. The friction of their bodies made her quiver, even in the bright afternoon Hawaiian sun. Every nerve ending from the tips of her toes up to the top of her head were firing and making her feel everything at once.

When Gav felt like he was able to get a handle on his body and mind, he gently pulled his head up so he could look into Abi's eyes. Seeing the indecision in her eyes made him hurt. It was okay for her to be scared, he was terrified of this...all of this. His reaction to her, their situation, how they would figure it all out; he didn't have a clue. But having Abi in his arms and feeling all of this with just a kiss made him want to sure as hell find out.

"Now," Gav said with a smile, "I'm here to be with you, that's it." He gave her a look when she was going to say something, "There are no expectations here, Abi."

Even though she nodded, Abi wasn't convinced. Maybe Gav didn't have any expectations but that didn't mean their parents didn't.

The afternoon was almost gone when they got back to Abi's barracks room. She still hadn't given Gav an answer about staying in Honolulu with him. She wanted to, she really did, but just being around him created chaos inside of her head. There was a part of her that just wanted distance from him so she could breathe and think clearly.

Gav didn't say anything on the drive back to the base. He knew Abi was in a crazy spot, having him show up unexpectedly and then asking her to go to Honolulu and stay with him. If it wasn't him doing this, he would've thought he was crazy. Being in the banking business, Gav learned how to play the odds and be practical. This situation was anything but practical.

They got out of the car and started walking toward her room when Abi looked up and saw her NCOIC standing at her door. Master Sgt. Phillips was knocking.

"Master Sgt." Abi said when they were close enough that she didn't have to shout.

Bill turned around to see his Crash Chief walking up and was thrown off kilter by her appearance. She certainly didn't look like that when she was at work. Between the hair being pulled back and the flight suit, he wasn't sure he would've recognized her dressed like she was.

Abi blushed when the Master Sgt. let out a low whistle. She stole a glance at Gav in time to see his jaw clench. Oh, she had a feeling that this was getting really bad really fast.

Bill smiled, "Well, Gunny, you sure do look good out of that uniform." He was leaning against the door to her room and didn't notice Gav off to the side so didn't see the punch coming.

Whack! Gav had to hit this ass. He wouldn't stand there and let him talk to Abi that way!

"GAV!" Abi shouted just as Gav's fist made contact with the Master Sgt.'s jaw.

Bill fell back against the door but recovered quickly. He was about to swing back at Gav when he heard the Gunny yell.

Abi would not stand here and have a fistfight break out at her room, "Inside now! Both of you!" She jerked the door open and all but grabbed the two men to get them inside.

Once she slammed her door she turned and glared at the two men standing in front of her. "You have got to be kidding me!" she yelled.

"Hey," Bill said while rubbing his jaw, "he hit me!"

Gav was clenching his fist ready to hit this guy again when he saw the look of murder in Abi's eyes.

Okay, she would need to be the mom...again. "Master Sgt., sit down!" she demanded, "Gav, sit over there!" She pointed to the couch.

When both men were seated Abi paced back and forth in front of them. "Okay, Gav, you just hit my boss." She glared at him waiting for an answer.

The reality of the situation was becoming clearer and Gav felt like a first-class jerk. "I'm sorry, Abi, he just was being so...suggestive."

Bill snorted and was going to laugh until he saw the look on the Gunny's face. "I'm sorry," he muttered.

Throwing her hands in the air, Abi was lost. What the hell did they do now? She looked back and forth between the two men.

Gav stood and walked over to the Master Sgt., "I'm sorry for hitting you, man," he extended his hand.

Bill took the offer of a handshake and stood as well, "Nice shot," he said with a smile. His jaw would hurt like hell the next day.

That's it? Abi wondered. They just shook hands and all was forgiven? Shaking her head, she plopped down into a chair.

Knowing she was otherwise engaged, Bill nodded and smiled, "Gunny, I'll see you at work."

Abi raised her hand to wave goodbye as the Master Sgt. left her room.

Knowing he was on thin ice, Gav walked over to where Abi was sitting. "I'm sorry I upset you," he said.

Looking up, Abi could see he was repentant. "Are you sorry you hit him?" she asked.

"Hell no!" Gav said loudly. Then, seeing her face, knew that wasn't what she wanted to hear.

He knelt down in front of her. He took her hand and brought it to his lips again. After kissing it he put it back where she had it resting on the arm of the chair.

It took all of Abi's resolve to keep from grabbing him and kissing him there in her room. Oh the man could melt butter with his eyes.

Gav smiled, knowing he was on his way to being forgiven, "I can't have some man looking at you like that in front of me."

"Were you jealous?" Abi asking in a teasing tone.

Nodding, Gav stood back up and walked to the sink to get a drink of water. "Yes, if you must know, I was very jealous."

Abi had to bit her lip to keep from smiling. It really wasn't funny but she so wanted to laugh. "I think that's nice."

Gav almost choked on the water he was drinking, "Nice?" he asked. "What's nice about being so jealous I wanted to rip a guy's head off for whistling at my..."

Standing, Abi walked toward him, "You're what, Gav?"

This was conversational quick sand and Gav knew it. "What was I going to say?"

"I don't know," Abi purred, "what were you going to say?" She knew he was flustered.

Gav knew Abi was enjoying his discomfort. Her eyes were bright and she was cornering him, "I was going to say my woman," he said softly.

Abi stopped, "Your woman?" she asked out loud.

He was blushing, "I suppose that is an antiquated way to put it."

The fact that he was embarrassed only made him seem cuter to Abi. "I," she moved closer to where Gav was standing, "happen to like antiquated."

She was letting him off and he appreciated it. "You do?" he asked sweetly.

Abi nodded, "Yes," she whispered and walked into his arms.

Gav held her and realized just having her in his arms was enough, for now.

Being in Gav's arms made Abi feel completely safe. It was so amazing to feel such a connection to someone she really didn't know. She tilted her head up and looked into his eyes. She wasn't alone in all of this; he was there too.

"I'll go to the hotel with you," Abi said.

Her acceptance made his chest swell. He gave her a quick squeeze and released her. He wasn't sure why he felt so off-kilter but he needed a little space.

Without looking at Abi, he murmured, "Excuse me," and went into the bathroom to splash some water on his face.

Standing in her room and watching Gav, Abi wondered what she did to make him so uncomfortable.

After a phone call to Eryn to explain the "incident" from earlier and let her know they were going to Honolulu, Abi put her bag in the car and started to drive to the hotel where Gav got rooms.

She turned on the radio to try and ease some of the tension in the vehicle. After their hug, he didn't seem as comfortable around her. Maybe it was just her imagination but he was very quiet.

"Jet lag?" she finally asked when she felt she needed to say something.

151

Gav nodded, "Yes, unfortunately." He grabbed onto the excuse she provided. Guilt racked his mind but he needed to get his footing emotionally.

Abi bit her lip as she drove, "Are you sure you want me to stay in Honolulu with you?" She wanted to let him off if he changed his mind.

"No," Gav said sharply. He didn't mean the word to come out sounding so harsh.

Abi glanced over at him. Good, she thought, he didn't want to run back to New York because she was a complete nut job.

Gav cleared his throat, "I just meant that I want you there."

She was surprised his tone sounded apologetic and replied, "I know what you mean. We're in some weird territory here and I'm not sure what I'm supposed to do or say."

Hearing Abi's honesty helped Gav. He smiled, "I know what you mean," he answered.

Abi thought about what he said while she drove. They were both silent but it wasn't awkward, at least Abi didn't think so. She felt better knowing they were both trying to find their way.

Instead of taking the H3 freeway, Abi decided to go through Kailua and take the Highway 63 route which cut through the mountains toward Honolulu. The drive was actually a bit more scenic in Abi's opinion and she thought Gav would enjoy it. She pointed out a few sights as they drove, trying to be somewhat of a polite tour guide.

Gav listened to Abi talking and was lulled by the tone of her voice. She was a capable woman but he could hear pride in the way she spoke about this place. It was a far cry from New York but he supposed that was the point of her joining the Marine Corps in the first place. He nodded in the appropriate places in the conversation and asked a few questions but he was really just focusing on trying to figure her out.

Once in Honolulu proper, Abi asked him which hotel he was staying at. When he gave her the name, her eyebrows raised in surprise. He just picked it based on a co-worker's suggestion. Seeing Abi's reaction, he wondered if he chose wrong.

"Gav," Abi said, "that is a gorgeous hotel and expensive from what I hear."

He smiled, "I wanted to choose something nice where we could enjoy our time together."

It shouldn't have surprised her that he chose the hotel; she could tell he had taste from his clothes and appearance. But still, she felt kind of bad that he, not only flew here to see her, but spent a small fortune on hotel rooms. Did she say something? Should she offer to pay for her room?

She pulled up in front of the hotel and gasped. It was amazing! She looked over to see Gav smiling at her and clamped her lips shut. She probably looked like an idiot.

Once the valet handed her a ticket for her car, she turned to grab her bag out of the backseat but saw that Gav already had the bag in his hand. He was waiting for her to come around the car and accompany him inside.

When they came into the elaborately decorated lobby, Gav motioned for Abi to have a seat while he got them checked in. He just dropped off his bags earlier and didn't actually check in.

Abi had a direct view of the registration desk so she could watch Gav as he spoke to the reservation agent. He stood very straight and was polite but definitely was all business. It wasn't tough to recognize the look of appreciation the agent gave him but he acted like he didn't notice the woman's efforts. Poor girl, Abi thought, then huffed. Nope, you better keep your hands off this one! Her eyes glared at the woman.

Gav got them registered and turned to see Abi looking ticked off. He wondered what she was looking at since she didn't seem focused on him. He walked over to her.

"Ready?" Gav asked her. "Are you okay?"

Jolting out of her mental list of punishments for the woman flirting with Gav, Abi smiled, "I'm fine," she answered.

They walked down the hallway after one of the bellhops. He carried Abi's bag, which seemed silly to her, but it seemed to be part of the service.

"They delivered my bags to my room earlier," Gav said to her as they walked.

She looked around and was taken in by the beautiful building. It was an old hotel but lovingly maintained over the years. It was pink and gorgeous and made Abi feel pampered before they even reached their rooms.

The bellhop showed Abi to her room first, explaining the amenities in the room and smiling when Gav discreetly gave him a tip and assuring the young man that they would not need his services. Once he left, Abi gave Gav a look.

"I'm fully capable of tipping, you know," she said in a motherly tone.

Gav walked over to her and turned her so she was looking out through the glass doors of her lanai, "I'm sure you are but you are my guest and I want to spoil you a little."

A girl certainly cannot complain about that, Abi thought to herself. "Only a little, okay?"

Smiling into Abi's hair, Gav wrapped his arms around her so they could both enjoy the view. "Okay."

She didn't believe him but felt too good to care at the moment. The ocean was in front of them, its blue horizon blending seamlessly with the sky above. There were swimmers out on the private beach the hotel maintained. They were playing in the sand and water and looked so carefree. It was hard to think about all the stress from work and this "arrangement" their parents wanted when there was such beauty laid out in front of them.

"Would you like to join me for some time on the beach?" Gav asked into her hair.

Abi smiled, "Mmmmm." Whatever kept him with her was a good idea as far as she was concerned.

Gav released her and regretted it immediately. "Okay, I'll meet you in about ten minutes, okay?" He grabbed his room key off the table.

Once she was alone in the room, Abi let out a breath. Boy that man packed a punch to her system and she loved it and hated it at the same time. Shaking herself, she turned to get her swimsuit out of her bag. She hung up her dress in the closet and shook her head thinking that this day was going to end a lot differently than she planned.

They met outside their rooms exactly ten minutes later. Abi wore her two piece swimsuit with a wrap she got in Honolulu when she was first stationed here. It was a beautiful blue with a variety of colored flowers on it. She smiled at the look of appreciation Gav gave her when he saw her. She was giving him one of her own.

If she thought he looked good in casual clothes, the man was amazing in a swimsuit! He was pretty built for a banker. His chest was defined with a dusting of hair. She wanted to touch it but kept her hands to her sides.

"Ready?" Gav asked and had to say the words around the lump in his throat. When Abi came out of her room in a two piece swimsuit, he thought he'd embarrass himself with his reaction to her.

Abi nodded and walked beside him on the way down to the beachfront. She would steal glances at him and wonder what his skin would feel like under her hands. Not good, Abi, she told herself.

The beach area was busy but not crowded. They found some chairs close to the water and Gav motioned for a waiter to come over. He ordered a drink and asked Abi if she would like something.

Once they were alone, Abi leaned back in the chair and sighed. This was so nice after the morning she had. She looked over to find Gav staring at her, an odd look on his face.

"I was just admiring the view," Gav said smartly.

Oh, he was teasing her, "Well I was enjoying my own," she nodded toward his body.

Her teasing was making his body react in a not-very-gentlemanly fashion. "You were?" he asked between reciting the words to the Gettysburg Address in his mind.

Abi turned her body so she was facing him, "Gav, you are hot! Let's be honest here, I'd have to be half dead to not notice and react to you."

He only got to 'Four score and seven...' in his head when every coherent thought left his brain. Abi was looking at him like he was crazy and he couldn't really get past the fact that she called him hot.

"Really?" Abi asked him and cocked her head, "No one has ever told you that before?"

Gav cleared his throat, "Well, I have to admit that I've heard some comments that were similar but having you be so open about your opinion of me is pretty hot too."

Touche! Abi smiled, "I aim to please," she said the words slowly and accentuated the word please.

Screw the Gettysburg Address, Gav said to himself. Sorry Abe. "If you keep saying things like that we may have a problem."

Why should she stop when it was so much fun? Without saying anything she jumped up from her chair and started walking backwards toward the water, "Well, let's see how much trouble we can get into?" She ran for the water and dove in.

Gav smiled and got up to follow her. He dove into the water and cut threw it in short time to reach her.

Being in good physical condition, Abi thought she'd give him some challenge but he surprised her with his swimming skills. She yelped when he grabbed her leg, swallowing a mouthful of salt water.

They swam and played in the water like kids. They played tag and even threw a soft football they borrowed from a group of teenagers nearby. When they dragged themselves back up to their chairs some time later, they were exhausted and laughing.

Abi wrapped her towel around her shoulders and took a sip of her drink. The cool, sweet liquid felt good on her throat and helped wash the taste of the saltwater away. "You surprised me with your mad swimming skills," she said to Gav.

Smiling, Gav turned to face her while he dried his arms. "Well, swimming five days a week keeps me in shape."

"You're a ringer!" she shouted and threw her towel at him.

Gav caught the towel and threw it back at her. It was easy to laugh with Abi, he didn't feel like he had to pretend to be powerful or polished or whatever he felt he needed to be in New York. Why couldn't everything be as easy as being with her?

Abi saw his facial expression shift and knew he was thinking. She didn't want to think right now; she was just focusing on having fun with Gav. Nothing else mattered right now.

They stayed out at the beach until the sun was low in the sky. They talked about the weather, other people on the beach, where they each traveled, and any incidental subject they could pick.

When Abi was back in her room, she wondered why she was so scared. If she thought about it, she would have to admit how much she genuinely liked Gav. Most of her friends didn't really say that when they talked about their boyfriends or husbands. It was always love stuff but never about how much they really liked the men in their lives. It was kind of sad when she thought about it.

After a shower and getting ready, Abi looked in the mirror. She was a good looking woman, not stunning or beautiful or gorgeous, although Gav would probably say she was something like that. Now why did she think that? How could she be sure of what Gav would think or say?

They decided to stay at the hotel and eat at the restaurant on premises this evening so they could get to bed early. Gav was pretty worn out from the trip.

She grabbed her bag and ran her fingers down the sides of her new dress, hoping it was nice enough. When she stepped outside she saw Gav coming out of his room too.

He was in dress slacks and a nice short sleeved shirt. His skin was already tanning from their afternoon in the sun. His hair was slightly damp, probably from a shower, and made her want to run her hands through it.

"You look beautiful," Gav said. He leaned in and kissed Abi's cheek.

Abi smiled, "Thank you, you look fantastic."

He was starting to blush. Her comments made him want to feel that way. "Thank you. Are you hungry?"

Nodding, Abi turned toward him fully and put her hands on his arms. "Yes, starving." She stood on her tiptoes and kissed him softly.

The kiss could be described by some as sedate but, to Gav, it was like a bomb of desire going off in his gut. Need spread through his body quickly.

"Well, let's get you fed then," he said and guided her down the hall toward the lobby.

Chapter 10

Abi woke up the next morning in her hotel room and turned over so she could stare out the window. She replayed the night before over in her mind.

When they walked over to the in-house restaurant, Abi caught Gav stealing glances at her as they made their way. She had to admit, she took extra time getting ready and made an effort to feel like a girl so it was nice that he noticed.

They had a quiet dinner, ordering dishes they could share, and continued to talk about everything and anything.

Smiling, Abi hugged her pillow closer to her chest.

She learned a lot about Gav, especially his upbringing. He was raised all over the world where she was raised in New York. It was fascinating to hear about the places he went to school and visited. He asked her about her travels while in the Corps and she was happy to let him into her little world of adventure. It was funny, when they talked, it was like they were the same people in their openness for exploring.

Abi turned over and saw it was only a little after six in the morning. Gav was probably still sleeping so she decided to get in an early run. It was a nice habit from being in the Marine Corps for so long.

After she got dressed and stretched, Abi left her room and paused in front of Gav's door. Not hearing any movement, she figured she would give him some time to wake up. She went out to the beach where they played the day before and started off on a slow jog.

While running, Abi's mind went back to the night before.

When they finished dinner, Gav walked her slowly back to her room. There was a beautiful outdoor corridor that went around the main hotel building with pillars about every six feet. The moonlight spilled over the stone walkway as they moved along, casting a magical glow over the whole area. They held hands as they walked.

"Thank you," Gav said.

She smiled up at him, even in her high heels, he towered over her. "For what?" she asked.

Gav stopped next to a pillar along the walkway. Its shadow provided a small patch of privacy. He leaned against it and pulled Abi closer. "For giving me such a great day."

Abi tried not to cry; his tone was so sweet. "You're welcome but I should really be thanking you."

Gav cocked his head to the side, "For what?"

Smiling, Abi leaned in closer, "For giving me some of the best kisses ever." Her lips found his and she proceeded to show him what she meant.

Abi was smiling while she was running down the beach. She could not remember when she smiled so much, especially while doing exercise. The man made her smile when she had no reason to.

Danette Fogarty

After the kiss, Gav walked her back to her room, kissed her chastely one last time, unlocked her door for her, and waited until she was tucked inside. Abi leaned against the door and waited to hear the sound of his hotel door close before she sighed.

Stopping, Abi sat down on the beach to rest. She didn't know how far she ran but she couldn't see the hotel anymore. That was okay since she ran three to four miles with Eryn so this was not a big deal. She just wanted a few minutes to think before she went back. The waves were a little rough this morning. A cloudy sky was overhead but she figured that would roll by pretty quickly. The waves and weather kind of mirrored her insides; they were feeling wild and a little unpredictable.

As she sat there, Abi wondered what it would be like when Gav wasn't here. After only one day with him, she wanted more. A lot more.

How was any of this even possible? She sat there contemplating for a few minutes more then got up to walk back to the hotel.

Gav woke up with a smile on his face. Oh, he was frustrated as hell but he still wore that damn smile. It was because of Abi and how she made him feel. He was a perfect gentleman last night but boy it cost him. Sighing, he turned over in his bed and looked at the alarm clock. It was seven thirty and he needed to get up and going.

After showering and getting dressed, Gav left his room and went next door to knock on Abi's door. He probably should've called but he wanted to see her as soon as he could. He smiled brightly when she opened the door. She was smiling too.

"Hi," Abi said in a breathy tone. Lord she sounded like an adolescent.

Gav entered her room and pulled her into his arms for a kiss, "Hi," he said quickly before his lips landed on hers.

The kiss was better than a cup of coffee and a run, its kick of adrenaline came much faster. Abi groaned, wrapped her arms around his waist while she drank in his kiss. It was like she was a starved person just given their first meal in weeks.

Oh man, he was in trouble, Gav thought. After having these amazing kisses, how did he leave her and go back to New York and back to his life? Not wanting to think about anything but this exact moment, Gav poured his heart into the kiss.

When Abi pulled away, she was out of breath and smiling like a dope. "Well, that was a great good morning," she said.

"You have four more of them coming," Gav said quietly. Just knowing there was a finite amount of time for them to be together didn't settle well inside.

Abi did not want to think about that. "Let's get breakfast," she said while stepping away to grab her purse. She didn't dare comment.

The two of them left Abi's room and went into Honolulu to find some breakfast and do some sightseeing. After grabbing a quick bite to eat, they walked along the main roads, peeking into shops and talking about the culture.

"It's so laid back here," Gav commented when they were strolling along the busy shopping district and peeking into the store windows.

Nodding, Abi smiled, "Yes, it makes us howlies seem so silly."

Gav looked over at her, "What's a howlie?" he asked with a laugh.

"Oh, it's a white person from the mainland usually who doesn't really have a clue how to live like the native Hawaiians." She smiled at some kids who passed by them heading into a surf shop. "It is not exactly an insult but pretty close, although it's pretty accurate."

Gav stopped in front of a Hawaiian store and looked inside, "Are you a howlie?"

Nodding, Abi chuckled, "Oh yes," she admired a beautiful beach wrap in the window display of the shop, "I am pretty uptight and all about the work."

He looked over at Abi and took her hand, "Is this all about work?" he asked. They both knew he was talking about their time together.

Abi shook her head, "No," she dropped her eyes, feeling a little shy, "this is most definitely not about work."

"Good," Gav said and leaned down to give her a quick kiss. He loved the way her lips felt against his. "Let's go."

Laughing, Abi followed him back to the hotel and wondered where they were off to now.

Gav gave the valet the claim ticket for Abi's vehicle and waited patiently for the young man to bring it to them. He did some investigating about the island last night when he went back to his room. He wanted them to do some fun things while he was here. If they didn't have a destination or something planned, he was pretty sure he would try to convince her to spend the days in his bed and, as awesome as that sounded, things between them were too unsettled to take that major leap.

The valet handed Gav the keys to Abi's car and he opened the passenger side door and gestured for her to get in.

Being one to have control in most situations, Abi was surprised by her quiet acceptance of him driving her to god-knows-where.

After he had Abi in the vehicle, Gav went around and got into the driver's side. He pulled out his phone and put in the address for their destination. He smiled at Abi and pushed start on the GPS.

The drive was nice, Abi thought, as Gav made his way through Honolulu. They turned east toward Diamond Head so she wondered if they were going to hike it. She kept meaning to do it but never got around to it. They past the turn off for it so she realized they were in for something else.

The drive around the southern part of the island was nice. They made their way out of Honolulu on Hwy 72 that wrapped around the very edge. Every time he looked out, he saw a stretch of the blue Pacific Ocean. Abi was quiet but he sensed she didn't really want to talk right now. That was okay, he would enjoy any time he had with her.

After about a half hour, Gav started to slow. Abi smiled when she realized they were going to Sea Life Park. It was a small marine park on the Windward side of the island. She talked about a couple of times with co-workers but never went herself before now.

"I hope you don't mind, I thought it would be fun," Gav said as he pulled into the park.

Abi shook her head, "No, I love to go to places like this."

They got out and went up to the entrance gate.

It was like being a little kid again; Abi was so excited. She wanted to see everything and not think about work or their parents or anything else. She just wanted to have fun. Isn't that what Gav told her in their emails? No expectations.

Once inside the park, they walked around and looked at all the animals there. It was so much fun. She read all the information placards posted on the outside of the exhibit areas. They mimicked the penguins and sea lions and watched the dolphins in fascination during one of the many shows the park put on.

A few hours later, they were walking back to the car with Abi carrying a large stuffed dolphin Gav got for her earlier. She loved it. They laughed as they drove back to the hotel. By the time they finished picking up lunch it was later in the afternoon.

They debated for a little bit about what to do and decided they both wanted to go back to the beach like they did the day before.

Less than thirty minutes later, they were out on the beach area looking for a place to sit. It was really crowded so finding some empty chairs took a bit but, eventually, they found a couple of vacant chairs. Off to one side there was a game of beach volleyball starting up and a guy was yelling for any takers.

Gav looked over at Abi, "I'm a little rusty but I'll give it a shot if you will."

Smiling, Abi tossed her towel onto the chair, "You're on." She jogged over to the sand court.

They ended up being on the same team with four other guys while their opposing team was made up of three couples.

The game was fast and furious with a lot of smack talk going on between the teams. Abi was used to being with guys and holding her own. She laughed a lot and was impressed with Gav's physical abilities. Looking at his body a lot certainly didn't hurt either.

His shorts hung low on his hips and moved when he did. She almost missed a ball aimed for her because she was so distracted with wondering what he would look like without the shorts. Luckily, her reflexes were quick and she recovered the ball fast without too much trouble.

They ended up winning two games to the other teams' one and everyone celebrated with a drink at the outdoor bar. The group pulled a couple of tables together so everyone could gather around and talk volleyball.

Gav offered to get the first round of beer for the group so he left to go up to the bar. While he was waiting for the bartender, he stood and watched Abi in the sea of men around her. She was so at ease with herself, not at all like most of the women he knew in New York.

In New York it was a game, on both sides, and he was tired of it. He watched her talk to the guys like they were old friends, not once did she worry about her appearance or act coy, she was just Abi. She was also the exact person he could see spending the rest of his life with.

The bartender came over and got his attention so he turned away from the thought of thinking too much into the future.

Abi watched Gav as he watched her. She was discreet and made sure she listened enough to the conversation around her to look like she didn't see him. It unnerved her to know he watched her like that so intensely, but it also created excitement inside of her. She was beginning to understand the dichotomy that was Gav and how he made her feel.

The group laughed and drank for a while and it was dinnertime when they decided to part ways. Gav walked Abi back to her room, wondering what they would do now. He didn't plan anything for the evening, wanting to follow however the time went.

Abi stood outside her door, "Thank you for today."

"You're welcome," Gav returned and wondered if she was saying goodnight.

Wringing her hands, Abi looked around, not knowing how to say it, "I was kind of hoping we could eat in tonight." The words sounded so weird, she was sure he would laugh at her.

Damn his mind for the thoughts her statement created, "Whatever you want," he wasn't sure what her meaning was, "what did you have in mind?"

Feeling bold, Abi raised her hand up and rested it on his chest, her fingertips feeling the strong beat of his heart. "I had a pizza and a movie in mind." She gave him a soft kiss, "In my room in about twenty minutes?"

The idea sounded better than anything he could think of at the moment, "Twenty minutes." He brushed his fingers across her cheek and smiled.

Abi stood at her door and watched him walk to his door. They both went into their rooms and Abi leaned up against the door inside her room and wonder how on earth she wanted a man so badly when she only met him just two days ago.

Running around her room, she grabbed a sundress and started the shower so she could hurry up. There was sand everywhere. After scrubbing her skin and washing her hair, she tried to blow dry it and put some lip gloss on at the same time. She was just spritzing on some perfume when there was a knock on the door.

Abi opened the door to a smiling Gav. "I've decided," she said as she stepped back so he could come in, "that twenty minutes is a little too quick for me to get ready."

"You look beautiful," Gav said as he stepped past her. Instinctively, his hand ran down her arm.

The tingling sensations his touch caused made Abi relax immediately. Her mind buzzed with thinking of other places she wanted him to touch. Blushing, she whispered, "Thank you."

Gav watched her flush and wondered if she was thinking the same thing he was. "So," he clapped his hands together, "what movie would you like to see?"

"I don't know," Abi said, her attention turning to the television.

They sat down on the sofa and Abi grabbed the remote. After a few minutes of looking through the options, they decided on an action movie they both thought would be good. There was a knock on the door and Gav got up to answer it.

Abi glanced over to see a room service attendant wheeling in a cart. There were several covered platters on it, which surprised Abi. She waited for the steward to leave and turned to Gav.

"I thought we were doing pizza?" she asked.

With a flourish, Gav lifted up the first cover, "Yes, here's pepperoni," he lifted the second one, "here's the sausage," and he leaned over the third cover and peeked inside.

Abi laughed, "What's under that one?" She started to get up but stopped when he put the cover back down quickly, as if he was hiding a secret.

This was a tough decision for Gav, he wasn't sure he was able to open up this much to Abi yet. After all, they really didn't know one another that well yet. Well...maybe he could risk it. He finally lifted off the cover, "This is my personal favorite, the dump pizza."

Shaking her head and loving his playfulness, Abi put her hand to her chest as if she were shocked. "Oh my, I'm not sure I can handle a man who gets everything on his pizza."

"I think you can handle just about anything," Gav said. He meant the words to be heard as he said them, slow and seductive.

Abi stood up and walked over to him. "You think so, huh?" she asked while running her hand up his arm like he did to her only minutes earlier.

Gav was finding it difficult to concentrate. He wasn't hungry anymore for anything other than Abi. He let go of the cover and turned to kiss her when she twisted quickly and dove for the tray. She grabbed the piece of pizza and ran around the serving table in no time.

"You tricked me," he said with a mock glare.

Taking a bite of the pizza, Abi smiled sweetly, "Yes I did."

If she didn't look so cute, he might've been a little put out. It was tough to even try to look offended when he wanted to laugh at her antics.

Gav shook his head and turned to open a bottle of wine he ordered with their meal. After he poured two glasses and handed one to Abi, he grabbed a couple of pieces of pizza and sat down beside her on the sofa.

Abi thought the pizza was awesome, or maybe it was that she was so happy eating it here with Gav. Now was not the time to open up that whole can of whatever. She grabbed the remote and turned to the movie they decided on.

The film was definitely action-packed but Gav didn't remember a lot of it. He spent most of the time watching Abi. She started to get sleepy and ended up snuggling up against him with her head on his shoulder. By the time the credits came up, she was sleeping peacefully and his body was on full alert.

Moving slowly, trying not to wake her, Gav turned so he could get his arm behind her. Shifting her onto his lap, he put both arms around her and sat there looking at her sleeping face for a little while. He didn't want to wake her but the urge to touch her was too strong; he traced her cheek with his fingertip. Her skin was so soft under his touch.

Abi was smiling, she was warm and safe and her skin tingled. Opening her eyes, she focused on Gav's face. It was smiling down at her.

"I'm sorry I woke you," Gav whispered.

Stretching out, and feeling every party of him that touched her, Abi looked into his eyes. "I'm not; it's a very nice way to wake up."

When she was like this, Gav thought they might have a chance to pursue a relationship. Of course, convincing Abi of that was a lot more complicated. "Do you want me to go?" he asked.

Abi shook her head, "No, will you lay with me for a while?"

The question surprised him. She was asking for a new level of intimacy. He was all for it; he just had to convince his body to settle down and not try for more. "Yes." He leaned down and kissed her softly.

When his lips met hers, Abi was truly in heaven. Her whole body settled into a cushion of contentment she never experienced before. Her eyes opened in surprise when he shifted position and picked her up as if she weighed nothing.

Not speaking, Gav walked over to the bed and laid Abi down on top of the covers. Then he sat down next to her and took off his shoes. Once they were removed, he laid down beside her.

They lay on the bed, facing one another, their hands entwined, and just looked into each other's eyes. There was a lamp on in the far corner of the room that cast a warm glow over their bodies.

While looking at Gav, Abi started to get tired again and closed her eyes for just a moment. She was drifting off into a dream in no time.

Watching Abi sleep touched some deep place inside of Gav he didn't know existed. Her fingers were entwined with his but that was the only part of their bodies that touched. He wouldn't leave her tonight; he would sleep here with her close and hope that she saw what they had a chance of figuring out with this unusual set of circumstances.

Sometime during the night, Abi woke up. She didn't know why she woke up, only that she did. When her eyes opened they found a sleeping Gav beside her. She didn't want to wake him so she stayed very still and watched him.

His features were relaxed, giving him a youthful look. Not that he was old by any means, he just looked more like a teenager like this. She remembered him on the beach for the last two days and liked that he had no problem having fun. Being as she was someone who tried to be very active, it was reassuring.

The last couple of days were great; unexpected, but great. Sometimes life surprises you...who said that? Abi didn't care who, only that they were pretty smart. The outside of her mind that originally didn't want to even consider an arranged marriage, started to think maybe it was something to think about.

A while later, as sleep was taking her away again, Abi hoped that Gav thought the same thing about her.

The phone was ringing and woke Abi. She jumped up from the bed and groped around for it, not remembering where she put it the night before. Damn it, where was it? Finally finding it on the other side of the room service cart, she held it up to her cheek.

"Hello," Abi said in a gravelly voice.

Eryn sighed, "Hey I'm sorry to disturb you but we have an emergency here."

Abi's senses went on full alert, "Shoot," she said and looked around for a pen and paper. You didn't spend this many years in Crash, Fire, Rescue and not learn how to wake up really quickly.

Eryn asked her NCOIC to hold on the other line, "We have a brush fire." She was making her way to her car; Chase was driving her to Crash Crew.

"Brush fire?" Abi asked, surprised. Usually base fire handled that.

Eryn buckled her seatbelt, "Yes, it's technically off base and Kailua Fire Department is asking for all available assistance. Don't know how it started but I'm on my way to the Command Center now. Two trucks from Crash Crew are going."

Abi was grabbing her clothes and stuffing them in her bag as Eryn talked. "Got it, be there in about thirty."

"Okay," Eryn said and hung up.

Abi went into the bathroom and splashed water on her face and brushed her teeth really quickly. She went back into her room and finally noticed Gav was sitting on her bed. How could she have forgotten about him?

Abi went over and sat down beside him, "You heard?" she asked him.

"Can I help?" he asked in return.

She shook her head, "Not now, we don't even know if it's anything big."

He could tell she was downplaying it for his benefit. "Okay, will you call me later?"

A smile formed, "Try to keep me from calling you," she dared him.

Gav leaned over and took a kiss. Lord, he wished they'd made love. Maybe he wouldn't feel so disconnected from her right now. Once he sat back, he smiled.

"I'll call you as soon as I have a time frame, okay?" She stood up and grabbed her bag.

He nodded and stood up behind her. He might as well go back to his own room. It was still dark out so he would try to sleep. "Be safe," he said behind her.

Abi left her room and smiled at him, "Will do." She hurried down the hall toward the lobby.

Gav wasn't a rocket scientist, never claimed to be one, but even he could tell that her mind was already on the task ahead. Once he couldn't see her down the hall, he went back to his own room.

Abi made quick work of getting her car from the valet. She tipped him and jumped in. The drive through Honolulu was quick since it was so early yet. She decided to take the H3 freeway back since the speeds were higher.

Coming through the tunnel that burrowed through the Koolau Mountains, Abi could smell the smoke. Not a very good sign. Once she rounded a bend that overlooked the valley above the base, she saw the smoke and the flames.

"Holy crap!" she said out loud.

This was no little brush fire. This was a wildfire that was burning up brush in the foothills above the base. It hadn't reached the highway yet so that was good. Traffic was going very slowly since the visibility was poor with all the smoke. She made her way toward the fire trucks parked on the side of the road. A police man tried to get her to keep going but she flashed him her badge and he allowed her to pull off next to the other vehicles.

Once out of her car, Abi asked the police officer where the Command Center was. He pointed to a RV and she nodded her thanks.

Abi entered the Command Center to find Eryn, Bill, Chase, and two other men dressed in turn out gear huddled over a map.

"Gunny," Eryn said with a nod. "Gentleman, this is my Crash Chief, Gunny Rochelle."

The men smiled and looked back at the map.

Listening to the conversation, Abi observed that there were some conflicts in the approach the different departments wanted to use to battle the fire. Chase leaned over so he could fill her in.

"Base fire is saying they have control since it is about to cross into federal land, but Kailua fire says it's technically in their jurisdiction. Eryn just wants to get the crews out there," he whispered.

Abi nodded. A testosterone match wasn't going to help right now. She cleared her throat. "Warrant Officer Johnson, why don't I get our crews out at this point," she pointed to the line the base land started, "and make a break."

Eryn nodded, "Do it," she said and turned back to the men.

Chase winked at her and watched as she went out.

Abi walked over to where two of their trucks sat and called the guys around her. The crews were to start making a break at the line near where the base would be affected. The bad part was that if it got to that point, there were about one hundred and fifty housing units just passed it. They really didn't want to evacuate all those residents so it was better to get the fire under control now.

The crews started setting up and Abi grabbed a set of turn out gear off of one of the trucks. She was impressed that her crews thought to bring it.

They would get this done and get it done right; nobody was going to have to leave their house. Grabbing a portable radio, Abi set the frequency so she could talk to Eryn and her crews and got to work.

Chapter 11

The clock said a little after one in the afternoon when Gav decided to try and call Abi. He didn't want to bug her but he was worried. He dialed her number and waited. No answer. Not wanting to leave a message, he hung up the phone.

An hour later, after pacing his hotel room like a caged animal, he decided to contact Eryn to see if she had any news. Again, he dialed and waited.

Eryn picked up her phone, "Warrant Officer Johnson," she said in a clipped tone.

"Eryn, this is Gav," he sounded pathetic to himself, "I was wondering if you had an update."

Even up to her eyeballs with stress and cranky men, Eryn managed a smile, "Hold on, Gav," she said and handed the phone to her husband. She mouthed Gav to him.

Chase took his wife's phone, "This is Chase Johnson," he said and caught himself before saying Master Sgt. Being retired was still an adjustment.

"Chase," Gav cleared his throat, "This is Gav Moslov," he was really unsure of what to say now. "I was wondering if Eryn had an update."

Smiling at his wife, Chase walked out of the Command trailer, "It's going okay, the fire spread quickly since there is mainly dry brush in the area and the crews are working to keep it from getting too close to the base where it could endanger some base housing." He looked over to see if there was any noticeable progress. Unfortunately he didn't see any. "We've got the local civilian fire department, base Fed Fire, and Crash Crew all working on it so hopefully it won't be a long process."

Gav appreciated the no-nonsense explanation. "Thank you," he answered, not knowing what else to say.

Chase had an idea, "Why don't I come and pick you up? You can hang around with me while we wait for the women to kick these guys' asses and get this done."

Not being able to help it, Gav laughed. It sounded like an apt description of both Abi and Eryn. "That would be great," he answered and told Chase where to pick him up.

An hour later the men were in Chase's jeep and going back over to Kailua to pick up some food. Gav felt better knowing he was going to at least see where Abi was and try to help out in some way.

"So," Gav turned to look at Chase, "Eryn said you recently retired."

Nodding, Chase smiled, "Yes, I happened to be in love and wanted to marry my boss. A very big no no in the Corps."

Gav didn't doubt that. "So they kicked you out?" he asked.

"NO," Chase said loudly, "I chose to go." He turned off the highway and down the road into Kailua. "I was on my last tour anyway and was eligible for retirement and Eryn's career is really going so it wasn't a hard choice to make."

Looking at the passing palm trees, Gav smiled. "What do you do now?" He was curious how it worked for Abi's friends.

Chase turned on the signal to turn into the restaurant they were picking up the food from, "I am a DOD contractor and work closely with the Marine Corps so I'm still in the loop." He pulled into a spot and turned off the jeep. "It nice, the money is good, and I got to marry Eryn."

They got out of the jeep and went into the small building. The order was called in to the restaurant in advance so they only needed to pay and pick up the food. Gav waited patiently for Chase to finish with the owner. He found he really liked Chase, the man was straight forward and not afraid to admit his feelings for his wife. Hell, he gave up his career for her.

They walked back to the jeep, loaded up with food, and started to go toward the base. Chase said it would be easier to get to the Command location from the base. The Military Police and local law enforcement closed off the roads that were close to where the fire was.

As they were leaving the base toward the mountains, Gav could see a lot of smoke up ahead. The smell of burning brush filled the air and made his throat sting. He saw the fire trucks only about a mile from the front gate of the base. No wonder they were working so hard.

Chase pulled off the road and hopped out. Gav followed him with the bags of food into a big RV trailer. Once inside, it was a little easier to breathe.

They put the bags down and Gav stood where he was. He could see a few other people in the trailer talking amongst themselves. They seemed to be focused on wind speed and direction from what he could hear of the conversation. The tension in the small area was palpable and he didn't envy Eryn for having to deal with it.

Eryn saw her husband and Gav come in and was relieved they were able to get back. "Hi," she said and kissed Chase quickly. She walked over to Gav and hugged him. "Thanks for coming," she said to Gav.

"Thanks for letting me," Gav answered.

Chase came over and stood beside Gav, "Any change?" he directed to Eryn.

"Unfortunately," Eryn said with a worried look, "no." She turned to the map, "The stupid winds have picked up and the crews are having a tough time getting it under control."

Gav was pretty sure he shouldn't say anything but he couldn't help it, "Where is Abi?" he asked them.

Chase and Eryn exchanged quick looks. This was Abi's job and maybe she told Gav about it and maybe she didn't. It wasn't for either of them to interfere.

Eryn spoke quietly, "She's directing the crews."

Being from a corporate background, Gav knew a line of BS when he heard it. However, he was also here as a courtesy and this was Abi's world, not his. He nodded and waited for Chase and Eryn to finish talking.

A few minutes later, Chase motioned for Gav to follow him out. They weren't really supposed to be there so it was time to go and leave Eryn and Abi to their jobs. Gav watched Chase and could tell that he missed this part of the job. They got in the jeep and backtracked the way they came earlier. Once they were back on the base, Gav had the nerve to ask a question.

"Is it always like this?" He was curious about what he should expect from Abi's career.

Chase shook his head, "It's a feast and famine kind of thing." He drove through the base and went out the back gate toward their house in Kailua. "A lot of waiting but then, all hell breaks loose."

Nodding, Gav figured as much. "Abi isn't just directing the crews, is she?"

Smart guy, Chase thought. "No," he replied. He wasn't going to lie, not even for Abi.

Gav sent up a silent prayer that Abi was safe.

The fire was turning and they were having a hell of a time containing it. Abi was standing next to a P-19 and getting pissed. They were almost out of water and called in the tanker. It was taking longer than anticipated and the fire was getting a little too close for Abi's comfort.

She could see the Fed Fire guys to the east of her and the Kailua Fire Department to the west and neither of them seemed to be making much progress either. The charred hills were spread out before her and smoldered behind the main fire line. If the damn brush wasn't so dry they might be able to get it out quicker.

Brush fires were not the norm for Crash Crew so they were going on training scenarios rather than actual experience. Her suit was hot and she was sweating like crazy underneath it but at least she wasn't burnt.

She was holding a booster line at the side of the P-19 while one of the guys on her truck was manning the roof turret at the front of the truck. The other P-19 was to the side and trying to make headway on their section.

This was a bitch of a day and she was tired.

One of her guys had to be sent to the base medical clinic for smoke inhalation and another was taken for exhaustion. Being in the gear and out in this heat was not good for any of them.

"Gunny Rochelle," Warrant Officer Johnson said over the radio.

Abi went behind the truck so she could hear better and answered, "Go ahead."

Eryn was outside the command vehicle and could see Abi's crews with her binoculars. "Your fresh crews are here and the tanker is making its way over to you." She nodded to Master Sgt. Phillips, "Master Sgt. is on his way to relieve you. Get back here."

Smiling, Abi responded quickly, "Yes, ma'am."

A few minutes later the Master Sgt. pulled up with the relief trucks and tanker. They positioned alongside Abi's crew and as soon as their water started, Abi's trucks pulled back to return to the Crash Barn.

When Abi got back to where Eryn was standing near the command vehicle, she was beat. She tried to shore up her reserves for her boss.

"Good job," Eryn said and guided her to a command truck. "Have some water; I have some food over here too."

Abi gladly accepted the water but shook her head at the food. She didn't think she could eat just yet.

They were sitting there when the radio crackled, "Warrant Officer Johnson," Master Sgt. Phillips said, "we've got it about twenty percent contained on our end. It looks like Fed Fire is making some progress on their end too."

Eryn listened and smiled, "Roger."

"Sure," Abi said sarcastically, "my crews get it all started and he swoops in for the touchdown."

Laughing, Eryn patted Abi's shoulder, "We're all on the winning team here," she said.

Abi nodded, "You're supposed to say that."

Eryn laughed again, "Yes I am."

An hour later the trucks were pulling back. Trucks from Honolulu Fire Department came over to relieve the crews and make sure there were no flare ups.

By the time everyone got back to Crash Crew and de-briefed, it was almost dark. The crews that responded were sent home and a relief crew was brought in to cover the airfield. Eryn promised to do something for the crews for their good job.

Bill, Eryn, and Abi were sitting in Eryn's office when they heard voices outside in the hallway. Chase and Gav filled the doorway with smiles on their faces.

Eryn got up and went to Chase, hugging him tightly. "Hello," she said and kissed him.

Abi was never really jealous of her friend's open affection until now. She could see Gav standing behind Chase and she would never have the nerve to kiss him and hug him in front of everyone here.

Master Sgt. Phillips stood and cleared his throat, "That's my cue," he nodded to Abi, "Gunny," and shook Chase's hand. When he came face to face with Gav, he stuck out his hand, "Gav," he said and left.

"Good to know you and the Master Sgt. aren't holding grudges," Eryn said and winked at Gav.

Oh crap, that's right! Abi blushed remembering that Eryn knew about their little scuffle the other day.

Gav smiled, "Nah, we both play well with others," he said lightly.

Eryn and Chase laughed which put Abi a little more at ease. If she wasn't so physically and emotionally exhausted, she might be able to carry on a conversation.

Gav stood there and watched Abi. She looked beat! He spent the better part of the afternoon and evening talking to Chase and learned a good many things about her. Some things surprised him and some didn't. They'd spent almost two full days together so he thought he had a pretty good idea about her. His thoughts stopped dead when her eyes met his.

Hi, Gav mouthed to Abi.

Abi smiled, hi, she mouthed back.

"Well, let's get a move on," Chase said and led his wife out into the hallway.

Confused, Abi stood and winced at the protest her muscles were making.

Gav was torn. Did he offer her help or not? This was where she worked and the one thing he did pick up from Chase's company today was that she had a major pride issue.

Seeing Gav keep his distance made Abi wonder if he was upset with her for leaving him in Honolulu at the hotel. "How did you get here?" she asked when she was beside him.

He nodded his head toward Chase, "Chase was nice enough to pick me up and bring me over here."

It wasn't tough to love Chase, the guy was sweet. She owed him. "I am filthy and I need to shower," she said to him as she picked up her bag.

Gav smiled, he could smell the smoke on her. Not that it made a bit of difference in his body's reaction to her nearness. He still wanted her with him.

They followed Chase and Eryn to the cars and stopped.

"Dinner at our place?" Eryn asked.

Abi looked to Gav, who nodded. She looked back to Eryn, "Yes, just give me time for a shower."

Chase put Eryn in the jeep, "No problem, that'll give us time to get the grill going."

Eryn and Chase pulled out and headed toward their place. Gav stood outside the car with Abi feeling a little funny. "Did you want me to go with them and give you some time?"

Looking at him, his face partially in shadow, Abi thought he looked a little mysterious. "I would feel better if you were with me," she smiled slyly, "besides, they already left; you'd have to walk."

Smart ass! Gav laughed. She was a handful. "Good point," He said and got in the car.

Abi drove them back to her barracks room and got out. She would definitely need some pain reliever.

Gav followed her to the door and waited for her to open it. He took her bag from her, getting a smile of thanks for his efforts, and set it on the desk. She went straight to the bathroom without saying anything. He watched the door close and turned on a light in the living area. He heard the shower start and searched the cabinets for some pain reliever. Finding a glass, he filled it with water and got out a couple of pills for her.

Not knowing what else to do, Gav sat down on the sofa and turned on the flat screen TV. He fell asleep while watching the news.

Abi came out of the bathroom in her robe. She turned the corner and saw Gav sleeping on the couch, the TV droning in the background.

After walking over to her kitchenette, she saw he put out some water and ibuprofen out for her. Smiling, she dutifully took them and went into her closet to get dressed.

Once she had on a pair of jeans and a shirt, she went back out to her living area and grabbed her phone. She texted Eryn to say Gav was asleep and they would need a rain check for dinner. Eryn texted her back saying okay, she and Chase were beat too.

Abi grabbed an extra throw blanket out of her closet and brought it with her to the couch. She sat down softly and leaned up against Gav, her hand resting on his chest. She watched the TV for a while until the exhaustion took her.

Gav woke up some time during the night. He looked over at Abi's phone on the table and saw it said a little after three. He'd fallen asleep on her; geez, some Romeo he was. He looked over to see her tucked in beside him, like she was the night before. She was sleeping soundly and didn't move when he woke up.

He moved his hand over her hair, loving the softness of it against his fingers. He shifted positions so he was stretched out and brought her with him so they were lying on the sofa together. It was comforting to have her beside him and it wasn't long before he fell back to sleep.

Abi woke with a start. She got her bearings quickly but a jolt of panic went through her system. Gav was here...in her room...he spent the night. It wasn't that she wasn't used to spending the night with a man; she just wasn't used to spending it in her room. That was one rule she never broke...until last night.

Trying to be quiet, she moved so she could climb over Gav's sleeping form. Even in sleep he was gorgeous. She had one leg on the floor beside the sofa when she felt him shift. Her eyes looked up just in time to meet his.

"Good morning," Gav said. He woke up when he felt movement.

Abi stayed where she was, half on and off of him, "Good morning."

Gav looked down at their bodies and smiled. She was nervous and he wondered if it was because he stayed or because he caught her trying to sneak away.

Her muscles were sore but she didn't know what she should do, "I, uh, was just getting up." She moved her other leg to set it down and brushed it across his leg and thigh when she did it. The friction, even with her clothes on, made her skin heat up with awareness.

When her leg slid across his thigh, Gav had to hold back a moan. Before she could finish moving over him, he put his hands up and held her sides, just below her rib cage. "Where are you going?" he asked. The teasing look in his eyes only thinly disguised his need.

Oh my, Abi thought to herself, if he keeps looking at me like that, I'm going to have to kiss him. "Uh, the bathroom," she said softly.

Knowing that was a no-win argument, Gav let go of her body and let her move off of him. He sat up and watched her walk into the bathroom. He would need to go in there after she came out to splash some cold water on his face and get his urges under control. She had a potent effect on him that was for sure.

Abi stood in the bathroom and looked in the mirror. What was wrong with her? She let a man stay over in her room, acts shy and looks like an idiot, and she can't stop thinking about making love with him. Even after all she was worried about with her parents and work, she couldn't stop thinking about seeing him naked and trying things she never even considered before.

She splashed some water on her face and brushed her teeth. When she came out, Gav was sitting up on the couch and looking great. Smiling, Abi wondered how he could pull that off with having slept on a couch.

Gav stood and walked over to her. "I have a question for you," he said in a soft voice.

"Yes," Abi replied, wondering what he was going to ask. Her pulse sped up in anticipation.

Taking Abi's hand, Gav brought it to his lips and kissed it softly, "Do you have an extra toothbrush?" He gave her a lopsided smile.

Abi closed her eyes and sighed, he was a trouble maker! "Yes, below the sink," she said as she stepped aside and let him go into the bathroom.

When Gav was in the bathroom, Abi walked over and picked up her phone. It was past eight so Eryn should be up. She pushed the contact and waited.

Eryn looked at her phone and smiled, "Good morning, I want details," she said in a rushed whisper. Her husband looked at her with raised eyebrows.

"Unfortunately," Abi plopped down on the couch, "there are no details." She peeked around to see if the bathroom door was still closed. It was. "We slept on the couch in my room."

Putting down the newspaper she was reading, Eryn pursed her lips, "Really...," she drew out the word.

Nodding, Abi answered, "Yes, and you know that's a rule I do not break!"

"I know," Eryn said back. "How about you two come over here? We'll grill out and have some fun."

The bathroom door opened and Gav stepped into the room. He saw Abi on the phone and walked over to where she was sitting at the desk. She pulled the phone down and covered it with her hand.

"Would you like to go over to Eryn and Chase's today or do you have other plans?" she asked him.

Gav cupped her cheek with his palm, "I'm wherever you are today."

Not wanting Gav to see how his tender words affected her, Abi just nodded and brought the phone back up to her cheek. She was still looking at Gav when she spoke to Eryn, "Yes, we'll grab some breakfast and then head over."

"Good," Eryn hung up the phone and put it down on the table. She looked at her husband, a gleam in her eye. "I think she's a goner."

Chase set down the sports section, "I can't speak for her but I spent half of yesterday with Gav and I like him."

Eryn nodded, she sensed he was making a point, "How do you think he feels about her?"

This is just the stuff Chase didn't want to get roped into. It was bad enough that this thing with Mitch and Katherine had them all spinning out of control. "I didn't ask," he answered honestly.

Looking at her husband, Eryn knew he wasn't saying everything but she wouldn't let her curiosity about Abi and Gav come between them. "Okay," she said with a sigh.

Oh, he knew that tone. "If I had to guess, I'd say he really likes her." He reached over and held Eryn's hand in his, "The guy flew from New York to Honolulu with like two days' notice, Eryn. I'm pretty sure he's crazy about her."

It was very nice when her suspicions were confirmed but Eryn would not gloat...much. "Thank you, sweetie." She leaned over and kissed him.

One kiss from his wife would not be enough; Chase wrapped his arm around her and pulled her onto his lap. "I want more of that please."

Eryn figured that if Abi and Gav were going to have some breakfast before coming over she and her husband had some time. "I think I can oblige you, Master Sgt," she said and wrapped her arms around his neck.

A few minutes later they were heading to their bedroom to explore their own wild attraction.

Abi decided it would be best if they drove into Honolulu so Gav could shower and change before they went over to Eryn and Chase's house. She felt awful that he paid for two hotel rooms that they never even used last night. When she was driving, she brought it up.

"Gav," she looked over, "I'm feeling really bad about you paying for the hotel rooms so I'd like to pay you for mine."

Sighing, Gav looked over at her. He was very content and having her say that immediately put him on edge. "No, thank you," he said with finality in his voice.

Suspecting he was stubborn was a little different than being face to face with the reality of it. "I'm serious," she said soberly.

"I am too," Gav looked over at her, "I chose to get the rooms before I even knew if you would stay in Honolulu so I knew how much it would cost." He tried to lighten his tone, "I'm not worried about it."

Abi wiped her face with her hand in frustration. It was also a last ditch effort to not say anything impulsive. "But it bothers me."

Turning so he could look at her, Gav clenched his jaw, "Well it would seriously piss me off if you paid for it so what are we going to do?"

After the intimacy of the last two nights, it was kind of a relief for Abi to be arguing with him. She didn't understand why that was but she went with it. "Fine," she returned in a snotty tone.

Gav turned away, deciding it was best to look out the window than argue with a woman who was driving and being unreasonable.

The rest of the drive was a test of patience for both of them. The tension in the car was like a tightly pulled string, it would snap at the slightest amount of pressure. Neither spoke, preferring to let the other sit and wonder what to do.

When Abi pulled up to the hotel, she was exhausted. Holding in the anger and frustration sapped her. She quietly followed Gav to their rooms and stopped at the door to hers. "I think I'll just lay down while you're changing if you don't mind."

Gav could see she was wiped, he shouldn't have picked a fight with her in the car. He felt bad about it. "That's fine," he said, his tone much gentler.

Abi nodded and used her room key to open the door. The room service attendant had been there so the bed was made and looked inviting. She crawled onto it and laid her head down, slipping into a deep sleep right away.

Gav knocked softly on her door but didn't hear anything. Maybe she wasn't in there? He knocked again but got no response. She gave him a room key for her room the day they arrived so he used it to go in.

Abi was on the bed and fast asleep, her hair splayed across the pillow like soft waves of honey. Her breathing was deep and even and he didn't want to wake her. Picking up his phone, he sent a text to Chase saying they would be late. After seeing the responding text of 'ok,' Gav walked over to the overstuffed chair next to the bed and sat down.

He answered some emails for work on his phone and sent a couple of texts to friends. No one except his boss and his parents knew he was here so there were a few comments. He was smiling at some smart ass comment a friend of his texted him when he looked up and right into Abi's eyes. She was awake.

"Hi," he said and put his phone down.

Abi woke up to see Gav sitting by the bed and texting on his phone. He was unguarded and smiling. She liked seeing the way his face showed his feelings. His features were really expressive. Seeing him like that only made him more attractive to her.

Sitting up, Abi smiled at him, "Hi," she looked around, "I'm sorry I feel asleep."

Gav was surprised, "Why? You told me you were going to lay down."

Leave it to him to point out the obvious. "I think I meant that you should've woken me up."

Shaking his head, Gav looked into her eyes, "Why? You looked beautiful." The statement was plain and it was the truth as he saw it.

Those words of his were going to get them into a lot of trouble. Abi bit her lip, "I'm sorry about being a jerk in the car."

It was nice of her to apologize, Gav thought. "I'm sorry I was offended." He was partly to blame for their stress.

"It's just," she started to say as she swung her legs over the side of the bed so she was facing him, "I'm not used to these "grand gestures" and I'm not sure how to take them."

Gav stood and moved so he could sit beside her on the bed. He wrapped his fingers around hers. "I'm sorry that you don't have them more often." He smiled when she looked up into his eyes, "The men in your life, up to now, have been asses!"

Abi laughed at the accurate description of her exes. "Yes, I guess they have been." She rubbed her thumb across the back of his hand, "How can I make up for my behavior?" she asked.

"Simple," Gav's eyes twinkled, "You can kiss me."

Nodding, Abi laughed, "I could...or I could just hug you and let it go at that."

Gav mocked sadness, "I suppose," he stuck out his bottom lip for dramatic effect, "or you could just kiss me and make it all better."

How could she possibly resist that puppy dog face? "Okay, one kiss," she said and pretended it was difficult for her.

He knew Abi was teasing him, but Gav didn't care as long as he got a kiss out of it. "Okay," he answered.

Abi leaned over and covered his cheek with her hand as she kissed him. It was meant to reassure him but it immediately burned her up on the inside. The heat crisscrossing between their bodies was making the room feel like a sauna.

Gav's tongue came out to gently touch Abi's lip and when she parted her lips for him to enter, he was lost on the ride of pleasure her touch took him on.

When Abi pulled away from him, it was not because she wanted to but because she needed to for her own sanity. The man reduced her to a pile of liquid on the inside and she needed to retain some sense of control here.

"Whoo," she breathed out.

Smiling, Gav knew just what she meant. "Yep," he responded and smiled into her eyes.

Getting up, Abi knew they had to go. If they didn't they would end up making love right there. She wasn't ready to open up that door just yet.

"Let's go," she said and pulled him up.

Gav was disappointed but not mad, he understood. "Okay."

The two of them left the room and walked toward the lobby in silence, giving each other a little space.

Chapter 12

As soon as Abi and Gav arrived at Eryn's and Chase's place, they could smell the delicious aromas of cooking meat drifting through the air. Abi led the way and knocked quickly before entering. Eryn always told her she didn't have to knock but Abi felt funny just walking into someone's home.

They went through the entryway and straight into the kitchen. Eryn was cutting up vegetables and smiled at them.

"Well hello there, you two," Eryn said.

Abi spoke first, "Hi, sorry we're late."

Eryn's eyes twinkled with mischief, "Oh, I'm sure you had a good reason," she answered in a knowing tone.

Abi blushed and shifted her position so there was a little more room between her and Gav. She didn't necessarily mind the teasing, she just knew it wasn't true and didn't want him to be mad.

"You," Eryn pointed at Gav, "can join the cook out by the grill as long as you grab two beers from the fridge and take one out to my husband."

He didn't have to be told twice. Gav nodded, grabbed the beers, and headed out to the lanai.

The women followed him with their eyes until the sliding door closed behind him.

Letting out a sigh, Abi slid onto one of the bar stools in Eryn's kitchen. "Thanks for inviting us." She smiled.

Something in Abi's tone stopped Eryn's movements. Her friend sounded sad.

Once she was sitting down, Abi propped her chin on her palm and watched Eryn work. When she stopped, Abi looked up and into her friend's eyes. They didn't look happy.

"What?" Abi asked, exasperated.

Eryn grabbed a towel to wipe her hands and went around the bar to sit next to Abi, "What do you mean what?" she asked in return.

Sighing, Abi sat up and said, "You look mad at me."

Shaking her head, Eryn smiled, "I'm not mad at you at all. I see that there is something there between you and Gav and I'm giving you a hard time about it but that's all."

Abi looked outside to see Gav and Chase discussing something over the grill. Guy talk she suspected. When she looked back at Eryn, she was trying to keep her emotions in check. "I know there's something there but we seem to be circling and neither of us knows what move to make."

Listening to Abi's words, Eryn was reminded of when she and Chase were first thrown back into working together. After ten years apart, the sparks were still there and it left them both reeling in a sea of insecurities and uncertainty. She could well remember that feeling was not a good one and pitied her friend for having to go through it.

"I like him...a lot...but it's not the way it's supposed to be." She looked back out for a moment then back to Eryn, "You know."

If Abi thought she would get sympathy, she was mistaken. "Abi, I know what you're saying but I don't agree with how it's "supposed" to be." She used her fingers to emphasize the word.

Abi slid off the stool and went over to the refrigerator to pull out a bottled water. She took a drink and turned back to Eryn, who was watching her expectantly. "It's supposed to be me meeting a guy and dating for a couple years then we decide to get married and have some kids."

Simple, Eryn thought, but not completely realistic. "So you think that Chase and I had this whole monumental blow up and so it's not supposed to be this way?"

Damn, Abi thought, now she'd insulted her friend, "No," she didn't know what to say.

"It's okay," Eryn said and walked over to hug her friend. When she pulled back, she led Abi back to the bar stool. "I'm just saying that we each have our own story, Abi. It's not a cut and dry kind of thing."

Gav walked inside and could feel the tension. He walked into a discussion, "I'm sorry," he said and went right back outside.

Eryn chuckled, "The man is good," she looked at Abi, "he's very intuitive and he seems to care for you."

"He can kiss like crazy too," Abi mumbled and felt like a first class dope when she realized the words were spoken out loud.

Looking dreamy, Eryn got back up to go back to chopping her vegetables, "I remember those days."

It was easy to talk about this with Eryn, Abi just didn't want to talk about it with anyone right now.

Gav and Chase both came in with a large platter of food and set it on the table. Chase went over and kissed his wife and grabbed some bowls from the counter to place on the table.

The four of them had a nice lunch and sat around the table discussing all sorts of things. Mainly Eryn quizzed Gav about his life back in New York. Abi was content to listen to him talk. His voice was very melodic for a man and it lulled her. She sat up when she noticed all three of them looking at her.

"What?" Abi asked, embarrassed that she zoned out.

Eryn grabbed her glass to refill it with ice water, "I was just asking when you thought you'd be going back to New York?"

Abi was caught, "I, uh, don't know yet," she answered and looked at Gav. His face was closed so she wasn't sure what he was thinking.

"Probably for the wedding right?" Chase asked. He took a drink of his beer and grabbed a roll from the platter, "Just so you know, Gav, I think the whole idea of an arranged marriage is kind of cool."

Gav looked at Chase when he heard the words and didn't really know how to respond. Abi didn't tell him that she'd discussed their situation with her friends. Knowing she had really upset him and he wasn't sure why. He looked from Chase to Eryn and finally to Abi.

Once Chase looked up, he realized he said something he shouldn't have. These women really needed to clarify these things with him. He turned to Gav, "I'm sorry, I thought you knew that I knew."

The four of them sat there just looking around and not knowing what to say.

Abi could see the transformation in Gav's features and she knew this was not going to end well. He was angry and she figured he had a right to be.

"Abi, why don't you and Gav go out onto the lanai and talk while Chase and I clean this up." She stood to grab plates and nodded to her husband to follow.

Without saying anything, Abi stood and moved around the table so she could go through the sliding glass doors that led out to the lanai.

She didn't even check to see if Gav was following; she sat down on a chair and waited.

Gav closed the sliding door behind him and walked over to where Abi sat, "You could've told me they knew."

Not liking his accusatory tone, Abi got defensive, "What does it matter? You seem to think this whole thing is great so why can't I tell me friends?"

Dropping his head for a second, in an effort to gain some control over his anger, Gav wanted to talk about this rationally. "You can tell your friends but I would just like a heads up."

"That's it?" Abi snapped back, "You need a heads up? How about me, Gav? I didn't seem to need a heads up for you to come here to Hawaii."

Damn, she had a point, Gav thought to himself. "You're right, but that was a little different."

Getting madder with each word, Abi had a hard time keeping the venom in her mind from spilling out of her lips. "Are you kidding me?" she said with a raised voice.

Gav stood there and looked at her. He was torn between getting mad and being fascinated at the way her eyes lit up when she was revved up with anger.

"You," she walked around the patio, her hands waving to emphasize her words, "just call one of my friends and surprise me so you can bully me into marrying you with kisses and words." She stopped and faced him, "And you say everything I want to hear but you don't follow up with it. How are you any different than the asses I've met up until now?" She didn't plan to throw the words he told her back at him but she couldn't help it.

Her comment was meant to hurt and it did, a lot. "I see," he responded.

Abi really didn't want to fight with him, "I know you think that comment was out of line and maybe it was." She sighed, trying to fight back the tears, "But I told you from the get go that this idea was ridiculous."

"Yes," Gav shot back, "and you've had no problems telling me that from the get go."

Feeling defeated and drained, Abi stood there and looked at him, "What did you expect to happen, Gav?"

His eyes lifted to meet hers. She was only a few feet away so he closed the distance between them in a couple of steps. Without thinking about anything, he grabbed her waist and pulled her to him. The feel of her body flush with his made him burn with something much hotter than anger.

Her mind was telling her to push him away but her body was telling her to go with it. Let him make her feel alive. She looked up and met his eyes with hers as he was lowering his mouth to take hers.

The kiss was like placing C-4 in a tank of gasoline. The heat between them was incinerating them both. Mouths melded and breathing mingled in with moans. Hands roamed and explored in a mutual need for more.

Abi pulled away awkwardly when she heard a sound behind them.

"Uh," Eryn said as she came out to the lanai and saw her friend in a pretty spectacular embrace with Gav. "Would you two care to come in so we can apologize or do you want to keep making out here on our lanai?"

Gav couldn't help but laugh. Abi looked embarrassed. Eryn was a very feisty lady who didn't believe in pulling punches. Without answering, he gestured for Abi to precede him back inside.

Chase was in the kitchen cleaning up when the three of them came in. He turned and looked at Gav and Abi with a sheepish smile, "Hey guys, I'm sorry if I caused a fight."

Eryn snorted, "Oh no, sweetie, these two weren't fighting when I went out there."

Abi blushed and stuck her tongue out at Eryn when she walked over to her husband.

Chase caught the look between Eryn and Abi and was relieved that everything seemed okay again. "I didn't know you didn't know we knew, Gav."

Nodding, Gav moved closer to Abi and put his hand on her side. "It's okay, Chase, the whole thing is a little unusual."

"A little?" Abi muttered in a flat voice.

The three others looked at Abi with a blank expression on their faces. Nobody moved.

"What?" Abi asked sarcastically. "I'm just saying this whole thing is pointless."

His temper was flaring again and Gav didn't like it. Why did Abi keep him on the brink of being pissed off so much? How could she kiss him the way she did and tell him that there was no point in them being together? He sure as hell didn't understand it.

Gav was about to say something to Abi when the doorbell rang.

Eryn and Chase left the room together to answer the front door. Abi turned around to say something to Gav but the look on his face kept her from speaking. Oh, he was mad. That might even be an understatement. She wanted to make it better but the others were coming back into the room. He moved away from her and went into the dining room.

Bill Phillips followed Eryn and Chase into the kitchen in time to see Gunny Rochelle standing there. She looked gorgeous in her shorts and tanned skin. "Hey, Gunny," he said with a smile, "you look gorgeous."

Before Abi could respond, Gav walked back in the kitchen and was about to take a swing at Bill.

Seeing what was going to happen, Abi stepped in Gav's way and maneuvered him around so they could go back outside.

"Hey, Gav," Bill said lightly.

Gav didn't respond, just let Abi direct him outside. Once she shut the sliding door she turned to him with fire in her eyes.

Abi kept a forced smile on her face until she turned to face Gav. "What the hell, Gav!" she almost yelled.

He didn't care if that jackass was her boss, Gav could hear the innuendo in his voice and he didn't like it. "What?" he asked back.

This whole thing was crazy, they were just teetering on insanity here and she couldn't stand it. "He's my boss, that's what."

"I don't care, he can't talk to you like that." Gav snapped at her. "He treats you like a cheap piece of ass or something."

The words knocked Abi back emotionally. Is that how Gav saw her? "What?" she asked in shocked frustration.

Gav pointed to the house, "I've taken sexual harassment classes, Abi. The man is a pig."

If this were anyone else, Abi was pretty sure she'd be laughing right now. It was all just absurd.

"Okay," she said more calmly, "I just want to clarify why you're mad." She walked over and sat down at the table nearby. "Are you mad because I told Eryn and Chase about the arrangement our parents made or are you mad that my boss is a flirt?"

Gav looked at her and knew she was calmer than he was right now. "Both," he spat out.

Abi had to clamp her lips to keep from laughing. "Well," she patted the seat next to her hoping he would sit, "I'm sorry that I told Eryn and Chase. I wasn't expecting you to show up here and meet them."

Nodding, Gav walked over and sat in the seat beside her. "I know," he mumbled. He wanted to feel bad about the fact that he just showed up but he couldn't after what they had between them.

"About the Master Sgt." She looked over and into his eyes. They were gorgeous and full of emotion. "I have handled worse so I think you should trust that I can see through a nice bit of BS."

She was right, Gav thought, he should trust her. The problem was he didn't want to think of any man touching her now that he had. It took every single ounce of restraint he had not to make love with her and he had to leave tomorrow and leave her here with the Don Juan wannabe. He was pissed. And he was taking it out on Abi.

Abi felt sorry for Gav. None of this could be blamed on anyone fully. "I've been in the Corps for over fifteen years now." She smiled, trying to lighten the mood, "Do you think this is the only time I've been hit on?"

The question prompted a feeling of protection as well as a healthy dose of jealousy. "I'm leaving tomorrow," he said softly.

Abi nodded, "I know."

He turned so he could face Abi fully and look into her eyes, "Listen, I know we didn't really settle all of this marriage stuff."

This was not something they were likely to settle either as far as Abi was concerned. "I know, I'm sorry I can't just fall in line like you and our parents want."

Gav took a breath, "You know, you keep lumping me in with them." He looked at her softly, "I wasn't really on board until I got here."

His words, again, made her think that all of this craziness was possible. "I still think its nuts and even if we do click, it just seems so wrong to just get married like that." She had to be honest with him. She owed it to herself and to him.

Nodding, Gav brought his hand up to cup her chin. He leaned in and kissed her softly. The kiss was quick but still packed a punch to his system. If Abi felt one half of what he did when they kissed, she wasn't as sure as she was telling him about not getting married. He would just have to bide his time.

"Okay," he said when he pulled away. Her eyes were large and as aroused as his were. "Let's go back in so I can make nice with the rock star inside." He couldn't keep the sarcasm out of his voice.

Abi giggled, "Okay, come on, Floyd Mayweather," she stood and offered her hand to him, "Let's see if you can keep control of your compulsion to punch somebody out."

Gav followed her and mumbled, "Not somebody, just Bill."

Laughing, Abi opened the door and walked through. They might just make it through the day after all.

That evening, they were driving back to Honolulu. The rest of the day did go pretty well. Gav promised to be nice and did a really good job at not punching her boss. She smiled while she drove down H3. She would worry about him leaving later on. Now she just wanted to enjoy the easy feeling they had.

"What are you smiling about?" Gav asked. He'd been watching her subtly since they left Eryn and Chase's place.

Abi looked over, the dimming light of dusk casting shadows in the car. "I was thinking how nice this is."

He could appreciate that since he was thinking the same thing. It was one thing to have a chemistry with someone and something else to like spending time with them. Some people didn't understand the difference. Before meeting Abi, he sure didn't.

She could feel the gears in his mind turning. "I am really glad you came to Hawaii to see me."

"Well," Gav looked over with a serious expression, "I was actually here to see Hawaii and thought you'd be okay too." He smiled so silly.

Abi laughed, "Okay, you go with that."

Reaching over, Gav took her hand in his, "I don't want to be serious right now, I don't want to think about tomorrow; I just want to focus on tonight."

The way his thoughts seemed to mirror hers really kicked Abi's heart into overdrive. It just amazed her at how much he could peg her thoughts with words. She squeezed his hand and nodded. Words were a little too tough to form right now.

They got to the hotel and went to their respective rooms to change. Abi mentioned that she'd like to go down to the beach again so Gav suggested they go down tonight. It was too dark to really swim but they could sit and talk.

After meeting up, they walked down to where the hotel had a beach bar and sat at it. Surprisingly, it was still open for those hold outs who didn't want to give up the gentle breezes and beautiful Hawaiian evenings.

Gav ordered for them and they sat and talked about the day. Gav asked more questions about her job and she answered them as best she could. After being in the Corps for so many years, you used the acronyms and forgot that civilians didn't know them.

They laughed about things and commented on some of the other patrons. The conversation was easy and sweet. After a while, Abi loosened up. She looked at him differently. Suddenly Gav wasn't some guy her parents wanted her to marry but he was a very interesting and very sexy man she wanted to be with more than anything.

Gav was talking about some of the guys they played volleyball with when he noticed the change in Abi's expression. Her eyes darkened and she looked at him very intensely. His body responded before his brain kicked into gear and he knew he wanted her.

"I was thinking," Abi said softly as she ran her fingers over his hand that rested on the bar, "that maybe we could go back to my room now."

Swallowing hard, Gav would have to be a complete idiot to miss the innuendo. "Are you sure?" he asked. He didn't want her to regret anything that happened between them.

Abi looked out over the dimly lit area toward the beach. Even in the darkness she could see the waves crashing against the sand. It was the same thing inside her, her feelings thrashing around and making her want the excitement she was pretty sure he could show her.

"Yes," she said softly.

Gav knew he should probably rethink the idea but he didn't want to. His whole adult life, he played it safe; with his career, his heart, he was always reasonable. Something about Abi made him want to just toss it aside. He nodded and motioned for the bartender to give him the check.

They walked back to the hotel in silence. Other than holding hands, they didn't touch. Abi was getting nervous and she wasn't sure exactly why. They were both adults and with the way his kisses melted her insides, she was pretty confident that anything else would be just as great. She would look at him almost shyly and then away.

Once they were in the hallway leading to their rooms, Gav's heart started beating loudly. He wondered if Abi felt the same way and realized she did when he could feel the hand he was holding shake a little.

"I'm nervous," he said when they got to the door of her room.

Abi chuckled, "Me too and I'm not sure why."

Gav shrugged, "Anticipation, maybe." He wanted to calm her nerves but didn't know how.

Looking down the hall to make sure no one else was around, Abi smiled, "Maybe if you kissed me now I wouldn't be so nervous."

The request was one he was glad to fulfill. "My pleasure," he murmured as he drew her close.

Just the act of being taken into his arms drove Abi's insides crazy. He wrapped himself around her to make sure they were flush against one another and slowly lowered his lips to hers. But the whole time, he looked into her eyes with such tenderness that she was helpless to do anything but answer the demands of her body and soul.

His lips touched hers tentatively, like they were sampling hers to see what the best part was. Every touch of skin sent shivers through them both, stoking a fire they both denied up until now. Neither knew who started what but they were both falling into the depths of exploring the other.

Gav heard something and slowly lifted his head. Abi's eyes were dark and wanting and he knew neither of them was going to back down but they needed to get inside before they embarrassed themselves or another guest. "Let's go inside," he whispered.

How on earth did she forget they were in a hallway of a hotel? Abi asked herself. She was just lost in what physical sensations Gav caused inside of her. It was crazy and addicting all at the same time. She couldn't speak so she nodded and turned around to open the door.

When Abi turned around, her bottom brushed against Gav's groin and the friction drove him mad. Without considering where they were or who could see them, he pushed against her and dropped his head so he could taste the delicate skin of her neck. She tasted sweet and a little salty from the ocean breezes. It was a fantastic sense of recklessness he never experienced before with a woman. He had her pinned against the door, his right hand holding hers against the cool wood. Her left hand was somewhere around the doorknob and his left hand wrapped around her to hold her breast.

In any other place, Abi was sure she would deck the guy who had her pinned like this but with Gav, the whole position felt wild. She moved her bottom against him, enjoying the feel of his hardness against it. His hand was on her breast, creating a stunning amount of shooting impulses through her whole being. His fingers were entwined with her other hand as it splayed against the door and held them in place. Enjoying his attentions, Abi let her head fall back against his chest and give him more access to her neck.

"Dear Lord, Abi," Gav said when he thought he would lose himself completely.

Turning her head just enough, Abi was able to capture his lips with hers. She didn't want to talk, only wanted to feel this incredibly messy and arousing feeling he generated inside of her.

They were kissing against the hotel room door when Abi felt the first pieces of her climax start exploding through her belly. What the hell! She couldn't understand how just kissing someone could make her body want to explode but it did. Being torn between letting the orgasm go and holding back she pulled her mouth from Gav's and leaned her head against the hotel room door.

Gav could feel the tremors run through Abi's body and didn't know if something was wrong when she pulled her mouth from his. "Are you okay?" he asked in a breathless whisper.

Nodding was the only thing Abi could manage. Her insides were like jelly and words weren't possible just yet. Somehow she managed to turn the knob and open the door.

When Abi moved inside the room and away from Gav, he felt lost. He followed her inside and looked at her. She was flushed from his impromptu lovemaking in the hall and he felt smug about making her look that way.

"Are you sure you're okay?" Gav asked after he closed the door behind him.

Abi blushed, "Yes, I'm fine, I never had an orgasm by just kissing someone before." The admission came out before she thought about it.

Just hearing Abi say the words kicked a shot of awareness into Gav's gut. "Really?"

Now he was just teasing her, "Please don't tease me about this, I'm embarrassed."

"Why?" Gav stepped closer to her, "I think you telling me that almost made me embarrass myself."

She wasn't sure she believed him but she appreciated that he was trying to make her feel better.

Once he was a step away, Gav smiled, "I think I want you so much that I'm not sure what the hell I'm going to do if you tell me we're not going to make love."

Abi could hear the want in his voice; it matched her own. "Luckily, you won't have to worry about that." She lifted her hands to his chest, "You will make love to me now and you will keep making love to me until I tell you to stop."

"I don't know what the Marine Corps response is to your order or else I would use it." He ran his hands up her sides, "But since I don't know I'll just say, hell yes."

With a wicked smile, Abi grabbed his face and brought it down to hers. She had no problems issuing orders in this case.

Chapter 13

As soon as Abi touched him, Gav was lost on the journey of pleasing her as much as he could. He brought his hands up and rubbed her back soothingly. Their lips were fused together, tongues dancing in the most sensational dance.

Abi wanted to feel more; she clawed at his shirt, not caring how she got it off of him, just that she could. Fabric gave and she was able to pull it up. Having to break the contact with his lips in order to get it off was frustrating but she made quick work of it. As soon as he was freed from his shirt, she was set on touching him everywhere she could. Her hands roamed up and down his chest. She loved that he only had a dusting of hair on his skin; giving her free reign over touching him only fanned her desire.

Gav was so hard, he thought he would burst before they even got their clothes off. Her mouth caused a rousing reaction throughout his whole body. Running at this level of intensity was intoxicating. He grabbed Abi around the waist and lifted her so she wrapped her legs around his torso.

Closer, Abi thought. She just wanted to be so close that she couldn't tell where they ended as individuals. "Yes," she moaned as Gav trailed seductive kisses over her shoulders and up her neck.

Yes, he thought, yes, he would do whatever she wanted.

Abi ran her nails down Gav's back and smiled at his intake of breath. She loved it that she could gain such a response from him. Her body almost felt like someone else's, having responded to Gav in this new and exciting way.

Gav stopped kissing her long enough to get her shirt pulled up over her head. He was able to get her bra unhooked with one hand, thank goodness, and sighed when the lacy fabric fell away from her skin.

"You are beautiful," Gav whispered when he set Abi back down on her feet. He was able to see her breasts and reveled in their fullness in his hands. His thumbs ran gently over her hardened nipples and caused little shutters to go through Abi's body. It was important that she enjoyed all of their lovemaking since he intended to do it all night.

Abi's head fell back, the sensations he built up in her were crazy and yet sooooo good. "I need you," she hissed through her clenched teeth.

Gav smiled, "Not yet, baby," he whispered and lowered himself to his knees so he could pay attention to her breasts properly.

Running her fingers through Gav's hair, Abi thought she would explode into pieces if he kept this up. It was a feeling of insanity and yet it was like the most perfect thing she ever felt. "More," she demanded.

"Yes," Gav answered and took one of her nipples into his mouth. He ran his fingers around the top of her shorts until they reached the button at the front. Not breaking contact with his mouth, he quickly undid the button and zipper and pushed the fabric down until it slid down Abi's legs to the floor.

Abi was standing there, her legs shaking, her breath ragged, and thinking that she couldn't think. "Ohhhh," she sighed when she felt the coolness of the room's air on her skin.

Gav pulled back from his ministrations of her breasts to look up and see Abi's dark eyes. She was looking down at him, her hair falling on either side of her face and making her look so beautiful. His hands were rubbing her lower rib cage and making gentle circles on her skin, down her sides.and back over her bottom. The same bottom that was firm and almost made him forget himself earlier. He didn't say anything, only stared into her eyes as his hands explored her body.

Watching Gav watch her was more erotic and more intimate than anything she'd ever done before. There was a moment's panic at the overwhelming feelings but she shoved them aside, preferring to focus on their physical contact.

His fingers finally found the scrap of lace that separated him from Abi's core. He could feel her heat against his skin. Leaning forward, he kissed her lower belly and darted his tongue into her belly button. He smiled at her little jump. So she was ticklish; good to know.

Abi felt weak, it was like she had no power over her body, and Gav controlled it all. Funny that she was the one who demanded but he was the one delivering. His fingers found the side of her panties and tore the lacy fabric away in a second. The lace dropped to the floor.

Gav could feel the shudders as they reverberated off of Abi. Such power in touch and feeling. He wanted to make it last all night.

"Up," Abi said sharply. She knew he would taste her and she would shatter and she wanted to wait for that to happen. She wanted to please him first.

Doing as Abi demanded, Gav stood. He gently ran his fingers up over her body as their positions changed. Every curve and dip of her soft skin was burning into his mind. The feel of her as she tried to catch her breath from his lovemaking only drove him on to do more.

Once Gav was in front of her again, Abi ran her fingers down his chest and belly until they encountered the tops of his shorts. With a quick flick of her fingertips, she had them undone. She forced the fabric over his hips quickly, loving the sounds he made in arousal. His skin was dancing across hers as their breaths mingled.

Gav didn't know how much longer he could hold out, "Abi," he pleaded.

She nodded, knowing that he was as close as she was. "I know," she said and pushed his briefs down. When her fingers encountered the tip of his hard shaft, she inhaled sharply. The feel of him was its own drug. Her fingers rubbed softly over the tip of him until he was shaking as badly as she was just a few minutes earlier. She wanted to explore more but they were to a point where release was a necessity.

Rushing, Abi pushed his briefs down lower and concentrated on kissing him. His lips were soft but his tongue demanded all she could give. The kiss took her breath away.

He kicked his clothes away and stood there, naked and wanting.

Suddenly the bed seemed too far away for Abi so she did what all Marines were trained to do; adapt and overcome. She moved him backwards until they hit the dresser. He was just tall enough to almost sit on the top of it so she jumped up and wrapped her legs around him tightly.

Feeling Abi's moist heat against him undid Gav in a thousand different ways. Her heat permeated his skin and covered his soul like the warmest blanket. He knew what she wanted because he wanted it too.

Abi used the top of the dresser to help keep her legs up and waited as Gav reached between them to position himself at the entry to her warmth. She was panting in anticipation and opened her eyes when she didn't feel him fill her right away.

Looking into Abi's eyes, Gav felt the last part of him fall away into the submission of someone who just found the other half of their soul. He was confused at the depth of his need for this woman. "Keep your eyes open," he said.

She did as he asked and kept her eyes open as he slid into her. The finality of their joining made her moan loudly; it was as sensational as she thought plus a thousand times better. "Yes," she breathed.

As his body manipulated his movements, his brain just checked out. He started moving, feeling her heat surround him and cause the kind of contact only two lovers could understand.

Abi's head fell back as she moved against Gav. His hands supported her bottom as she rode him fast and hard. It was like someone else was taking over, leaving only the shell of her person behind to try and decipher the feelings and sensations their joining created.

"Baby," Gav said in a raspy voice, "I need you to come with me."

Nodding, Abi lifted her head to look into his eyes, "Yes!" she yelled.

Gav held back as she rode him. He wanted to wait until they could tumble over the edge of insanity together. Once he could feel the shudders start, he allowed himself to let go.

"Abi!" he yelled out.

Abi lifted her head to watch him as they both let go, "Yes, Gav, let's go together!"

Her body exploding from the inside out, Abi threw her head back and rode the wave as it tumbled over her.

Gav leaned against the dresser and held Abi as they both fell into the last remnants of desire. He pulled her to him so her head was leaning on his shoulder and he could hold her close.

Without realizing it, Abi started to cry. She only noticed the tears when Gav brought his hand up to the back of her head.

"Are you okay, baby?" he asked.

Pulling away just enough so she could look at him, Abi smiled, "Yes, I've never cried before."

From what he knew, Gav thought it was a good thing. He wanted to make sure he hadn't hurt her. "I was afraid I'd done something."

Shaking her head, Abi kissed him on the cheek, "Only gave me the best orgasm I've ever had," she answered.

Gav's chest puffed up in male self-satisfaction. "Well, I think we can do better," he said softly.

Holding Abi securely, Gav pushed away from the dresser and carried Abi over to the bed. He dropped her unceremoniously onto the bed and smiled wickedly at the shocked expression on her face.

"Nice," Abi said dryly.

Laughing at her response, Gav motioned for her to back up on the bed, "I'm just trying to show you who's in charge here."

Even with his teasing tone, Abi knew he was baiting her, "Reeeaaalllyyy?" she asked slowly, "You think you're in charge?"

Again, Gav laughed, "Hell no!" he returned, "I just want to give the illusion of me being in charge."

Abi nodded, "Good." She crooked her finger, "Now get your ass over here and we'll see who's in charge."

It was not a question, but a demand, and Gav absolutely loved it when she said it. "Yes, ma'am," he answered and crawled onto the bed to be beside her.

Scooting over, Abi pushed the comforter out of the way and pushed the extra pillows onto the floor. She didn't want anything impeding her access to Gav and wanted to feel the soft, cool sheets against her skin.

When the bed was how she wanted it, she stretched out, her body facing Gav's. They held hands between them, having that as the only connection between their bodies just re-ignited the flames of need.

"I guess this is a silly question," Abi said shyly, "but was it good for you?"

Gav was shocked, "Baby, I hope you could tell that it was fantastic for me." He reached up and brushed her hair back from her face. "Why are you so worried about that? I knew it would be awesome, I guess I just have to prove it to you."

Abi smiled, "I guess you do." She was worried. For some reason her and Bryan's sex life wasn't that great since he had to cheat and now Gav was leaving tomorrow.

He could read her mind, "Don't think about tomorrow, let's just make love tonight and find out everything we can about one another."

It was astonishing that he knew the words that would soothe her, "Okay," she answered and reached over to feel his skin.

With Abi's hands on him, Gav forgot about everything except them, here, in bed, making love.

They made love once again and drifted off into a deep sleep. Gav woke up some time in the night with Abi snuggled against him. Feeling her soft skin, his body reacted immediately and he woke her up with kisses down the inside of her thighs.

The room was silent except for the sighs between them. The blinds were open and the moonlight snuck in between the slats, giving the room an otherworldly glow. Gav was positioned over Abi, ready to join them when he saw the moonlight and how his cast across her eyes, making them shine like green gems. She was the most beautiful creature he ever saw and his heart flipped at the sight of her poised beneath him for their joining.

"Gav," Abi said, "love me."

Gav nodded and kissed her gently. When he lifted up and filled her with his hardness, he whispered, "Yes, always."

There were no other words uttered as they made love again. Their bodies feeling in the semi-darkness of the room. Sighs of discovery and pleasure were heard and returned.

When Abi woke up in the morning light, she was alone.

Sitting up in the bed, she looked around the room and took a moment to get her bearings. The night before ran through her mind, bringing a smile to her face. As she moved, her body felt a little achy in places. Another reminder of the night she and Gav shared. The door opened and she smiled when she saw it was Gav.

"Good morning," Gav said as he entered Abi's room and saw she was awake. He woke up an hour earlier and didn't want to disturb her so he went to his room to shower and pack for his flight.

Abi stretched, "Good morning," she said.

Just watching her body move and knowing what she could do with that body made him hard with want. His eyes must have given him away because she put up her hands and shook her head.

"Give me a few minutes," Abi said and jumped up to go to the bathroom. She saw the look of want in Gav's eyes but there were certain bodily functions that had to be attended to first. When she was in the bathroom and looked at herself she wondered why romance books and movies never really addressed those things. No one ever seemed to have morning breath or had to use the bathroom.

She giggled to herself at the silliness of her thoughts. She washed up quickly and came out of the bathroom in time to see Gav hanging up the phone.

Gav just finished ordering room service when Abi came out of the bathroom. Looking at her, naked, made his breath hitch in his chest. She leaned up against the wall. Trying to be calm, he smiled, "I called for some breakfast," he said in a cracked voice.

Abi nodded and kept staring at him, "How long did they say they'd be?" She asked.

"Um," Gav couldn't get his mind to work. "About twenty minutes."

Nodding, Abi pushed away from the wall and sauntered over to where he stood. "I think we can manage some PT in that amount of time."

There was something about the way she said the words that drove Gav's body into overdrive. "I'm sure we can," he countered and took her into his arms.

Their lovemaking was hurried, as if they were teenagers who were hoping they didn't get caught but helplessly driven by their crazy hormones.

As Gav lay there afterwards, his breathing labored, he smiled and looked over at Abi.

"What?" Abi asked him with a smile on her face.

He shifted so his body was facing hers. He ran his hand up and down her arm in a soothing motion. "Nothing, just thinking how lucky I am."

Abi laughed, "I'm not sure lucky is how you'll be when that room service attendant knocks and you're buck naked."

Nodding, Gav sat up, "Okay, I'll get dressed if you do."

Putting a fake pout of her face, Abi sighed, "Okay, if I have to."

Gav put up his hands, "Not my rules, that's just so the room service person isn't slammed with want for seeing you and I have to kick his ass."

How was it that Gav could make her smile so much? "I don't want you to kick anybody's ass so I'll get dressed." She moved so she could get clothes out of her bag.

Gav came up behind her and put his arms around her. How could having her close be such an addiction in such a short time? One of the hundreds of questions he'll have to answer during his flight back to New York.

There was a knock at the door so Gav turned around. Abi ran with her clothes into the bathroom.

They enjoyed breakfast on the patio off of Abi's room. Gav ordered a bit of everything because he wasn't sure what she would like.

Finishing her omelet and stealing bites of Gav's french toast, Abi was relaxed. She was famished after their sex-filled night. When her belly was full, she got up and walked over to Gav's chair and plopped down on his lap.

Gav smiled and kissed her. He could taste the syrup on her lips and drank her in. He cupped the back of her head with his hands so he could hold her too him. The kiss was tender and relaxed but still held the hint of repressed pleasure.

Reluctantly ending the kiss, Abi sighed. "What time does your plane leave?" she asked Gav. The words were catching in her throat.

"A little after two," Gav answered.

Abi looked at the clock on her phone. "We have about three hours before I have to get you to the airport so what would you like to do?"

Was this a trick question? Gav thought it was pretty obvious what he wanted to do. Pulling her to him, he kissed her soundly.

The only reason Abi ended the kiss was because, if she didn't, she would pull off his clothes and attack him right there on the patio. This intense need for him was tough to handle and she didn't seem to have any control over it. She stood up and took him by the hand to lead him back into her room.

Abi was walking backwards into the room and undoing her shirt to throw it to the floor. Next was her shorts; she popped the button and shimmied out of them as she made her way to the bed. She stopped when the backs of her legs felt the bed, peeling off her bra and panties and throwing them somewhere in the room.

Gav followed her, taking off his clothes along the way. When they were both naked and standing next to the bed, Gav lifted her up so she was once again wrapped around him. Going slowly, he bent down to place her on the bed and sank his hard shaft into her wet core as he pushed her up onto the bed.

The feeling of Gav entering her and the bed shifting behind her almost took Abi over the edge. The constant bombardment of pleasure shot into her, lifting her up into the sweetest oblivion she ever experienced.

Increasing his rhythm, Gav started feeling the clawing need reach its climax. "Abi," he whispered.

"Yes," she answered, "yes, Gav."

That was all they needed to say. They both crashed into the wall of desire together. The fragments of their bodies falling to the bed in a heaving lump.

Abi looked over at Gav who was half on top of her, "Whoa," was all she could say.

Gav chuckled but didn't move right away, "Yes," he said.

They laid there on the bed, Abi's hands running through his hair and down his shoulders and back while his fingers ran up and down her side. The movement was soothing and only increased the connection between them.

A while later, Gav's phone started going off. He opened his eyes and was shocked that he and Abi fell asleep in the same position they were in after they made love. Slowly, he got up and went over to shut off the phone. It was the alarm that said he needed to get ready for his flight. He stared at the phone, wishing it was lying to him. When he looked over at Abi, he knew she felt the same way.

Abi got up and went in to shower. She needed a few minutes of distance from Gav. She washed her body and was pissed that tears made their way down her cheeks. They only knew each other for a couple of days so she shouldn't be acting like this. She scrubbed her scalp in the hopes that the process would scrape away the raw emotion she was feeling. Once she was done and dried her hair, she put on a dusting of makeup, and came out into the room.

The first thing she saw was Gav's suitcase. Seeing it was like being slapped in the face that he was actually leaving. Shoring up her resolve, Abi took a breath and followed the sound of his voice onto the patio.

"Thanks, Chase," Gav said as he looked out over the water. The different blues mixed with the white caps of the waves was soothing to his nerves.

He hit disconnect and turned to see Abi standing in the doorway. Just seeing her made his heart flip in his chest. He put on the best smile and walked over to her. Lifting his palm, he slid it down her cheek and tried to make them both feel better.

"Chase?" Abi asked. It was a silly question but she didn't know what to say.

Gav nodded, "Yes," he smiled, "he was just wishing me a good trip and said thanks from him and Eryn."

Abi stared up into his eyes, "That was nice."

"I think," he leaned down and kissed her softly, "I owe them a lot more thanks for letting me come here to see you."

Those words again. Abi nodded and quickly wiped the stray tear across her cheek.

He didn't want to see her cry; he wouldn't be far behind if she did that. "Baby," he murmured and pulled her into his arms.

They stood there for a while, just holding one another and wondering how this all happened so fast.

Finally, Abi stepped back and tried to smile, "We should get going."

Gav watched her grab her bag and walk toward the door of the hotel room. For some reason he felt like this was more of a goodbye than he hoped it would be. A feeling of uneasiness started working its way through his belly.

After Gav got his bag, they walked to the lobby of the hotel. Gav checked out while Abi went to the valet to have her car brought around. Gav met her out front just as the valet drove up. They put their bags in the trunk and got in.

Driving to the airport wasn't bad because it was a Sunday and traffic was a little lighter. Abi drove quietly, not really sure what they should be saying. She didn't want him to go but knew he couldn't stay. This was a nice little vacation but they each had their own lives to get back to. His was in New York for crying out loud; this was probably as far removed from what he knew as it could get.

Gav watched Abi as she drove. Her mind was busy mulling over things like his was. He was pretty sure it wouldn't have been as hard if he left before last night, but he had to get home.

Abi parked in the airport parking and got out of the car. She opened the trunk with the remote and stood there while Gav came around. He was about to reach in and grab his bag when she spoke up, "Stop!" she almost shouted.

Gav turned, wondering what was wrong, when she grabbed him and kissed him.

The kiss held everything that Abi wanted to say to Gav. She wanted to tell him that she loved their time together, that she was happier than she ever was before when they made love, that she appreciated him coming all this way just to see her. She wanted it to say everything except the one thing he needed her to say, that she would marry him.

After a kiss like that, Gav was off-balance. His system was in chaos and he wanted to do a lot of things except go into the airport to board his plane.

Gav grabbed his bag and they walked across the street to the terminal. He checked in online so he only needed to drop his bag at security and get through the check point. Abi was right beside him as he made his way up to the check point line. He turned to her and smiled.

Abi didn't know what was appropriate so she went with her gut, "Thank you for coming to see me."

Smiling, Gav cupped her cheek in his palm, "Thank you for not kicking me back to New York and for giving me a great time here."

"I-" Abi started, then stopped. "I hope you have a good trip."

He would have to be the one to say it, he knew that. "I'll call you when I land." He smiled at her nod. "I'll email you too."

Nodding again, Abi sighed, "Okay, go get on your plane."

Gav leaned forward and kissed her softly, "Goodbye, sweet lady," he whispered, then turned to get into the line.

Abi stood, rooted to the spot until she couldn't see him any longer. Knowing things were now inexplicably changed, she turned and walked toward the airport exit. The damn tears were running down her cheeks the whole way.

Chapter 14

Abi woke up Monday morning and felt hung over. She spent the night before catching up on emails and watching TV, trying to find something mind-numbing to do. It kept her from thinking that letting Gav leave was the worst thing she could've done.

Getting ready for work, she listened to her radio and a song came on that she and Gav listened to in the car. During the news she heard a story about the Sea Life Park, where she and Gav visited. By the time she got to work, she was frustrated and didn't know what to do.

After opening up her office, she went into the Mess to get a cup of coffee. She said hi to a couple of the guys from the Section, came out, and headed to Eryn's office.

Eryn just set her bag down when she heard someone behind her. Abi stood in the doorway and looked almost miserable. It wasn't a stretch as to the reason. Lord knew she had quite a few bad days when she and Chase broke up all those years ago.

"Good morning," Eryn said while motioning for Abi to have a seat.

Abi sat down across from her friend's desk and took a sip of her coffee, "Morning," she grumbled back.

It was a friend's prerogative, boss or not, to feel bad for someone they cared about. It also was a friend's prerogative to say 'I told you so.' Eryn sat down behind her desk, "Did Gav get off okay yesterday?"

Looking as if the question came out of nowhere, Abi's brow furrowed, "Yes, why?"

Okay...Eryn thought. "Maybe I was asking because you look like you lost your best friend."

Abi shook her head, "Nope, just the Monday blues," she answered and stood up. "I'll see you at the meeting." She stood and left Eryn's office.

Eryn watched her Crash Chief walk out and thought that she had the worst case of denial ever.

The morning passed quickly. They had a muster in the Truck Bay and did Section relief. There were a few things to address but nothing too bad. The two guys Abi counseled the week before were put on additional duty as part of their punishment so they were disgruntled but Abi didn't care. If somebody screwed up, they had to take the consequences.

After the relief she went back to her office and heard the phone ringing. She quickly grabbed the receiver, "Gunny Rochelle," she said in a breathy voice.

"Hi, it's Gav." He said then felt stupid that he had to introduce himself on the phone.

Abi smiled, the first genuine one she had today, "Hi, how was your trip?" she asked as she sat down behind her desk.

Gav was unpacking his bag as he talked to her. He got home and felt restless. He wanted to talk to Abi to feel better. "It was long, but okay."

"Good," she responded. What else did she say? "Um, I wanted to thank you again for coming."

He stopped walking into his closet at the tone in her voice. Gone was the woman he made love to yesterday. In her place was this cool stranger. He spent the flight thinking about their night together and how this changed things. Now it felt like the first conversation they ever had. What was going on?

Gav sat down in the overstuffed chair in his room. "Abi, I was glad to do it. I miss you."

Hearing the emotion in Gav's voice made Abi mad and she couldn't figure out why. "I'm at work so I have to go." She played with the pen on her desk.

"Okay," Gav said quietly. "I'll talk to you soon."

Abi nodded, "Yep." She hung up the phone and sat at her desk for a long time wondering why her hands were shaking.

Gav disconnected the call and sat there staring into space. Here he thought they took a giant leap forward but maybe his leaving only pushed them further back.

Abi got through the rest of the day quietly. She left right at sixteen thirty and drove directly to the gym. It didn't matter that it would most likely be packed with other day workers; she needed something to use up the pent up energy she had.

She must have beaten a lot of the crowd because there were machines available. She did an hour on the elliptical then worked on some of the weight machines. She forgot her boxing gloves and tape so she couldn't use the punching bag which sucked. She could've used that to relieve some of this stress.

After running herself ragged, she walked out of the gym. She was at her car when she noticed her ex, Bryan, walking a few rows down. He had his arm looped around some woman's shoulders. Abi thought maybe she would be jealous but she didn't feel anything. The guy didn't even sit at the same table as Gav in the lovemaking department. Shaking her head, she got into her car and went back to her barracks room.

The rest of the week was identical to Monday. Abi got through the day with minimum effort and went to the gym to wear herself down. She only slept out of physical exhaustion. Nothing really held any appeal. She received two emails from Gav but hadn't read them yet. She didn't have a clue why, but she just couldn't.

Eryn walked into Abi's office Friday afternoon and sat down. "Dinner with us tonight," she said coolly.

Abi looked up from her log book and nodded. "Okay."

That was it? Eryn was frustrated. She'd been telling Chase all week that Abi was depressed now that Gav went back in New York. Chase tried to get her to be patient but they both knew Eryn didn't really possess that particular trait. Nodding at Abi, she got up and left her Crash Chief's office.

After work, Abi skipped the gym. She didn't get a time from Eryn for dinner but decided she should go home and get changed. They usually planned it around six-thirty so she'd just show up then.

Showered and changed, Abi saw that she had some time before she would leave. Deciding it was finally time to read Gav's emails, she opened up her laptop and logged on. The first one was dated on Tuesday.

Abi:

I was pretty tired yesterday when I called so I didn't ask some questions I should have. You sounded very distant and it threw me a little. Given our last night together in Hawaii, I think I expected some of that closeness to stay. I would be lying if I didn't say that I wasn't disappointed. Maybe you were having a bad day at work and I shouldn't be so sensitive.

I am going crazy thinking about you! There I said it. I know it's probably not very cool to just admit it but it's the truth. I think about you being under me and me making love to you until we're both spent. I think about your lips and how they taste against mine. I need to stop typing or I'm going to be in some trouble.

Anyway, I hope we can still email and call one another. Granted, nothing is really changed in our situation but I'm okay with that for right now. I had a great time in Hawaii, even after hitting your boss. Please email me back.

Gav

Abi sat back in her chair, a smile on her face. He seemed at ease with saying, or typing, that stuff. It made her feel uncomfortable for some reason. Maybe it was because even though they had a great couple of days, they wouldn't get married and live happily ever after. She was expecting a phone call from her parents any time now to interrogate her about Gav's visit. In the end, nothing was different.

Yeah right, her inner voice screamed, you're an idiot if you think that! She looked down at the screen and opened the second email dated the day before.

Abi:

I noticed that you haven't read my first email so I'm sure you're busy or something. I just wanted to drop a line to say that I miss you. I hope your week is going well. I'll call you this weekend if that's okay.

Gav

Much shorter but no less sweet in Abi's opinion. She figured she should respond but when she looked at her clock, it was time to go to Eryn and Chase's for dinner. She logged out of her email, planning to answer Gav later when she got home.

She drove to the Johnson's and was surprised that the Master Sgt.'s car was parked out front. Eryn hadn't mentioned Bill was coming too. It didn't matter to Abi; she didn't mind him and he proved to be very good at his job. So he was a bit of a flirt, that didn't make him a bad boss, only a little annoying.

After knocking, Abi walked in and went straight to the kitchen. Eryn was setting the table and smiled when their eyes met. "Hi," Abi said and went over to help place the dishes.

"Hi," Eryn said back, she nodded out onto the patio, "the guys are out back talking grill stuff."

Abi looked out and waved to the guys before turning back to Eryn. "I didn't know Bill would be here tonight."

Eryn walked into the kitchen to pull out the salad she put together earlier. "Yes, I wanted you both here."

Nodding, Abi helped Eryn put the rest of the dinner fixings on the table before the guys came in. A few minutes later everyone was seated at the table and about to begin eating when Chase cleared his throat.

"I wanted to thank you both for being here," Chase said to Abi and Bill. "My lovely wife thinks you're both great and has a little announcement to make."

Eryn smiled at her husband, "I thought you should be the first to know that Chase and I are expecting our first little Marine."

Bill reached over and shook Chase's hand and Abi got up to give Eryn a hug.

After hugging her friend, Abi whispered, "I suspected as much when you couldn't get out of the bathroom before nine o'clock in the morning."

Eryn winked at Abi and wiped at a tear. "Thanks," she said, knowing her friend would support her through this.

They started eating and talking about babies. Abi was surprised at how knowledgeable Bill was. He mentioned he had thirteen nieces and nephews. Whew! Abi wasn't sure how she could handle keeping them straight much less, remembering birthdays, etc.

After dinner was done and she started back to the base, Abi started thinking about being an only child. She wondered how disappointed her parents were at only having one daughter. The fact that she didn't have any plans on giving them grandkids must be hurtful.

That thought made her think of Gav for some inexplicable reason. What would their children look like? Probably bubbly little terrors but she would love them so much. Funny, she thought, that she would consider children with him but not marrying him. Shaking her head to clear the personal thoughts she didn't want to have, Abi pulled into the parking lot and got out.

After settling in for the night, she sat down at her laptop and started an email to Gav.

Gav:

I am sorry for not writing back sooner. I was just busy this week. I wanted to let you know that Chase and Eryn announced they were expecting a baby tonight at dinner. Like I hadn't already guessed, but I was happy for them and knew you would be too. Bill and I both support her so it will be easy enough to handle. Bill has 13 nieces and nephews so he's the most prepared for this. I'll keep you posted.

I was distant on the phone earlier this week and I'm not sure why. Being together was really great but we're both back in our real lives so it's tough for me to go back and forth. Perhaps I'm not as evolved as you are in that respect.

I really like you and had a great time during your visit. My boss seems to harbor no ill will so I hope you're relieved.

Have a great weekend. I will be in and out so you can call. Not sure if I'll have my phone on me but, if I do, I'll pick up. Take care.

Abi

Abi hit send and smiled. She didn't really know what to say in the email. He was right, their situation was really no different now. They just slept together. How did that leave them really?

She went to bed and dreamed about Gav and children and Eryn telling her, "I told you so."

New York was lively, even on a Saturday morning. Gav woke up a little later than he did on weekdays but still pretty early compared to most of the people he knew. He didn't use the weekend for an excuse to go to a club and drink excessively; he didn't see the point. After running a couple of miles and picking up the paper at a newsstand near his brownstone, he went home and made a quick breakfast.

After reading the paper, he showered and changed into shorts and a polo shirt. The New York summer was in full swing and he planned to take advantage of it by being outside as much as possible. He had plans for a baseball game with friends later in the afternoon.

Deciding to check his email before he left, he opened it up quickly and smiled. Abi emailed him. Great! He started reading her email and the smile faded once he was three sentences in. Bill again! For some reason, the mere mention of the man's name irritated him and sucked the happiness right out of him.

He ended up reading the email three times, hoping to catch some glimpse of Abi's feelings but he was only let down. She didn't seem as affected by their intimacy as he was. He was having dinner with his parents tomorrow night and hoped to give them some good news.

Getting out of his email, Gav decided to just let it go for now. He had a good life here in New York; a great job, friends, his parents.

There were many people who had much less. So how come not having Abi here with him made it all seem empty?

Abi spent Saturday cleaning her room, dropping off dry cleaning, doing laundry, and having lunch with some friends. She got back to her room just before dinner and checked her email. There was nothing from Gav. The hurt she felt wasn't so bad. She knew he was busy like she was.

Sunday, Abi attended church on the base and visited with some friends she hadn't seen in a while. They just returned from a deployment. It was a lot of fun catching up on the excitement of their mission and reminiscing about their pranks when they were younger.

The visit was a much-needed distraction from her current worries about the situation with Gav.

Mark, an old friend, asked her, "Abi, what's up with your love life?"

She and Mark dated on and off over the years and she was thinking that maybe it was an invitation to rekindle something. After being deployed for a year, she figured it wasn't that odd for him to ask. She smiled and didn't answer right away.

"Okay," Mark put his hands up, "I get it."

Abi touched his arm, "No, I'm not seeing anyone, Mark. I'm just not looking for anything right now."

Mark nodded, "Okay."

That was it. No further conversation was needed. Abi appreciated that about Mark; there were no complications. It was a yes or no thing. Too bad everything couldn't be that easy.

Gav got out of the cab in front of his parents' house and took a deep breath. This "summons" was about one thing. They wanted to know if he and Abi were getting married and when. Of course, his parents never said that but they all knew his going to Hawaii was for one purpose. Now, he felt like the trip was technically a failure but he sure didn't regret it. That one night with Abi was more than he could've hoped for. Of course, the rest of the trip was nice too; it was just intense on a lot of levels.

Climbing the stairs to his parents' front door, he was always surprised at the beauty of their townhouse on the Upper East Side of Manhattan. Here, the properties were a lot more expensive than where he lived. He always thought his parents were pretty frugal, except when it came to their home. Here, they flourished and enjoyed entertaining on a grand scale.

His parents' housekeeper, Helen, answered the door and smiled. "Oh, Master Gavriil, how are you?" she asked.

Helen was the rock of this place. He was pretty sure his mother didn't plan a whole lot when it came to entertaining. It was Helen who took over and ran it like a precision military exercise.

Smiling, Gav leaned in and kissed her cheek, "Good, Helen, how are you?"

Helen loved it when Gavriil came home. They were all instantly taken with his charm and good humor. She blushed when he kissed her, "I'm good, come in. Your parents are expecting you."

Gav walked in and made a sharp turn to the left. He was used to being invited for dinner and finding out his parents were actually throwing a party so it wasn't surprising to see other people there. He actually appreciated the fact that he wouldn't have his parents' undivided attention.

"Gavriil," his father announced when he walked into the room.

Knowing the drill, Gav walked over to where his parents' guests stood. A woman turned around and smiled. She was Abi's mother, he was sure of it. The hair was different and the skin was a little paler, but she looked like Abi would probably look like in thirty years. Still stunning. Dammit, he thought, Abi would still be gorgeous.

"Gavriil," Elena Rochelle said in a quiet voice. She was somewhat startled when she saw Gavriil for the first time in person. His pictures did not do him justice.

Gav put on his best smile, "Mrs. Rochelle," he said and kissed her hand.

Abi's father, Andrei, stepped forward and offered his hand to Gav, "How are you?" He didn't know the boy all that well even though they worked for the same bank.

"Mr. Rochelle," Gav nodded. Why did he feel like he was being interviewed?

Isaak Maslov came over and handed his son a glass and clapped him on the back. "Let's eat, shall we?"

The group went into the dining room and sat down. Gav sat across from Abi's parents and his father sat at the head of the table and his mother was between him and his father. It was an intimate dinner but Gav still felt way too closed in.

"So," Andrei Rochelle said once the first course was served, "how is our girl?"

Gav took a drink of water and was so thankful Helen provided it. "Well, sir," he started, and was stopped by Abi's father.

Andrei shook his head, "Please, call me Andrei."

Nodding, Gav smiled, he appreciated that they were all trying to make him feel more comfortable. But basically that wasn't going to happen if they were all going to watch him.

"Andrei," Gav said, "she's good. She's busy at work," he explained and caught the look of disapproval from Mrs. Rochelle. Interesting.

Picking up his fork, Andrei seemed to consider his words before he spoke. "Does she like you?"

The hundred million dollar question was just thrown out into the room.

All eyes were focused on him and Gav wanted to run away. Even as an adult, he could still be made to feel pretty small under the intense gaze of his parents.

Gav cleared his throat, "Yes, sir, I think she does."

Andrei leaned back and clapped his hands together. He winked at his wife, who smiled, and nodded to Gav's father.

Feeling his mother's hand squeezing his shoulder, Gav felt her support. But they all had to understand that this wasn't something that was going to be solved with one impromptu visit. How did he explain all of this?

"Sir," Gav said after a few minutes, "even though Abi likes me but I don't think she wants to marry me."

Elena Rochelle eyed Gav with concern. She'd been watching him and knew he was handsome and smart and accomplished, but his world was so different from their daughter's. Not to mention, Abi's stubborn streak; she would not be swayed easily. Being a woman herself, Elena could sense there was something Gavriil was not telling them.

Andrei did not want to hear this, "But she likes you, yes?" Whenever he was upset or emotional, his Russian accent came out.

Gav nodded, "Yes, I believe she does, sir."

Glaring at Gavriil, Andrei asked, "Do you like her?"

It was the easiest question Gav had all evening. "Yes, sir," he smiled, "I like her very much."

Klara and Elena exchanged looks. Some things were easier for women to understand. It was obvious something was between the youngsters but, as women, they understood that it wasn't as black and white as their husbands happened to believe. Especially not in this day and age.

"Well," Klara Maslov said, "let's eat and leave Gav in peace for a bit."

The couples followed Klara's suggestion and ate in comfortable silence. Both of the fathers talked about work and Abi's mom was commenting on the dish and asking Gav's mother for the recipe. Everyone seemed relaxed except for Gav. He felt like he was walking on a tightrope without a net and he was starting to get a little resentful of Abi for leaving him here to face the parents alone.

They got through dinner and took after-dinner drinks in the living room. Abi's mother asked him some questions about Hawaii and he was happy to answer. He left out a few of the details, there was no need for the parents to know everything. As soon as he felt it was acceptable, he announced he had to get home.

Isaak and Klara came over and hugged their son goodbye. They made him promise to come and visit soon. He kissed Abi's mother, Elena, on the cheek and commented about how he now knew where Abi got her beauty. He went to shake Abi's father's hand and was surprised when the man avoided it.

"I'll walk you out," Andrei Rochelle said. He clapped Gav on the back and walked with him.

Gav went out the front door, not knowing what to expect Abi's father to say. He went down the stairs and stood on the sidewalk.

Andrei didn't want to speak to Gavriil in front of the others. "I wanted to say that I respect you for even considering this arrangement." He looked down the street as if the words would come his way, "I also know that my daughter can be stubborn and I hope you won't give up on her, even with her chosen career."

First, Gav was shocked that Abi's father was so understanding. Second, he was kind of offended that the way her father put it was that she had some inferior job or something. Of course, he didn't want to argue with someone who could, hopefully, become his father-in-law. Instead he nodded.

"Thank you, sir," Gav replied and waved for a cab.

Once he was inside the vehicle and speeding away from his parents' home, all the feelings he tried to repress during the last couple of hours played through his mind. By the time he got back to his brownstone, he was pissed.

He dialed Abi's number.

Chapter 15

Abi's phone rang when she was putting away some groceries she purchased. It was late in the afternoon and she was thinking about dinner but wasn't sure what she should make.

"Hello," she picked up.

Gav smiled. Hell, even the sound of her voice made his body react. "Abi, it's Gav."

She stopped what she was doing and went to the sofa to sit down. "Hi."

He was trying to be nice but he was all mixed up inside, "Are you busy?"

Abi felt something funny, he didn't sound quite right, "No, what's wrong?" she asked.

Funny that she picked up on it. "Oh, I just had dinner with my parents...and yours."

"What?" Abi asked loudly. Was it possible for your stomach to drop out of your body? She was pretty sure hers just did.

Gav sighed, "Yes, all four of our parents." He sat down on the edge of his bed. "And, let me tell you, it wasn't exactly a great time." Keeping the sarcasm out of his voice was a losing battle so he didn't even try.

Abi became defensive, "Are you mad at me?" she asked.

Considering her question, he answered, "Yes, sort of."

Now she was really defensive, "Why? I didn't do it!"

"Well, I'm not sure that would be an accurate statement." He was getting downright pissed now. "You weren't there."

Abi's mouth was tight, her jaw set, "Listen, I'm stationed here for my job, don't try to blame me for not being there." The words were said coldly.

Something was becoming clear to Gav, "Is that how your parents always made you feel?" he asked softly.

Letting out a breath, Abi geared herself up. "Listen, Gav, I didn't ask you to come here. I didn't ask our parents to tell us we had to get married." She took a breath, "I didn't ask you to have dinner with them. I didn't do any of this!" Her voice rose a little more with each word.

"You know what, Abi," he clenched his jaw, "I didn't ask for a lot of it either but its happening and I'm here dealing with it!"

Abi didn't honestly expect him to go up against her. She wasn't exactly used to it. Most people knew she would keep pushing and gave in. Gav surprised her by pushing back.

She knew he was right about some of it, "Fine," she answered sharply. "I'm sorry, is that what you wanted me to say?"

Gav shook his head, "No, Abi, I want you to quit hiding."

Ramping up again, Abi stood up and started pacing, "I'm not hiding, Gav!" she all but yelled into the phone.

"I don't believe you," he said softly and hung up the phone. He couldn't talk to someone who wasn't willing to even invest in the conversation.

Abi heard the dial tone and tossed the phone onto the sofa, "Ughhhh!" she yelled to no one.

Monday morning Abi woke up with bruises under her eyes. She went to bed early and tried to sleep but her argument with Gav kept playing over in her mind. She got into work a few minutes earlier and poured herself a cup of coffee. Bill was coming into the Mess as she was leaving.

"Good morning, Gunny," Bill said lightly.

Abi tried to avoid contact, "Morning," she grumbled.

Whoa, Bill thought, something was wrong. "Gunny?" he asked before she got out of the room.

Turning around, Abi hoped she looked better than she felt. When she locked eyes with Bill, she figured she didn't since he immediately looked worried.

"Gunny," Bill said, "my office in five minutes." He left without anything further.

Abi went to her office and squared her stuff away. She was in his doorway in exactly five minutes.

Bill looked up and nodded, "Sit," he ordered.

When Abi was seated, Bill got up and closed his office door. "Now," he said when he was seated again behind his desk, "you want to tell me what the hell is going on?"

The most embarrassing thing about this situation was she was usually the one saying those words to one of the crewmembers. She always spouted off about not letting your personal life come into work. If there was a problem, let someone help you fix it so it didn't distract you. And now, after all this time, it was a spiel she was being given.

"Master Sgt.," Abi started, "I didn't sleep well. That's all."

Bill leaned forward and clasped his hands together, "Gunny, you can try to dish that bullshit out somewhere else but not here." He looked at her with concern. "I'll help if I can."

Well, well. Underneath that flirtatious and cocky attitude was a genuinely nice guy. A welcomed relief to Abi. "I would rather we not talk about it, Master Sgt. Phillips."

"Abi," Bill said, "I'm sure you would but frankly, I need to know you're in the game here." He sat back. "I'm thinking it involves a certain man from New York with a killer right hook."

She couldn't help it, Abi smiled. "Yes."

Nodding, Bill smiled again, "He doesn't support your career?" He wasn't sure what the deal was but he was willing to help her out. Abi was one of the first nice people he met here and he valued his friends.

"It's not that," Abi started, "he said I was hiding." Thinking of their words, Abi got upset again. "I'm not hiding, this is my job, dammit!" She got up and started pacing. "This is what I chose to do and I'm not giving it up, not for my parents, and not for him!"

It amazed Bill at how a few sentences could reveal a lot about a person. Abi just told him a lot and, although he could listen, he couldn't provide the answers she needed. Those she would have to find herself.

Bill waited for her to sit back down, "I don't know Gav all that well so I'm just going off of an observation here." He put up his hand to gesture for Abi to wait when she wanted to comment. "I saw a man that respected what you did...a lot."

Nodding, Abi thought about what Bill said and what Gav himself said to her when he was here. He always asked questions when he didn't know what something was or if he wondered about something. He listened intently when she talked about work and let her take off for a day to help with the brush fire and didn't complain one bit.

"Now I feel like an ass. Thanks," she said to Bill.

Laughing, Bill shook his head, "There is no pleasing you, is there?" He meant it as teasing.

Abi shook her head, "Apparently not." She stood, "Thanks for the talk, Master Sgt."

"Anytime," Bill answered.

Walking out of her NCOIC's office, Abi figured she owed Gav an apology but had absolutely no idea how to do it.

At the end of the day, Abi poked her head into Eryn's office. "I'm out of here, you almost done?" she asked.

Eryn looked up and smiled, "Yes, I had meetings all day regarding RIMPAC and the first planning meeting for the Ball."

Abi scrunched up her face, "Not so much fun, hey?"

Shaking her head no, Eryn straightened her desk up and motioned for them to go out. "Not really, they were fine, just not my favorites."

"Did you tell the Captain about the baby?" Abi asked.

Eryn nodded as they walked out of her office. "Yes, everybody knows."

It was easy to be happy for Eryn. She was a great friend and really wanted a family. Abi never really gave a whole lot of thought to the idea of kids until recently. Thanks to Gav. Thinking of him, Abi frowned. She still had to figure out what the heck to do to apologize.

"Are you thinking about Gav?" Eryn asked when they were walking out to the parking lot.

She saw Abi's face go from relaxed to tense and figured, with what the Master Sgt. said to her about this morning, that he was on Abi's mind.

Guilt piled up on Abi's shoulders, "Yes, I had a fight with him yesterday."

Eryn hugged her friend quickly, "Anything I can do?" she asked. Abi was always a rock when she and Chase were going through their tumultuous reunion.

Shrugging, Abi smiled appreciatively, "Not right now, but thanks."

They each got into their cars and waved as they pulled out of the parking lot at Crash Crew.

Abi got home and plopped down on the couch. She didn't even bother to take off her flight suit; she just wanted to shut off her mind. Stretching out, she closed her eyes for a few minutes, the sound of the news humming in the background.

Waking up with a start, Abi looked around. Something woke her up but she didn't know what. Looking around, Abi noticed it was dark outside. One of the late night talk shows was on the TV so she must have been sleeping for a while. She was still tired so she went into the closet and changed into her pajamas.

Shuffling along, Abi thought maybe she should eat something but her bed looked way too comfortable so she decided to just get some sleep. She turned off the lights and slipped into bed, letting sleep carry her away.

Tuesday morning, Abi woke up feeling better. She was up before the alarm, probably from sleeping so long. She decided to eat breakfast and then check her email quick before she took off for work.

There were some solicitation emails that she deleted right away. Stupid spam! There was an email from Katherine's assistant asking her to RSVP to the fashion show this coming weekend. Crap! She couldn't believe she missed that. She sent off a quick email to the woman saying that she couldn't make it. Such a shame since it probably would've been a lot of fun. There was no email from Gav. Deep down, Abi didn't really think he would. She was just hoping he would and that would make it easier on her.

A few minutes later, Abi was walking out the door of her room wondering how she would figure this out.

When Abi walked into work, she was in a better mood than the day before. One of the Section Leaders caught her as she was going down the hall to her office. He had some concerns about an upcoming training class she scheduled. After answering his questions, Abi set her stuff down and got to work. She had to start making recommendations on some fitness reports that would be submitted by both Master Sgt. Phillips and Warrant Officer Johnson.

She was halfway through them when she heard a page for her to report to the OIC's office. Frowning, Abi got up and went to Eryn's office.

Even from the hallway, Abi could smell the aroma of flowers. She came around the corner of Eryn's office door and stopped in her tracks. On the desk was a humongous arrangement of flowers. They were gorgeous and Abi was immediately envious of Eryn for getting such a lovely gift. She never thought of herself as a flower girl until she received the ones from Gav. Darn it, she didn't want to think about him right now.

Eryn could see Abi's expression and knew her friend was having a tough time reconciling her feelings about Mr. Maslov. This probably wasn't going to help. She stood up and walked around her desk. Once she got to Abi, she handed her the card that came along with the flowers.

Abi looked down and read the card...

Eryn & Chase –

Congratulations on your wonderful news.

Gav

Abi looked at Eryn and then re-read the card. Oh he was good, that man! How was she supposed to figure this out when he was doing such nice things for her friends? She gave the card back to Eryn and went over to the arrangement.

It was a mix of tropical flowers with a wide variety of colors. The ribbon around the vase was done up in pink and blue. It was a thoughtful thing to do and completely like Gav. She looked from the flowers to Eryn and started crying.

Closing her office door, Eryn took a deep breath. She figured this was coming. You didn't fall in love without losing it a little bit. If anyone knew that, it was Eryn.

"Why don't we sit down," Eryn said soothingly and guided Abi over to the sofa.

Once they were seated she rubbed Abi's hand until she was done letting it all out. She grabbed some tissues and handed them to her friend.

Abi was spent emotionally and she couldn't cry anymore. She looked at Eryn with an apologetic face, "I'm sorry. I'm not sure where that came from." It was a lame excuse but it was the best she could give.

"I'd say," Eryn said softly, "it came from being in love."

Shaking her head no, Abi didn't believe it. "I don't think so."

Eryn laughed, "Why don't you think so?" She always thought Abi was really in tune with her emotions.

Looking out the window, then back to Eryn, Abi said, "Because if I was in love with him, I'd marry him."

Now Eryn really laughed. "Are you kidding me?" she asked in astonishment. "That's when you know you are in love; you're so flippin scared you can't see straight!"

None of this made sense to Abi. She shook her head again and got up to check her face in a little mirror Eryn kept in her desk. Once she figured the guys wouldn't see that she'd been crying, she smiled at Eryn and left the office.

Eryn watched her friend and wondered if she'd been as lost and dense as Abi was right now......ABSOLUTELY!

The rest of the day Abi stayed in her office. She brought a lunch so she ate alone and tried to avoid talking to anyone. She wasn't in a bad mood or anything, she was just confused and didn't want anyone else to see her in her current state.

After work, she went to the gym and worked out. She spent a little time with the free weights and was on the elliptical when she saw her ex-boyfriend, Bryan, come into the gym. Oh great, she thought, this would be fun. Maybe he wouldn't see her.

She watched as Bryan went over to the treadmill and ran. When her time on the elliptical was up she got off the machine, grabbed her stuff, and tried to get out of the gym without having to talk to him. She was mere feet from the door when she heard Bryan call her name.

Turning around, Abi tried to paste a smile on her face. "Hello, Bryan," she said with a lot more confidence than she felt.

"Abi," Bryan said when he was closer, "you look great."

The compliment used to make her happy but not it only made her nauseous. "What do you want?" she asked impatiently.

Bryan looked at Abi and thought she looked different, "I was hoping we could hang out."

Was he dense? "I'm pretty sure I gave you that answer when I kicked your ass in the parking lot the last time. How about we just nod when we see each other and let it go at that."

He looked at Abi and wondered what happened since he last saw her. "Fine," he said and nodded before he walked away.

Good, Abi thought, another chapter closed.

The rest of the week passed with little change. Abi would work all day and spend the nights wondering what she should do to apologize to Gav. Although, truth be told, she wasn't so sure she was the only one here who should apologize. She checked her computer religiously in the hopes he would email her but he didn't.

On Friday night, she was up late going over a surprise training fire schedule she and Master Sgt. Phillips were going to spring on the Sections the next evening. It wasn't something that was easy to do but it was a great training tool. They were going to meet at Crash Crew and recall the Section.

It was after midnight when she got ready for bed and she had an overwhelming need to call Gav. It was almost seven in the morning there but it was also Saturday and she didn't know if he got up early. Taking a chance, she dialed his number.

Gav's phone rang and brought him out of restless sleep. He hadn't slept well since he had that fight with Abi.

"Hello," he said groggily.

Abi cringed, feeling bad because she woke him up. "Gav," she said weakly, "it's Abi."

Gav woke up immediately, his heart wanted to pump out of his chest. "Are you okay?" he asked.

She wanted to laugh because he sounded so cute. "I'm fine." She paused, not sure how to say what she needed to say.

"Abi," Gav yawned, "baby, why are you calling me when it's in the middle of the night there?"

Hearing Gav using the endearment was almost her undoing. She kept the tears at bay but it was a challenge. "I just wanted to say I was sorry about being mean on the phone with you."

Sitting up, Gav wiped his hand down his face. This was a start. "I know, me too," he answered.

She was relieved, "You were right; I have always felt like my parents thought I was running away and I guess I was."

The revelation was a complete surprise to Gav. He did a lot of thinking about Abi and figured it wouldn't be easy for her to admit her fears and the impact of her parents on her career choice. Having met the Rochelle's, he knew they were good people; they just wanted something different for their daughter than what she chose.

Abi was nervous since Gav wasn't saying anything. "Are you there?" she asked.

"Yes," Gav said, "Abi, I just want you to be happy." It really was that simple. If she chose to continue a relationship with him, he'd be overjoyed but, if not, he would survive.

Smiling, Abi brushed a non-existent fuzzy from the arm of her sofa, "I'd be happy if we weren't fighting."

When Abi sounded vulnerable, like she did now, his chest squeezed tight. "Then we won't," he said firmly.

Abi couldn't help it, she laughed, "Okay then."

Gav smiled, "Now you need to get to bed, young lady."

"Okay," she said softly, "could you stay on the phone with me a little longer while I snuggle in?"

That thought brought up images of his last night in Hawaii and his body responded immediately. "Yes," he said in a raspy voice. "But this could be a short phone call."

She picked up on his tone right away and smiled bigger. "Okay."

A few minutes later, Abi was in bed, the phone cradled to her cheek, and a smile on her face. Gav was telling her about his week, mostly about the crazy things he encountered at work. It was such a relief to be talking again. Abi didn't realize how much she missed talking to him. She yawned.

"Time for bed, young lady," Gav said when he heard her yawn. He was now wide awake but it was worth it. "Call me later?"

Abi smiled, "Yes. Good night, Gav."

"Good night, Abi," he said back and hung up.

Saturday morning Abi woke up in a great mood. Not a surprise since she dreamt about making love to Gav all night long. Not a bad way to spend the night as far as she was concerned.

She got all of her errands done and spoke to Master Sgt. Phillips a couple of times about last minute preparations for tonight's surprise training fire.

At nine o'clock, she pulled into the Crash Crew parking lot. Trying to be quiet, she got out of her car and nodded to the Master Sgt. who just pulled in. They went into his office and met up with the Training NCOIC, Gunny Williams.

They met for a quick run-through of the planned exercise then allowed Gunny Williams to call the emergency.

Abi and Master Sgt. Phillips stood near the command vehicle and observed the response of the after-hours crew. They timed the arrival of the recalled personnel and made notes. The training fire itself was in a controlled pit area so the crews rolled and put it out without incident.

They finished up with the crew at about four in the morning and Abi was beat. She actually rode back to the barracks with the Master Sgt. because she was afraid she'd fall asleep while driving.

Bill dropped her off, "Hey," he said when she got out of the car, "are things better between you and Gav? You seem better."

Abi appreciated his concern. "Yes, thanks," she answered and waved when he pulled away. She barely made it into her room when exhaustion overtook her. She managed to get out of her flight suit and went to bed in just her bra and underwear.

It was about noon when Abi woke up. She was in the exact position she fell asleep in and that told her she was really tired and slept hard. Her muscles were a little achy but not bad. She was glad she had the day off because she intended to be a slug and stay in her room all day.

After a quick lunch, she showered and changed the sheets on her bed. That was extent of her planned activity for the day. There were some chick flicks on cable that she intended to watch. She was curled up on the sofa in a comfy t-shirt and shorts when her phone rang.

Seeing it was Eryn and thinking she was probably going to ask how the training exercise went, "This can't wait until tomorrow when we're at work?" she answered in a sarcastic tone.

"Abi, its Eryn. Listen, Katie's in the hospital," she said in a rushed voice.

Sitting up straight, Abi's thoughts went into overdrive. "What's happened?"

Eryn explained that apparently Katherine had fainted after having an argument with Mitch after the fashion show and was in the hospital. Katherine's assistant, Suzanna, called Katherine's parents but wouldn't give them any information so Eryn ended up calling and getting some news from the girl. Eryn was beside herself with worry so Abi tried to be strong for her friend. After Eryn was done talking, Chase got on the phone.

"Abi, I'm sending Eryn to New York and I can't go. Can you go with her?" he asked.

It didn't take any time for Abi to answer, "Of course," she said. "Tell me when."

Chase gave her some information and they would need to make sure Master Sgt. Phillips was okay with both of them being gone for a good week. As long as that was good, they would leave in just a few days.

When Abi hung up the phone she was reassured that Katherine was okay and felt better. Chase was relieved that she would be with Eryn on the flight. It wasn't until a while later that she realized she would be in a position to surprise Gav.

Chapter 16

Eryn was able to get the plane tickets on Monday. She and Abi had a lengthy debate about who would pay for Abi's ticket. Since it was last minute, they weren't cheap by any means but Abi still thought she should pay her own way. Eryn said that Chase insisted since Abi was accompanying his wife, he would pay for them. Because they were at work, and Abi didn't want to upset Eryn, she conceded.

They met with Master Sgt. Phillips to go over everything that was going on in Eryn's absence. Abi went over all pending training exercises that were scheduled for the next week and gave him any necessary paperwork.

Eryn and Abi were walking out when Bill called after them, "Gunny, can I have a word please?"

Abi came back in and sat down, "Yes, Master Sgt."

Bill leaned back in his chair, "I know this comment may be out of line but I'm thinking that if you're going to New York, maybe you and Gav can patch things up. I know you said that everything was okay the other day but I got the feeling that wasn't the whole story."

"You're right," Abi stood, "that comment was out of line." She started to leave the office but turned around at the doorway to face him. "But, I will take it under advisement."

Laughing as she walked down the hall, Bill started to read over the paperwork he was given. "You do that, Gunny," he mumbled to himself.

Their flight was leaving late Tuesday night. Eryn called Katherine about every six hours and Abi felt bad for the woman. Between Eryn and her parents, Abi doubted Katherine was allowed any time to recuperate. They still weren't told what caused Katherine to faint so it was important to Eryn to be there for her cousin as soon as possible.

Abi packed Monday night and had to fight the urge to send Gav an email. She didn't think she could keep from telling him that she was coming to New York. It was important for her to surprise him; a little payback for his impromptu visit but she also wanted to make sure he was going to be home. It would suck if he was out of town for business or something like that.

When her phone rang later that night, she jumped. At first she thought it might be Gav but, with the time difference, she decided that probably wasn't it. After looking at the caller ID, she saw it was Eryn.

"Hey," she said as she turned the sound down on her TV, "is everything okay?"

Eryn was walking around her bedroom and throwing clothes into her suitcase. Her thoughts were in chaos. She assumed it was a mixture of concern for her cousin combined with the pregnancy hormones. Finally, she thought she had to call and talk to someone who understood.

"I'm fine," Eryn answered, "I'm just amped up about the trip."

Abi nodded into the phone, "Understandable, just remember, she's okay."

A tear slipped down Eryn's cheek, "Thank you again for going with me."

Chuckling, Abi sat down on the couch, "Not a problem, I had a ton of leave and I could use the trip."

Eryn knew her friend well, "You mean you could use the trip to see Gav."

Just hearing his name set Abi's nerves on alert. "Maybe," she answered but knew Eryn was right. It was the truth but that didn't mean she had to admit it just yet.

"I just needed to talk so I hope I'm not interrupting you." Eryn felt kind of bad being so out of sorts. Chase had a dinner meeting with his boss and was kind enough to let her bow out so she could get ready for the trip.

Sometimes, Abi thought, it wasn't easy being alone. "Eryn, it's not a problem at all."

Picking up a jacket she set out, Eryn bit her lip. "Well, what did Gav say when you told him you were coming to New York?"

Abi felt kind of guilty, "I didn't tell him," she responded.

"Ohhhh," Eryn said, "you are a brave woman."

Laughing, Abi shook her head, "Not sure about that. I'm just looking forward to a little payback for his surprise here."

Eryn cleared his throat, "Not entirely his fault."

"I know," Abi said dryly, "you'll get your payback later when you let me babysit the kid and I feed him or her a ton of sugar then send them home to you."

Sighing, Eryn smiled widely, "I can handle that."

The two of them talked for a little while longer until Eryn said that Chase was home. Abi hung up and thought about how nice that must be, waiting for someone to come home to you. Another thing she didn't consider much before Gav.

Tuesday flew by. There were department meetings and orders given about what was going on. They were lucky that there was nothing big on the docket right now. Only Master Sgt. Phillips knew the women were travelling together; everyone else just assumed they took leave around the same time.

After work, Abi drove back to her room to shower and change for the flight. She checked her email and was surprised when she saw an email from Gav. Crap!

Abi:

I thought you were going to call me Sunday. I wanted to call but I'm still not sure what you're up to and I don't want to call when you're sleeping. I just wanted to say hi and let you know I've been thinking about you. I know, not a guy thing to say but I think we've moved past that.

I am going out tonight for dinner with my parents and don't know when I'll be home, just in case you decide to call. Work is finally caught up from my little vacation so it's been a little lonely around here.

Take Care,

Gav

After reading the email, Abi sat back in her chair. His email was kind of simple but it felt like he was saying a lot anyway. He says he's lonely so is that an invitation? She'd find out soon enough.

Chase knocked on Abi's door an hour later. He smiled when she opened the door, "Ready?" he asked.

"Yep," Abi answered and shot him a smile of thanks when he grabbed her suitcase.

They were on their way to the airport a few minutes later.

Chase looked over at his wife, "Now you girls don't have toooo good of time without me."

Eryn snorted, "Right, I'm knocked up and Katherine is sick; should be a riot."

Abi bit her lip to keep from laughing. She caught a glance from Chase in the rearview mirror and he winked at her.

"How is Katherine doing?" Abi asked.

A look of worry fell across Eryn's face. "She's at home resting but there's still no word on what's wrong." She squeezed Chase's hand, "I'll get some answers when I'm there."

It must be nice to be so confident, Abi thought. Eryn just said it and it happened. Not all the time of course, but enough for Abi to admire her friend's determination. She, on the other hand, wasn't sure about any of her decisions where Gav was concerned.

The flight was on time so they said goodbye to Chase at the line for security. Abi rubbed Eryn's shoulder when she saw her friend's tears. It touched Abi that her friends were so in love. She cried when Gav left and that was the only time she could remember doing that. It was tough to say goodbye.

Once they were seated on the plane, Eryn settled in and tried to get some sleep. It was a red eye so they were both hoping to get some rest. It would be early afternoon when they arrived in New York and each of them had to sleep in order to be somewhat alert when they got there.

As the plane took off, Abi drifted into a half sleep of wondering what Gav would think of her showing up in New York. Would he be as happy as she was to see him? Would he be pissed that she didn't email or call him? Would her parents and his parents start something? That was the one variable Abi was really unsure about...their parents.

The flight was pretty routine. They had a layover in Los Angeles for a few hours so they left the airport and headed to a nearby restaurant for a bite to eat. Abi checked her email on her phone while they were in the taxi.

"Any word from Katherine?" Abi asked Eryn when her phone was pulling up her emails.

Eryn shook her head, "No, and that assistant of hers is going to get her ass kicked when I get there," she said sharply.

Oh, that assistant of Katherine's didn't know what was going to happen to her today, Abi thought. "Kick her ass!" Abi said in support.

They had a nice breakfast and walked a few blocks to stretch their legs before hailing a cab to take them back to the airport.

The flight to New York was, again, uneventful. Any other time the flight would drag by and Abi would be fidgety thinking about her visit. Now she was fidgety and wondering what she was going to say to Gav.

During the descent into JFK, Abi started to feel nauseous. What was going to happen?

Sensing her friend's indecision, Eryn squeezed Abi's hand. "It'll be fine."

Abi looked over and smiled at her friend. Yes it would.

They landed, got their baggage, and hopped in a taxi to head over to Katherine's place.

It took a good hour to get to Katie's apartment from the airport and Abi could see that Eryn was exhausted. They had hotel reservations and really should have gone there first but Eryn was insistent about seeing her cousin right away.

The cab pulled up and Eryn got out, "Are you sure you don't want to come up?" She asked Abi.

Abi smiled but shook her head, "No thanks, this is a family thing." She winked at Eryn, "I have a family thing of my own to contend with myself so I'll try to work that out and meet you at the hotel later."

Eryn nodded and waved as the cab pulled away from the curb. With a sigh, she squared her shoulders and prepared to find out just what the hell was going on around here.

Abi directed the cab driver to take her to the hotel she and Eryn made a reservation at. It was a little more upscale but Abi sure didn't mind that. She could've stayed with her parents but this trip wasn't really about them and she didn't want them to confuse the situation. Plus it was a power move on her part to set her own terms and boundaries.

She checked in and went up to the room. It took very little time to settle hers and Eryn's bags inside and freshen up. On a whim, she called Gav's office before she left.

"Mr. Maslov's office," a very professional voice said.

Abi smiled, he had an assistant. Whoo hoo. Stop it, she told herself. Now was not the time for teasing. "Yes," she said in a shaky voice. "Is there any way I can get an appointment with Mr. Maslov today?"

The woman hesitated, "One moment please," she said directly.

Even though she only waited a minute or two, Abi could have sworn it was an hour, she was so nervous. Finally the woman came back on the line.

"Thank you for holding, Mr. Maslov has a three forty-five appointment available," the perky voice said.

"Um," Abi said, "can I please take that?" she asked.

Gav's assistant asked, "Your name please?"

What did she do? Well, she didn't need to lie. She said, "Ms. Rochelle."

The perky voice was back again, "Well see you then, Ms. Rochelle."

Abi smiled, said, "Thank you," and hung up.

Looking at her watch, she had two hours before she had to meet Gav so she figured seeing her mother was a good way to pass the time and put a limit on how long she would have to visit. Grabbing her room key, she headed out.

Fifteen minutes later, the cab pulled up in front of Abi's childhood home. It was a lovely building with twelve different apartments. The neighborhood was upper middle class and a very welcoming. She got out and paid the driver.

After walking up and greeting the doorman, Mr. Simms, she went inside and pressed the button on the elevator.

The ride up to her parents' floor took a few minutes and she was feeling as though she was regressing into their little girl on the way up. She was really nervous about what her parents would say about her visit and especially about Gav.

Abi took a deep breath as the elevator door opened to her parents' floor. She stepped out and nodded to a young woman and her son who were getting on as she was getting off. She got to the door and pressed the doorbell quickly before she lost her nerve.

Elena Rochelle was surprised by the sound of the doorbell since she wasn't expecting anyone. She peeked through the peephole and saw soft, green eyes looking at her. She opened the door quickly and gasped at the sight of her daughter, Abi, standing there.

"Hello, Mama," Abi said.

Grabbing her daughter, Elena pulled her in for a fierce hug. Oh, she missed her little girl so much! After a moment, she whispered into Abi's ear, "Mah-yo Sohl-neesh-kah."

The lovely endearment of "my sunshine," brought tears to Abi's eyes. She hugged her mother tight. It had been too long since she'd been home.

"What are you doing here?" Elena asked as she finally stepped away to pull Abi inside.

They walked into the apartment and Abi smiled. It was the same and yet different since she was here last. There was a fresh coat of paint on the walls, new furniture, but some of the same furnishings she remembered as a child. The smell of food wafted through the air and made her stomach growl.

Elena heard her daughter's tummy and smiled, "Let's go into the kitchen so I can feed you. You're too skinny."

Abi laughed at her mother's comment, the woman probably weighed nothing and was only an inch or two shorter than Abi. "Mama, I'm hungry but I'm not too skinny."

Clicking her tongue, Elena guided her daughter to the table and turned to the stove, "I can say you're too skinny; I'm your mama."

She had a point, Abi thought, and smiled, "Yes you are."

After dishing up a bowl of stew for Abi and slicing some freshly made bread, Elena always preferred to make her own, she sat down next to her daughter. There was something very soothing about feeding your baby, even when they were no longer a baby.

"This is delicious, Mama," Abi said between bites.

Elena tried not to cry, "I don't know why but I wanted to make it today. Now I know it was for you."

Abi wanted to cry now, "Thank you, Mama," she said in a soft whisper.

They ate the lunch and Abi helped her mother clean up. It always amazed Abi at how humbly her parents lived. Her father was a successful manager in the banking business and yet, they never moved to a bigger place or bought fancy furniture or cars. They lived comfortably but not lavishly and Abi appreciated that her parents were still the same.

Elena made tea and carried the tray out to the living room where Abi was looking at pictures. "Sit," she said as she placed the tray on the coffee table.

The tone her mother used was one she remembered too. It meant that they were going to talk seriously. Some things really never did change.

Abi sat down and served them both tea. Once she was re-seated, she turned to her mother, "I'm only here for a couple of days." she didn't want her mother to get the wrong idea. "My friend, Eryn, had to fly in to see her family and I came with her," Abi said in a rushed voice.

Elena nodded, "Did you come to see Gavriil?" she asked. Elena felt there was no point in tiptoeing around the issues.

Looking down at her cup of tea, Abi tried to figure out what the right answer was. "I think so."

Wanting to tread carefully with her daughter, Elena nodded, "Do you love him, Abigale?"

Abi took a sip of her tea in an effort to buy some time. There was no easy answer to that question either. "I don't know."

Appreciating that her daughter didn't try to rebuff the question or evade it, Elena patted Abi's hand. "I have to tell you that I admired the way Gavriil stood up to your father."

Her head popping up, Abi frowned, "What do you mean?" she asked her mother.

"Oh, Gav didn't tell you," Elena said. "Your father was ready to burst when Gav told him to mind his own business, although Gavriil did it in a very polite way."

Abi didn't know what to say. She didn't know much, Gav said that he was dealing with the parents but he didn't mention her father's bullying tactics. Now she felt guilty for leaving him with it.

Seeing her daughter consider the information, Elena decided it was time to come forward with a few facts her daughter probably didn't know. "Do you know why we arranged this marriage between you?" she asked.

Shaking her head slowly, Abi gazed over at her mother. The beautiful hair, a little grayer, but still soft and styled to accentuate her mother's lovely face. The set of pearls her mother wore every day because they belonged to her grandmother. The smiling eyes that always loved Abi, no matter what. All of these things were beautiful.

"When Klara and I sat there and watched the two of you," Elena sniffled and grabbed a handkerchief from the table to dab her eyes, "we saw Gavriil pick something up for you and hand it to you."

Abi smiled and nodded.

Elena gazed into the distance, tapping into the lovely memory, "It was the gentleness he had when being with you, even at such a young age." She dabbed her eyes again, "It was if it was a sign."

Wanting to cry herself, Abi placed her hand over her mother's, "He is still very gentle with me." She smiled at her mother's look.

"Oh, my sweet love," Elena said to her daughter, seeing her for a woman now, a woman in love. "He is a truly great man."

The tears were falling now, Abi could see what her mother was saying. It didn't matter now that her parents "arranged" this. It only mattered that she and Gav felt the love they needed to make their life work.

Abi looked down for a moment, then back up to her mother, "I think I love him, Mama, but I'm just so afraid."

Elena pulled her daughter close so she could hold and comfort her. It was like when Abigale was a baby and snuggled close to Elena's heart. No matter what her baby did, she would always be Elena's little girl.

"I know you are afraid," Elena whispered into Abi's hair. She stroked the soft strands with her fingers. "That is the wonderful part of love, Abigale. It is very scary and very risky."

Elena pulled back enough so she could see her daughter's eyes. "You have always been a strong and independent woman, Abigale." Elena dabbed her baby's tears. "Now you have someone who is willing to share that journey with you."

Abi nodded but wasn't convinced. "You say that but I have a job that isn't one I'm willing to give up."

Sighing, Elena tipped her face down to give her daughter a serious look, "Abigale, no one is asking you to."

Shaking her head, Abi couldn't quite accept it all. "He lives and works here and I live and work there."

Elena sat back and thought about what her daughter said, "Yes, you do. But love and marriage are about compromise."

Frustration was warring inside of her and Abi wanted to keep it there but it still snuck out into her voice, "I think I would need to do all the compromising here."

It hurt to see her daughter so confused and Elena wanted to reassure her but that couldn't happen. "Did you ask Gavriil what he was willing to compromise on?"

The question threw Abi a little. "No, I haven't."

"Then you cannot possibly know what he is willing to do for you," Elena said sternly. She would not baby Abigale on this matter.

Abi nodded. "I know."

Elena was about to say something when the front door opened.

Andrei came home, expecting to have a late lunch with his darling wife when he saw her on the couch with their daughter. He stopped in the doorway, "Abigale," he whispered.

Abi smiled and stood up, "Hello, Papa."

Closing the space between them, Andrei hugged his daughter tightly. He looked over to see his wife and knew he walked in on something.

When her father stepped back to look at her, Abi blushed.

"You are too skinny," Andrei said and laughed when his daughter rolled her eyes.

Her parents would never change and maybe that wasn't such a bad thing. Abi would always love her parents and they would always love her, even if she ran away to do something they considered a little crazy.

Andrei waited for his daughter to sit back down and leaned down to kiss his wife.

Abi watched her parents and noticed yet another thing that never changed. They loved one another more than most people did and it was so nice to see that.

Once Andrei was settled, he looked over at his little girl, "Why are you here, Abigale?"

Elena answered for her daughter, "Her friend Eryn is here seeing her family and Abigale came with her."

Nodding as he sipped his tea, Andrei listened. "It isn't to see the Maslov boy, then?"

Abi shook her hand. The man was incorrigible. "That's part of it too, Papa."

"I knew it," Andrei put down his teacup and stood abruptly. "I knew as soon as I asked him at the dinner." He smiled at his wife.

Lips pursed, Abi looked from one parent to another. "Papa," she said in a voice full of warning, "you should not interrogate Gav."

Andrei waved his hands in a dismissive gesture, "The boy can take anything I can dish out; he's tough."

Abi laughed, thinking her parents were insane. And yet, she was touched that they would think they needed to butt in and determine her life for her.

"Now, you two, listen," she said to her parents, "we're going to talk about this and you're going to listen."

Surprisingly, her father sat back down and both of her parents did listen. When Abi left their apartment a while later, she felt like they'd come to an understanding.

Chapter 17

Gav sat at his desk and sulked. It was a Wednesday and he felt like it was Monday. The day seemed to drag on and he was irritated for no apparent reason.

Well, that wasn't exactly true. He was irritated because he hadn't heard from Abi. When they talked over the weekend, everything seemed good. But now, nothing. What did he say? He was trying to give her space but it was a lot tougher than he thought it would be.

Every night he would dream of them together and wake up hard and aching for her. If that wasn't enough, he would see women who, apparently, looked like her walking around the city. Twice now he'd walked up to strangers and called them Abi. It was humiliating and he hadn't told anybody about it. Maybe he should see a psychiatrist or something.

Still daydreaming, Gav didn't even look at the papers his assistant, Lorraine, set down in front of him.

Lorraine stood next to her boss' desk and sighed, "Are you going to tell me what's going on with you?" she asked her boss. The guy was a whiz but these days he was downright flaky. Ever since that little trip to Hawaii.

Gav looked over at Lorraine, irritated by the question. "There is," he scowled, "nothing going on with me."

"Okay, keep saying it and maybe it'll be true." She stuck her tongue out at him and left the office. They'd worked together for over five years so she knew how he was.

Yelling after her, "Whatever!" Gav said in a snotty voice at the closed door. Not very professional but he didn't care.

When Abi got out of the cab, she looked up at the tall building in Manhattan where Gav worked. Her father worked for the same bank but at a different branch so she'd never been here before. He told her what he did but she was still nervous about showing up at his work. Of course, he did it to her and payback was most definitely a bitch.

More resolved, she smoothed the skirt she was wearing and made her way inside. She spent the cab ride from her parents' apartment trying to freshen up her makeup and smooth her hair.

She had to look for his name and finally found it. He was on one of the upper floors of the building. Great.

Once the elevator doors opened and Abi stepped out, she wore her best game face. It was like she spent the ride up reminding herself that they were either going to work out or not. She was scared, no, she was downright terrified because Gav could decide that she didn't deserve a chance with him.

Abi walked up to the reception desk and asked for Gav's office. The lovely receptionist pointed down the hall and asked her to stop at the desk there. She made her way down the corridor, seeing lots of doors with executive's names on them. It was really no different than walking into the Colonel's office at her command. Equating it to something she was familiar with made her calm down.

She came up to the desk and saw a smiling woman there. "Hello," Abi said. "I have a meeting with Mr. Maslov.

Lorraine looked at the calendar, "Ms. Rochelle, right?" she asked.

Abi nodded, her anxiety building up again.

The woman was lovely, Lorraine thought, although she looked really nervous for some reason. "Mr. Maslov was called up to a meeting upstairs, I'm afraid," Lorraine said. "I'm not sure how long he'll be; would you like to wait?"

What did she do? Abi asked herself. "Okay," she said in a shaky voice. This was not how she thought this would go at all.

An hour later, Gav was leaving the office of one of the Vice Presidents and was ticked off at, what he thought, was a complete waste of time. The meeting could have been put off and he was forced to miss some of his appointments. He didn't like that and thought it was bad business. Pressing the button for his floor, he swore under his breath.

Abi was too nervous for this. She decided, after an hour, that she couldn't wait. She got up and went over to the desk, "I'm sorry but I think I need to leave."

Lorraine was discreetly watching the woman. There was something about her that made Lorraine wonder why she was meeting with Gav. "Would you like to reschedule?" she asked the woman.

"No, thank you," Abi responded. She smiled and made her way to the elevator.

Abi pushed the down button and stood in front of the elevator coming down from the upper floors. But then, the elevator coming up from downstairs pinged so she turned as the elevator opened and stepped inside.

Gav stepped off the elevator and smiled to the people getting on the one going down. For a second, he thought he saw Abi out of the corner of his eye. Oh great, now he was seeing her at work too. Fantastic, he thought sarcastically. Maybe Lorraine could recommend someone for him to see.

He walked up to Lorraine's desk, "Hello, sorry that took so long."

She looked up at her boss and sighed. "Well, there was a very nervous looking young lady that waited until just a few minutes ago." She nodded toward the elevator.

"Really?" Gav asked, "What was her name?" He didn't look at his meeting calendar for the afternoon.

Lorraine shuffled some papers on her desk, "Uh, a Miss Rochelle," she said and was shocked when she looked up to see Gav running for the elevators. "Gav!" She hollered down the hall.

Gav heard Lorraine but didn't care. He did see Abi, she was getting on the elevator as he came downstairs. Dammit! She was in New York! His heart pounding, Gav pushed the down button on the elevator constantly until the door opened.

The ride down to the street level took forever and Abi was already stretched to her limit. Everyone was quiet, a few people would greet one another, but it was the forced silence between strangers that grated on what little nerves she had left.

Finally, the door opened and Abi stepped out, finally able to breathe easier. She wasn't sure if she should be relieved that she wasn't able to see Gav or not. Hailing a cab, she stood there and pondered what she should do next.

Gav was ready to yell by the time the elevator hit the bottom floor. He pushed his way off as politely as he could. Once in the lobby, he practically ran for the doors.

Abi was getting into a cab; he could see her through the glass doors. She was gorgeous! "Abi!" he yelled as he ran through the lobby area, garnering stares from the other people in the area.

The cab pulled up to the curb and Abi got in. She was about to close the door when she thought she heard her name. Looking around, she didn't see anyone she recognized so she closed the door and gave the driver the address for the hotel. Maybe she would take a nap and try to call Gav later.

Gav reached the street as the cab pulled away, "Abi!" he yelled as loud as he could.

Standing there, on the sidewalk, he watched the cab drive away with the woman he loved.

Twenty minutes later, Lorraine brought two bottled waters into Gav's office and sat down across from him. She placed one on his desk for him to drink and opened the other for herself.

"Are you going to tell me what that was about?" she asked expectantly.

Gav didn't want to talk to anyone but Abi right now. "No," he said sharply.

Lorraine chuckled, "Oh so that's why you've been so distracted." She wasn't swayed by his nasty look in her direction. "Very pretty but seemed a little timid for you, though."

Gav almost choked on the water he was drinking. "What!" he said. "Abi is not timid in the least."

Eyebrows raised, Lorraine wasn't convinced. "Could've fooled me. I thought she was going to jump out of her skin every time that elevator door opened."

What was his assistant talking about? Gav couldn't believe it. They must be talking about two different women. Abi was confident and kicked ass on everything she did. He didn't, for one minute, think she would be nervous in his office.

Once he was able to talk Lorraine into going back out to her desk, he tried calling Abi. Her phone must've been off because it went straight to voicemail.

Not knowing what to do, he called his mother, getting Abi's parents' home number from her. He didn't want to explain why he wanted the number and he was thankful that his mother didn't ask. He called their house and got the answering machine. Dammit! Finally, he called Chase's cell number.

"Hello there," Chase answered his cell when he saw it was Gav calling.

Gav smiled, glad Chase was a nice guy, "Hey, I was wondering if you knew that Abi was here."

Chase chuckled. What was he? The go-between for everybody? First he talked to Mitch about Katherine and now Gav about Abi. "Yes, I asked her to fly with Eryn."

Surprised and confused, Gav asked, "Why is Eryn here?"

"Her cousin is sick and Eryn needed to fly in to see her so I asked Abi to go with since I needed to stay here for work." He nodded to one of his co-workers as he walked into his office.

Gav was still confused. "Do you know where they're staying?" he asked, a little embarrassed at the desperation he heard in his own voice.

Aha, Chase thought, Abi hadn't seen him yet. Geez, this whole love thing was tough on everybody. "Yes," he answered.

Feeling exasperated, Gav, tried not to growl into the phone. "Are you going to tell me where she's staying?"

It was too much to resist, Chase couldn't help but bait him, "Oh, you want me to answer the question."

"Dammit, Chase," Gav growled.

Poor guy, Chase thought, "Okay, okay."

They talked for a few more minutes and, when Gav hung up, he felt a little better. Now he just had to figure out how to catch up with Abi. In a city this big, that could be a little tough.

Abi went back to the hotel. She was exhausted. Her parents wanted her to come over for dinner but she declined at the time because she figured she and Gav would have plans. Now what?

Back in the hotel room, Abi flopped down on the bed. She kicked off the heels she wore. She wasn't used to heels and her feet were screaming now. Absently rubbing them, she clicked on the TV and laid down on the bed. It didn't take long for the jet lag to kick her butt and she drifted off to sleep.

Eryn unlocked the hotel room door several hours later and frowned. Abi was there. She honestly expected Abi to go find Gav and not see her for the remainder of the trip. Wishful thinking maybe on Eryn's part. She tried to be quiet as she set her carry-on bag down and went over to the vacant bed. The TV droned low in the background. Looking over, Eryn saw that Abi's phone was shut off. She must've forgotten to turn it on when she got off the plane.

Sounds woke Abi up slowly. She wasn't alone in the room and cracked her eyes open. They were scratchy. Once they were focused, she saw Eryn smiling at her.

"Good morning, sleepy head," Eryn said brightly.

Looking around, Abi was confused, "What do you mean good morning?" she asked.

Cocking her head, Eryn clamped her hands on her hips, "Usually, when one says good morning, it means that the morning has come and it's good."

She didn't need the sarcasm, Abi thought. "Ha ha." She looked out the window and her eyes shot up. "Did I sleep all night?"

"Yes," Eryn answered, getting her clothes set out, "and thank goodness you don't snore."

Thinking her friend was a comedian, Abi snorted. "I don't snore," she said defensively.

Eryn came out of the bathroom, dressed, "That's what I said."

Abi got up and headed into the bathroom with her toiletry bag. She turned on the shower and set out her soap and shampoo. She heard Eryn knock on the door and yelled, "Yes."

"There's coffee in the pot and I'm off to see Katie. You have a good day," she said loudly into the door.

Eryn's thoughtfulness made Abi smile, "Thanks," she answered.

After she was showered and felt somewhat human, Abi came out to get dressed. The weather was only slightly cooler here than in Hawaii so she was glad she brought a couple of skirts and pairs of shorts with her.

Choosing a cotton skirt in darker pink and a stretchy t-shirt top in lighter pink, she did her hair and makeup lightly and got ready to go out. Not seeing Gav the night before was upsetting now that she thought about it. He didn't even call her!

Abi walked over to the night stand where she set her phone the day before and frowned. It was turned off! Great, she was an idiot!

She turned on the phone and went to brush her teeth. When she came back she looked at the screen and cringed at the six missed calls she had. Even better, she sighed.

The first call was from Gav and he didn't leave a message. The second was from her mother saying that Gav called their house. The third was from Eryn saying she was on her way back to the hotel. The fourth was from Gav again but he didn't leave a message. After the fifth call was a message from Gav so Abi pushed the button on her phone and listened.

"Abi," he said softly, "I'm sorry I missed you at my office. What are you doing here?"

Frowning at the tone in his voice, Abi wasn't sure what to make of it. Was he upset with her for coming to his office?

The sixth call was another message from Gav.

"Abi, I don't know why you won't call me back but I'm getting upset here." He paused, "Please call me."

Abi sat down on the bed and wanted to cry. What did she do now? Before she could think, the phone went off in her hand. She looked down and saw it was Gav. Don't be a chicken, she yelled at herself before she clicked the accept button.

Taking a quick breath, Abi said, "Hello,"

"Abi," Gav sighed in relief, "are you okay? I was going nuts when I saw you at the office and then you wouldn't return my calls."

His voice sounded funny to Abi, "I'm sorry. I shut off my phone and fell asleep right after I got back to the hotel room." She was feeling shy for some inexplicable reason.

Gav smiled, "As long as you're okay I'll forgive you for making me have one of the most sleepless nights ever."

Now that sounded like Gav, Abi thought to herself. She laughed. "Okay."

Her shyness was sweet and made Gav want her more. "When can I see you?" The question came out rushed and sounded anxious, even to him.

"I guess the question is, when can I see you?" She answered his question with her own.

Gav was at his office, a curious Lorraine checking in on him every ten minutes or so to see what was going on with the mysterious woman from yesterday. "I have some meetings this morning, unfortunately, but I can be wrapped up here around one this afternoon."

Looking around, Abi wasn't sure what she could say. "That's great actually, then I can meet my mom for lunch or something."

Turning away from his door, in case Lorraine walked in, Gav whispered into the phone. "Yes, make sure you're full because you may not get a chance to eat for a while once I get my hands on you."

His words were an invitation and a promise all rolled into one. She loved it and her body reacted fast. "I see."

She was quick, he'd give her that. "I'll call you when I'm done to see where you are."

"Okay," Abi said in a breathy tone. She could make a few promises of her own. "Bye."

Gav heard the dial tone and hung up his cell. Oh, the woman was going to kill him. That was okay. He turned around to see Lorraine standing in the doorway of his office with a 'You better spill,' look on her face.

A few minutes after hanging up with Gav, Abi called her mother. She wanted to spend time together if her mother had time. Although Elena was surprised by her daughter's request, she was all too happy to meet with her for a late breakfast.

During the cab ride to meet her mom, Abi watched the city pass by in fascination. It was sometimes hard to forget all the craziness that was New York when you were in a laid back place like Hawaii. Buildings buzzed by, people were walking in every direction. Horns were honking and the noise was everywhere. She realized she missed it.

They were meeting at an upscale restaurant uptown that Abi hadn't been to before. It shouldn't surprise her that her mother would have other "favorites" now. When Abi was little, they would go to late afternoon tea on Saturdays. It was always at fancy restaurants that had frilly tablecloths. Abi loved the girl time with her mother. This kind of reminded her of it and made her smile. She walked into the restaurant and gave the hostess her name. The smiling young lady led her around tables to a corner booth. Her mother was there with another woman.

Funny, Abi thought, her mother didn't mention anyone else joining them.

As Abi neared the table, her mother stood and held out her hands. Smiling, Abi held them and kissed her mother on the cheek. "Hello, Mama," she said.

"Abigale," Elena said smiling, "I'd like you to meet my very good friend, Klara Maslov."

Maslov? Abi asked herself. As in Gav's mother Maslov? Oh mama, Abi groaned inwardly. Not now.

Klara smiled at Abigale and motioned for her to sit. Obviously, Elena didn't tell her daughter that Klara would be joining them. The poor girl seemed about as scared as Gav did when she and Isaak sprung Abi's parents on him.

"Mrs. Maslov," Abi said and shook the woman's hand politely.

Klara liked her already, she was able to hide her discomfort pretty well, "Abi," she said, then stopped, "is it okay to call you, Abi?"

Smiling, Abi sat down, "Of course. My parents and people from work call me Abigale but I'm Abi to everyone else."

The waiter came over and took orders for coffee and tea.

It was a little awkward at first, "Mrs. Maslov," Abi finally said, "My mother didn't tell me you were joining us so I apologize for my nervousness." Gav's mother's warm demeanor certainly helped put Abi at ease. "I just wanted to say thank you for your letter."

Well, the elephant was addressed and Klara was relieved. "I'm glad you weren't offended." Klara winked at Elena, "There were a few people who weren't very happy that I sent it to you."

"I happen to think," Abi said lightly, "that we're all taking on something very different and trying to make our way through it."

She was a lovely woman, Klara thought, no wonder Gav was in love with her. If the dinner didn't confirm it for Klara, then Abi's reaction this morning did. If Gav meant nothing to Abi, she wouldn't be so nervous in front of his mother. Relief filled her heart.

Klara nodded her thanks to the waiter. "Remember, this was something that was part of my upbringing."

Abi flinched inwardly, "I'm sorry, I didn't mean to offend you, Mrs. Maslov." She looked over to see her mother nod reassuringly.

"Oh, you misunderstand," Klara said sweetly, "you most certainly didn't offend me, Abi. I was just saying that I know how odd it seems to be when you're told you *WILL* marry someone you don't know."

She was right, Abi nodded, there was someone who did understand what she was going through. "May I ask you some questions, Mrs. Maslov?"

Klara nodded, "Yes you may, Abi, as long as you call me Klara," she answered.

Abi smiled, "Okay, Klara," she answered.

When their breakfast was over, Abi found she was a little disappointed. Gav's mother was amazing! She was put in a marriage that could have made her miserable but she chose to love the man she married. For Abi, it was a little different, but only in the semantics. Although, Klara didn't have any choice in the matter when she was promised. As much as Abi knew her parents wanted this marriage between her and Gav, they wouldn't disown her if she refused.

Her mother and Klara asked if she wanted to go to a meeting they were attending for a local volunteer organization. Abi declined, feeling like she really needed some time to herself to do some heavy-duty thinking. After she put the other two women in a cab, she called Eryn. Getting voicemail, Abi left a message letting Eryn know she was meeting Gav at one this afternoon and she didn't know when she would be back at the hotel this evening.

Having a couple of hours to kill before Gav called her, Abi walked a while. She listened to people as they passed by and window shopped for a few blocks. She found a cab and gave him the address and sat with a smile on her face.

The Metropolitan Museum of Art was a favorite place of Abi's when she was growing up. Her father, for all of his business sense, definitely had a love of art. He would take Abi there at least three times a year to see the new exhibits and study the classics. "There is something very moving about art," he would tell Abi.

She paid the cab fare and turned around to see the gigantic building in front of her. She climbed the steps and went inside.

There were children, probably on a school field trip, roaming around. She watched the teacher round up a few stragglers as their guide led them into the main exhibition area. Abi paid her ticket price and entered.

It was just as she remembered it from her childhood. The sounds, the smells, and the art, were like old friends waiting for her to come back for a visit. She leisurely strolled through the galleries, stopping here and there to admire a piece. There were sculptures from Rodin and paintings by Monet. There was contemporary art that made Abi question the artist's sanity and moving pieces that brought her serenity.

Going through the main building, Abi fondly remembered asking her father a million questions about art and artists. He was very kind in answering all of them. She and Gav would have to bring their children here.

The recurring thought of Gav and "their children," swept the air out of Abi's lungs. She sat down on the nearest bench and tried to calm herself down. For all of her epiphanies, she really had no idea of how Gav felt about her. Sure, he said the right things in the emails and made her feel like the most special woman in the world when they were together, but he never said the words she needed to hear the most...I love you.

Gav was ready to chew his arm off by the time his last meeting wrapped up. How could executives find so much to talk about? Normally he would have been in the thick of any meetings, but today the only thing on his mind was Abi. As soon as the meeting was adjourned, he was on his phone calling her.

"Hello, Gav," Abi answered her phone. She was still sitting on the same bench.

Her voice sounded a little off to Gav, "Are you okay?" he asked as he punched the elevator button. "Where are you?" he followed up quickly.

For all of Abi's insecurities, he certainly sounded happy to talk to her and excited to see her. "I'm at the Met," she answered.

Another surprise, he wouldn't have pegged her for an art enthusiast. "Can I meet you there?" he asked as he grabbed his briefcase from his office. He nodded to a smiling Lorraine as he walked out.

"Yes," Abi answered, "I'm sitting in the main gallery."

Gav nodded to one of his co-workers and got onto the elevator, "Okay, I'm on my way."

Abi hung up her phone and smiled. Knowing he was on his way settled her down.

It seemed to take forever for Gav to get to the Met but the cab pulled up in front of the building about twenty minutes later. He threw money at the driver, not caring that it was like a one hundred percent tip.

Getting inside, Gav started to look for Abi. She said she was in the main gallery but the place was huge. He was about to text her when he saw her sitting on a bench, looking up at a large painting. He wasn't sure of the artist because as soon as he saw Abi, everything else faded around them.

Abi knew when Gav was there. Her body felt it. She looked around and finally found him. He was standing about thirty feet away and looking at her intensely. His fitted suit gave him an imposing air. His hair was mussed, probably from running his fingers through it. She noticed he did that when he was in Hawaii.

She couldn't move; she just sat there and looked at him.

Gav moved toward Abi, a smile plastered on his face. She was like a lighthouse, guiding him to someplace safe amidst all the chaos around them. His heart flipped over and over in his chest, making it hard to breathe.

When he was standing next to her and looking down into her eyes, Abi found the courage to speak, "Good to see you, Gav."

Gav wanted to growl. "Good," he said sarcastically and sat down next to her, "I'm telling you I am so crazy right now and you say good?"

Abi laughed, not at him, but because she was so happy too. "I'm sorry I made you crazy."

He shook his head, "No you're not."

"You're right," she said softly, "I'm not."

Gav looked around them, as if noticing the museum for the first time. "You fit right in here."

Abi looked around and back at Gav, "Why would you say that?" she asked.

"Because," Gav's voice hitched. "All beautiful pieces of art should be right here."

Her breath hitched. Oh, he was going to get her with those words of his for sure. "Thank you," she answered.

Gav shook his head, "No, Abi, thank you."

Her tears were starting, "For what?" She asked so softly, she wasn't sure he heard her.

His eyes were filling up too. "For being who you are and showing me there's so much more."

"More what?" she asked him.

Gav took her hand and brought it to his lips, "More everything."

Her chest was heaving with emotion and Abi couldn't help it, she leaned over and kissed him. "I love you," she whispered as her lips touched his.

Oh thank god, Gav said to himself. "Well," he said softly as he looked into her eyes, "that's wonderful because I love you too."

Gav scooted off the bench and onto his knee in front of Abi. He would remember this moment just like he remembered their first night together, the way the moonlight shone on Abi's skin, and he knew he would love her forever.

Abi's hand flew to her throat. She was so surprised by his gesture and a little scared too but mostly she was happy in the knowledge that someone loved her and was willing to be with her for the rest of their lives.

"Abigale Rochelle," he started, "I know I was picked for you, in more ways than I can express. Please love me and be with me and I'll try to never give you a reason to doubt your choice in loving me."

As far as proposals went, Abi was pretty sure she got the best one ever. She nodded, tears streaming down her cheeks. "Okay." She tried to sound tough, "I'll marry you but you better put your money where your mouth is, Maslov."

He should never have doubted that Abi would accept his offer but make it on her terms. "You got it," he answered.

Nodding, Abi stood and waited for him to stand up next to her. "Okay," she said when they started walking out of the museum, "now we just need to go and tell our parents."

Gav rolled his eyes, "There'll be no living with them now," he said sarcastically.

Abi nodded and smiled, "It's a good thing that I live in Hawaii. We can run away if need be."

"Good point," Gav countered, "You think they can use a banker in Hawaii?" he asked.

They were now outside and Gav raised his hand to catch a cab, his other arm around Abi. She thought it was the best place in the world to be; beside Gav, wherever that was. "I think they can," she said and kissed him there on the sidewalk in front of the museum.

A few minutes later, they were tucked in a cab on the way to Abi's parents' place. They were discussing their future and kissing like there was no tomorrow.

Look for the final book

in the

Semper Fi in Love Series........

A Marine and Her Sensibilities

Out for release on

March 5, 2014